W9-BNX-124

ONE NIGHT
with a
BILLIONAIRE

JESSICA CLARE

BERKLEY BOOKS, NEW YORK

BERKLEY

An imprint of Penguin Random House LLC
375 Hudson Street, New York, New York 10014

ONE NIGHT WITH A BILLIONAIRE

A Berkley Book / published by arrangement with the author

ISBN: 978-0-425-27579-5

PUBLISHING HISTORY
Berkley mass-market edition / June 2015

PRINTED IN THE UNITED STATES OF AMERICA

10 9 8 7 6 5 4 3

Cover art: *Glass of Champagne* © CulturaLimited/Superstock.
Cover design by Sarah Oberrender.
Interior text design by Laura K. Corless.

Penguin
Random
House

continued . . .

For all the fans who have been following along
with my billionaires and can't wait to read
Cade's book. This one's for you!

Also, for Mel aka Mistress M, who recommends my books
to everyone and always makes me feel like the world's
best writer. Everyone should have fans like you. ♥

ONE

⟨~⟩

If there was a gift Kylie Daniels wished she could gift to the world, it would be the ability to pencil in a great pair of brows. The woman sitting across from her? Her brow game was terrible. She looked as if she'd Sharpied her thin black brows on in the dark while intoxicated and it overwhelmed her narrow face. And what were those little comma things she'd drawn at the end? Jesus, Mary, and Joseph.

Not that Kylie was an expert on makeup, but . . . well, okay, she *was*. An expert on makeup, that is. She was a licensed cosmetologist, had worked with several singers and stage productions, and could make even the most heinous pores disappear with the right brushes.

And that was why she was sitting in the office of Dirty Dollar Records this lovely July afternoon, sweltering her large ass off as she waited to be called in for an audition. A friend who styled hair for several celebrities had mentioned a record manager who was looking for a makeup artist who was discreet, inventive, and ready to tour with his client. Through a friend of a friend, Kylie had gotten the job interview and now sat, waiting, and hoped that her own makeup didn't sweat off by the time she got in there.

No one wanted to hire a fat makeup artist in L.A., but they really, really didn't want to hire one if she looked like hell. Makeup was Kylie's calling card, after all. She had to look damn good at all times or people questioned her ability. So instead of going for low-key and demure as one normally would for a job interview, she went all out. Kylie wore a tight navy dress with a square sailor top and clinging black mermaid skirt, along with bright red heels. The entire look was retro, and she'd curled half of her dyed blond hair into two fat sausage rolls that perched atop her head like a forties movie star, letting the rest dance on her shoulders. Her makeup was bold, too. Her brows had been penciled into a sweeping line above eyes that were lined with a deep black eyeliner extended to a dramatic point, and the rest of her eyes highlighted with a bright white to make her cat's eyes pop. Her lashes had been stacked with fake ones to create a thick fan. She'd gone light on the blush to highlight the porcelain look of her skin and picked a dark, cherry red for her lips. Two cherry earrings and a cherry-decorated necklace completed the ensemble.

It was a little kitschy, but she was interviewing to be the makeup artist for Daphne Petty, and Daphne Petty wasn't exactly demure herself. Known in music circles for her wild lyrics, her nutty stage costumes, and her party-girl attitude, she looked like she'd be a lot of fun to go on tour with.

Kylie hoped so, anyhow. Anything had to be better than the diva she'd recently toured Asia with. Chanteuse had insisted that her crew wear all white and not speak unless spoken to. Kylie couldn't wait to get away from that job. She'd gotten the boot when she'd returned to the States because, as it had been explained, Chanteuse didn't like that Kylie "didn't take care with her appearance" and she felt it reflected poorly on her to have someone like that in her staff.

AKA, your fat butt embarrasses me. It still stung, but Kylie was doing her best to get over it. After all, she questioned the sanity of someone who had a diamond-encrusted toilet seat that she took with her on tour.

So here Kylie was, unemployed once more and hoping for the best.

"Miss Daniels?" a voice called, and Kylie got to her feet, her old-fashioned circular hatbox suitcase in hand.

She sucked up her nervousness and straightened her clothing as she strode forward, then offered her hand to the frowning man waiting for her. "Kylie Daniels," she told him, keeping her voice cool and confident despite the look he was giving her. This man was clearly conservative, but hopefully his client wouldn't be.

"Thank you for coming," he said, and led her back into the office. "I'm Mr. Powers. Please follow me."

She hefted her case of cosmetics and trailed after him, biting back her annoyance when he passed by the elevator and headed for the stairs instead. *Oh sure, take the fat chick in high heels carrying thirty pounds of makeup up the stairs.* She hoped he wouldn't mind her being a little sweaty when they got to the top, then.

Mr. Powers's office was on the fourth floor, so by the time they arrived, Kylie was breathless and perspiring. Not the look she wanted for her interview, but too late to do anything about it now. Mr. Powers hadn't said a thing as he led her upstairs, but pointed her into a conference room and smiled politely.

She entered it, set her case down on the table, and sat down on a chair, waiting. Powers left and returned a minute later with a stack of papers and a pen. "We ask that you please sign these non-disclosure agreements, Miss Daniels, as the label is extremely concerned about public image."

"Of course," Kylie murmured, taking the pen. She'd had to sign something similar when she'd worked for the diva Chanteuse. She quickly signed and handed the papers back with a smile. *See how accommodating I am?*

Mr. Powers didn't sit down at one of the eight empty chairs next to her. Instead, he hesitated, then tucked the paperwork under his arm. "Before you meet Miss Petty, you should know a few things."

"All right." Kylie clasped her hands in her lap and kept the smile on her face. She was ready for anything they could throw at her after working in Hollywood for a while. *The client doesn't like for her right side to show up in photographs. This client feels the color green offends her chi so doesn't wear it. Don't look this client straight in the eye. Always ask this client open-ended questions as she feels that her staff should challenge her. This client is in character at all times, so please play along.*

"Miss Petty fired her last makeup artist due to personality conflicts." He double-checked the signatures on the paperwork and then gazed down at her, though she got the impression he was fidgety. Uncomfortable. Weird. "The label is quite concerned that Miss Petty is happy. You understand this, yes?"

"Of course." Where was he going with this?

"However, the label also likes to maintain Miss Petty's image. In fact, we are concerned with that above all things. Miss Petty's image *must* be maintained. That is where you come in."

"O-okay?" *What was the answer he was looking for?*

"In short, people pay lots of money to see a vibrant, beautiful Daphne Petty on tour. I expect you to do your part, of course."

"Of course," she repeated. This entire conversation was bewildering.

"Which is not to say that Miss Petty has the liberty of firing you. That will be at the label's discretion."

Ooookay . . . Daphne wasn't going to be allowed to fire her if they didn't get along, but the last person was fired because they didn't get along? It was all very confusing. She kept smiling, though she was starting to feel a little worried. "I think I can handle that?"

"Good. I see you brought your tools with you?"

She patted her bag. "Of course."

"We would like for you to do Miss Petty's makeup for her. Think of it as a screen test."

It wasn't the strangest request she'd gotten. "That's fine. Any particular look you're going for with Miss Petty on this new tour?"

A strange look crossed Mr. Powers's face. "Healthy. Just healthy will be fine."

Healthy? "I'm sure I can give her a natural glow."

"Great." He gave her a tight little smile. "I'll let Miss Petty know that you're here."

"Thank you," Kylie murmured, and Mr. Powers left her alone in the conference room. The air was on upstairs—thank goodness—and so it wasn't quite so hot. Her sticky forehead dried, and as she waited for Daphne Petty, she eyed the posters on the walls of prior tours, the platinum and gold records. This was a big break and a good job, and she crossed her fingers under the table that Daphne wouldn't have a problem with Kylie's non-Hollywood-sized butt.

Eventually, though, she got bored. Time ticked away and the clock showed she'd been sitting in the conference room for a full forty-five minutes without someone stopping in. She freshened her own makeup, and then dug through her kit, mentally trying to put together a look for Daphne Petty. From what she remembered, Daphne had bright eyes, so she could highlight those. Eye makeup and lip color would depend on the shade of Daphne's hair, and from what she'd seen in tabloids, Daphne tended to dye it all kinds of strange colors. Unless she went for a totally nude palette? She dug through her tubes of glosses and shadows, thinking. Of course, if Daphne's hair was pink again, the colors would have to be really subtle—

Someone crashed into the door behind her, and Kylie jumped in her chair. She spun around, startled. A moment later, the door opened, and someone stumbled in. It was a woman with big round sunglasses that covered most of her face. Her platinum blond hair was cut into a short, messy bob that looked as if it hadn't been washed in at least a week. She wore an old Ramones T-shirt over a pair of faded capri jeans and wobbled as she stood in the doorway. "You the makeup girl?"

It was Daphne Petty.

Her voice was slurred. *Drunk. Lovely.* "That's me." Kylie stood up and extended her hand. "My name is Kylie Daniels. It's very nice to meet you, Miss Petty."

Daphne looked her up and down. "You look like a fat Marilyn Monroe. Or Bettie Page. You know they don't like big butts here in L.A.," she mock-whispered. "Careful that my trainer doesn't see you. He won't let me eat anything but lettuce." She dropped into a seat next to Kylie and pulled her sunglasses off, rubbing her face. "All right. I'm here." She waved a hand in the air. "Make me beautiful."

Kylie just stared. The once-lovely Daphne Petty was skeletally thin. Track marks lined up one arm and down the other, along with scars at her wrists from cutting. Her skin was blotchy and broken in a few spots, a bright red patch on the corner of her mouth. Her eyes were sunken and her color was extremely unhealthy.

She looked like hell.

And now, Kylie understood all the corporate-speak that Mr. Powers had given her. Daphne couldn't fire her because *she* was a mess. And the label didn't want a "look" for Daphne for her tour. They wanted Kylie to hide Daphne's ill health. They wanted her to paint her up and make her look normal.

They didn't need a cosmetologist—they needed a goddamn magician. Kylie gave Daphne a pitying look. Daphne, whose dilated eyes were glancing around the room but focusing on nothing. A magician, Kylie amended, or a miracle worker. She was neither, but she'd do what she could. She pulled out her airbrushing kit and plugged it in, then handed Daphne a face-cleansing wipe. "Once your face is clean, we'll begin. Let's start with a primer, shall we?"

An hour later, Daphne Petty's thin face had been contoured to make her appear more robust. Her sharp cheekbones were disguised, her too-thin nose widened with a bit of shadowing, and then she'd pretty much airbrushed every possible inch of Daphne she could reach. The track marks on her arms were covered. The red spots on her face—dear lord, Kylie hoped they weren't from meth—were concealed. Her eyes were art-fully highlighted and emphasized to bring out their color, and Kylie picked out cheery, warm colors for her eyes and her mouth. When she was finished, she showed Daphne—who'd sat in a dazed high the entire time—the mirror.

At the sight of her face, Daphne had smiled and seemed to notice Kylie again. "Wow. I really like this. You do good work, Fat Marilyn."

Wow. Was that nickname supposed to be a compliment? Kylie wasn't sure. She snorted. "Thanks. I try."

She gave Kylie a shrewd look. "So can I ask why you want this job? Touring is hard and brutal, and I'm going to be a raging bitch pretty much ninety percent of the time."

"I like traveling," Kylie lied. "I like seeing new places."

"Bullshit," Daphne said. "This is my fourth national tour, and I know the only thing you're going to see is the back of the tour bus and my greenroom. So why not spit a little truth for me?"

Fair enough. "You're high profile, and this'll look good on my résumé." Not entirely the truth again, but a little more mercenary.

That seemed to make Daphne happy. She touched the side of her nose in an *aha* moment and then pointed at Kylie. "Now I get you. All right, then," Daphne said, getting to her feet. She seemed to be coming down off of whatever high she'd been on, and was almost normal. "I suppose I should get that fussy dick Powers and see what he thinks." She winked at Kylie and gave a toss of her limp platinum hair.

And Kylie found herself smiling. When Daphne was playful like this, it was easy to see why she was so popular.

Daphne opened the door to the conference room and stuck her head out. "Powers, get your ass over here," she bellowed down the hall, and Kylie winced. But Daphne's method was effective. A moment later, Mr. Powers appeared in his stuffy little suit and took a look at Daphne. He eyed her critically, and then grabbed her chin and turned her face, checking it from the right and the left.

To Kylie's surprise, Daphne was docile and stood for the humiliating treatment. When Powers grabbed one of Daphne's arms and examined it, then peered into Daphne's eyes, it reminded Kylie of someone purchasing a horse. Kylie couldn't help but murmur, "Do you want to check her teeth, too?"

Daphne giggled.

Powers looked over at Kylie, his brows drawing together. "Did you do something to her teeth?"

"Inside joke," Daphne said, and then held her skinny arms wide. "So what do you think?"

Powers looked over at Kylie, then back at Daphne, then back at Kylie again. "You're hired. Send your salary demands to the personnel office."

"You and me are gonna be great friends, Fat Marilyn," Daphne announced, and then pulled out a flask.

Somehow, Fat Marilyn doubts that, Kylie thought to herself, but she couldn't help but feel sorry for Daphne, just a little. She had to be miserable as hell on the inside to be such a mess on the outside.

———

Once Kylie had accepted the offer, she was steered toward the Human Resources offices. There, she'd signed contracts and talked salary and all the nitty-gritty details of her job details that both Mr. Powers and Daphne were too important to go over. To Kylie's surprise, no one batted an eye at her salary demands, just agreed and set a start date. The money was a sum that made her happy, even if it meant touring for the next four months. The fact that they paid her demand without haggling told her she'd have to earn every last penny, though.

———————

Still pleased with her new employment, she packed up her gear and headed back out to the street. Instead of returning to her friend's apartment, though, she took a cab to the outskirts of L.A., deep into the quiet suburbs. "Wait here," she told the cabdriver. "I promise I won't be more than twenty minutes."

"The meter keeps running," he told her.

Kylie didn't have a car, so it wasn't like she could argue over the price. "Fine. Just stay, okay?"

He turned up the radio and gave her a thumbs-up.

Sucking in a breath, Kylie headed into the nursing home.

As soon as she stepped through the doors, the cool waft of air-conditioning touched her sweating brow. The sterile white tile floors were a blinding white, the walls a comforting pink. It almost distracted from the big locked automated glass doors that were only accessible via a keycard.

Kylie went to the visiting window and signed in. She handed the clipboard to the attendant. "I'm here to see Sloane Etherton."

"Just a moment," the girl at the window said. She turned in her chair and pulled a folder that was tagged with a yellow slip. "I'm supposed to remind you that your last payment didn't go through." She gave Kylie an apologetic look. "Do you need to talk to the billing department to make arrangements?"

She shook her head. "No, I can make a catch-up payment now. I . . . had some financial difficulty for the last few months." Kylie pulled out her checkbook and began to write. "Everything should be fine now. I just signed a contract for a new job and I get my first advance payment on Monday." Or as soon as she could finagle something from Mr. Powers. "Can I postdate the check?"

"We're not supposed to accept postdated checks."

"Well, I'm leaving the state in a few days to go on tour, so I won't be here to pay in person," Kylie snapped, annoyed. "So either you take a postdated check or you take no check."

But it seemed she'd said a magical word. The receptionist's head lifted, her eyes wide. "Tour?"

"With Daphne Petty," Kylie said, writing out the dollar amount for two months of fees. It'd wipe her account, but she was low on choices. "And I'm sure I could get you tickets." She ripped the check free and held it out to the girl. "If you can take a postdated check."

"I'm sure I can misplace it for a few days," she said with a grin, plucking the check from Kylie's hands.

Five minutes later, she was admitted to the back and down a quiet hall. The attendant at her side held her Nana's records. "Miss Sloane has been a little difficult lately, Miss Daniels."

"You know my nana," Kylie said tightly. "She's never been an easy woman." Heck, *difficult* was probably one of her good days.

The attendant didn't crack a smile. "She keeps trying to leave. You know that sort of thing is frowned upon."

"She can barely walk and she's senile," Kylie said, unhappy. This wasn't the first time she'd been told this about Nana Sloane. "I don't see how she is attempting to escape."

"Unfortunately we get that a lot with the elderly dementia patients," the attendant told her. "They get confused as to where they are and try to leave. It's why we have to keep the place locked down. Sometimes they get creative, though, like your nana, and that's when things become a problem."

"I'll talk to her," Kylie said, a tension headache threatening to crush her. "But—"

"I know. She has dementia. We know it's a losing battle," the attendant said gently. "But we still like to try and drive the concept home if possible."

She understood, even if she knew it was impossible. No one came out a winner where Nana Sloane was concerned. Kylie nodded. "I'll see what I can do. Is she okay otherwise?"

"Other than the usual ailments that an elderly demented woman has? Sure. She's unhappy when she's lucid, she's confused when she's not, and she frightens the other patients."

"Sounds great." She grimaced, picturing her bitter grandma railing at the other residents. "What about today?"

"Today was a bad day," the attendant said. "She's heavily sedated at the moment, but if you stick around for a few hours—"

"I can't," Kylie said, relieved to hear that there wouldn't be a messy confrontation. Not today. "I'll just pop in to see her and go."

The man nodded and opened the door. "Let me know when you're ready to leave and I'll take you back out."

Kylie stepped into her grandmother's room, feeling the weight of responsibility on her shoulders. The room was utterly silent and clean. A picture of Kylie's mother, long deceased, was next to the bed. There was no picture of Kylie's father, or of Kylie. But that didn't surprise her—she'd never been Nana Sloane's favorite person.

You're a burden, Kylie Daniels. I have to work two jobs just to put enough food on the table to feed your fat ass. The least you can do is be grateful. If only your mother were here.

She squelched the hateful memories and pulled up a chair next to her grandmother's bed and took the woman's hand in her own. Nana's hand was fragile and so utterly small in her own, her skin dry like paper.

"Hi, Nana," Kylie whispered. "I hope you're doing well. I just got a job going on tour, so I'm not going to be able to visit much for a few months." Not that her nana noticed if Kylie was there or not. Most days she was lost in her own mind, or looking for her long-dead daughter. Kylie rubbed her fingers against her nana's palm. "But the good news is that you're all paid up and my new job should allow you to stay here for a long time. I know you don't like it at this place, but they have the best care. They really do. I'm going to make sure that you're taken care of. It's my responsibility, and I'm not going to shirk it." She pressed her mouth to the old woman's limp hand. "Be good while I'm gone, okay?"

She held her grandmother's hand for another minute, lost in thought and worried about burdens and family, and the weight of responsibility. Nana Sloane didn't wake up. It wasn't a bad thing. When Nana was asleep, she was peaceful. Almost sweet. She wasn't spitting nasty words at Kylie, screaming that she didn't belong here, or sobbing uncontrollably. Kylie could deal with the snide comments about her weight. She could deal with the jabs about her hair, or her slutty clothing. But when Nana wept as if her heart was broken, her dreams shattered? It nearly broke Kylie, too.

Thankfully, her nana's lined face remained slack, a bit of drool pooling at the corners of her mouth.

So Kylie left.

Seeing Nana Sloane was good for her, though. It helped Kylie focus. Made her determined. It was a reminder of what she was working for. She might hate touring and never having a place to call her own, but as long as her nana was safe and looked after, well, that was all Kylie could ask for. She'd been a burden to the woman in her younger years, and now it was Kylie's time to return the favor.

No matter how much it sucked the life out of her.

TWO

If Cade Archer could have predicted how he'd spend his thirtieth birthday, he'd have only been part right. Surrounded by the Brotherhood, the secret society he'd been in since college? Check. Playing a hand of poker in a smoky cellar beneath a club he owned? Check. The men chewing on cigars and discussing business strategies as usual?

Not so much.

"Check this shit out," Reese Durham said, pushing a sonogram picture toward the center of the table. "He's got a dick like a baby's arm."

Griffin Verdi picked up the photo and squinted at it. "You sure that's not, in fact, the baby's arm?"

"Nope." Reese chewed on the end of his cigar, looking quite pleased with himself. "Reese Junior's packing some major heat."

Griffin rolled his eyes and tossed the picture back down. Undeterred, Reese snatched it up and offered it to Hunter. "So when are you and Gretchen thinking about children?"

"Maybe next year," Hunter said, studying the photo. "After the wedding."

"No children for us yet," Logan said. "Brontë wants to finish her degree first. I'm certainly in no rush."

"Amen," Griffin said. After a moment, he added, "Though I wouldn't mind if Maylee and I had a happy accident."

At his side, Jonathan Lyons dropped a handful of chips onto the pile. "Violet and I are hoping for a happy accident. Maybe sooner than later."

"Ha," Reese said, and punched Jonathan in the arm affably. "Go for it. Raw-dog her, man. Our kids can nanny swap."

"That is a horrid term," Griffin said. "Raw . . . dog?"

"Bareback—"

"I know! Good grief, I know."

Cade just shook his head and picked through his cards. Definitely not what he'd have expected for his thirtieth birthday. He'd pictured spending it with his friends, of course, but talking about babies and marriages? Not exactly. Hardened bachelor Reese had turned from ladies' man to future daddy and expert on everything husband-related.

In fact, everyone in their small circle had more or less settled down in the last year.

Everyone except Cade.

It wasn't that he didn't date. Okay, maybe he didn't. It wasn't that he wasn't interested in women. He was. Actually, there was one in particular he'd been messed up over for the last, oh, fifteen years or so. He was just waiting for the right one to come around to the idea of being with him.

He thought of Daphne, her wicked smile and devilish attitude, the way she'd draped her arms around him so sweetly . . . and then he thought of the time she'd OD'd in his arms, limp and cold, her lips tinged with blue.

Maybe marriage and a happy-ever-after just wasn't in the cards for someone like him. He pushed a handful of chips into the center of the table. "Raising you, Jon."

"Bastard," Jon said with a grin, and the topic returned to cards once more.

Cade checked his phone discreetly as the others put in their bids. Daphne was supposed to text him when she was out of her practice session. The last time they'd talked—via hastily typed texts—she'd told him she had long dance-routine numbers she had to endure for her upcoming concert and this weekend were dress rehearsals. But she wanted to do something for his birthday, she'd said. She'd buzz him and let him know her schedule.

But that was days ago, and Daphne had never called.

And here he was, thirty and alone. That should have told him something right there. That when it was convenient for Daphne, she liked Cade around. And when it wasn't . . . he wasn't even on her radar.

Maybe someday he'd learn. With a small sigh of disgust, Cade tossed another set of chips into the pot. "In."

———————

When poker wrapped up for the evening, Cade found himself walking out with Reese, who'd won the majority of hands that night and had also been celebrating the success of his celebrity cruise line and his plans to partner with a movie studio for character cruise lines based off of popular TV shows and movies. He was in a great mood as they walked out, while Cade was quiet, lost in thought.

"Hey, man," Reese said, catching Cade's attention. "Everything all right with you?"

"Always," Cade said, smiling. Really, he didn't have much to complain about. Business was great, his charities were having a record year, and he was healthy. There was nothing that should make him discontent or unhappy.

And yet, he felt unsettled. Moody. Envious of his friends and their happiness, perhaps.

"You're just kinda quiet lately."

He shoved his hands in his pockets. "Just thinking. Nothing important."

"You busy this weekend? Me and Audrey are heading up to the cabin. Hope that's okay with you."

Cade's getaway cabin? Where they'd met? He grinned. "You know I gave you carte blanche when it comes to that place."

"Yeah, Audrey's been having a bad week. Hormones." Reese grimaced. "Thought I'd bring her back to the love nest and let her relax this weekend. You're welcome to come."

And be a third wheel? Watching as they cuddle? He was happy as hell for Reese, but he had a hard time looking at healthy, joyful Audrey, because every time he looked at her, he saw Daphne. Or rather, who he wanted Daphne to be.

Because once upon a time, Daphne had been plump and beautiful and lighthearted. And he'd loved her. Now? Now he didn't know how he felt. Obsessed, maybe. Desperate? Maybe that, too.

He checked his phone again. Still no text from Daphne. No missed calls. Nothing. Damn it. He knew she was busy, but he was, too. Didn't she give a shit? At all?

"Hey? Hello?" A hand waved in front of his face.

"Sorry." Cade gave Reese a sheepish look. "Just distracted lately."

"Cabin? This weekend?"

Cade shook his head. "Pass. You and Audrey have fun. I have plans." Hopefully.

"You're spending time with Daphne, aren't you?" Reese's tone was disgusted.

For a moment, he thought about denying it. He knew Reese didn't understand Cade's fixation with the pop star. Maybe he thought it was a fling that Cade was hoping would resurge again. But the truth was, Cade had been in love with Daphne since he was fifteen, when they were both trailer rats without a nickel to rub together. And now that she was in trouble, it was hard to just cut her off and wish her the best. Not when they'd slept together eight months ago . . . and then she'd tried to kill herself.

Hell, he was still messed up over that himself. So he said, "She needs me."

"She needs a reality check," Reese said.

"It's difficult," Cade told him. Difficult to talk about, and difficult to understand. Sometimes he got it. He understood why she'd succumbed to the fast-paced lifestyle. Like Daphne, he'd grown up as trash. The poorest kid on a dirt-poor block, he'd run barefoot with the neighborhood kids and had always kept a close eye on the Petty twins, pretty redheads a few years younger than him. Daphne Petty had been his first kiss, his first love, his first, well, everything. She'd been so special—talented, funny, smart, and with a way of drawing people in and making them notice her. When Cade left for college on a scholarship, he'd asked Daphne to wait for him. He'd make his way in the world and he'd come back and rescue her from their small town. Except Daphne hadn't waited. She'd met a music producer, and the next thing Cade knew, the girl he'd been in love with was on the radio. She'd slimmed down to nothing, dyed her hair an outrageous shade, pranced around on TV in bikinis, and sold millions of albums.

He'd been so proud of her at first—Daphne had a fun sense of humor, and it came through in her quirky songs. But as time passed and he became busier with his own business, they drifted apart. Daphne grew more and more ensconced in the music business, and even though she'd been a healthy redhead at one point, now she had wild hair, a stick-thin figure, and fake breasts. And a coke habit.

He still loved her. Always would. But when her "quirkiness" started showing up in tabloids with pictures of her doing lines and trips to rehab? He worried about her. Tried to help her stay on the straight and narrow as much as he could, from afar.

But it was never enough. Eight months ago, things had come to a head. She'd promised him that if he'd give her one more chance, she'd clean up. Not in rehab. She'd be in every tabloid imaginable if she went to rehab. Couldn't he go away with her someplace private and get her a personal doctor? She didn't need a life coach, she just needed Cade and Audrey at her side, encouraging her.

He'd fallen for that—hook, line, and sinker. He'd done his part, all right. He'd hired the best doctors and ensconced them nearby. He'd ensured she had the easiest drugs to wean herself off, and doled out her new prescriptions carefully. He'd supported her every step of the way . . . and then she had a fight with Audrey over him. She'd seduced Cade, stolen his meds, and overdosed while lying in bed next to him.

That had required a lot of therapy to get over.

Things between them were complicated all right. And tangled. Because how was he supposed to feel about his childhood sweetheart that slept with him one day and then reached for pills the next?

"You know Daphne's my sister-in-law," Reese said, clapping him on the shoulder as they walked out of the club. "And Audrey would be hurt to hear me say it, but Daphne's a train wreck. She was clean for what, three whole weeks last time?"

"She says she's clean now."

"She says a lot of things," Reese retorted. "I've seen how she hurts Audrey with her promises. If you can disentangle yourself, man, do it."

Sound advice. He knew it, and yet it was harder to practice. "I need to talk to her, regardless." To see where "they" were, or if they were anywhere. If her label was sending Daphne out on tour, she had to be clean. If she was clean, maybe they could start again.

If not . . . maybe it was time for Cade to move on. Either way, he needed to know.

THREE

⌒

On opening night of Daphne Petty's North American tour, the star was a raging bitch, and the staff was running in fear. Kylie herself was hiding out with the costumers until she was needed. The next room over, she could hear Daphne screaming at her assistant. "Didn't I say I wanted boneless buffalo wings? What, you expect me to eat these things with bones in them? For fucking real? Didn't *anyone* read my goddamn tour rider?"

Kylie winced in sympathy. She'd been working for Daphne for a week now, and as the Teacher's Petty tour got underway, she learned that Daphne could either be the sweetest, most fun person in the world . . . or a complete nut job. She'd been warned by everyone in the crew to not take anything Daphne did or said personally, and to just ride out any sort of confrontation. Give Daphne the right of way and the arguments would disappear.

So far, to Kylie, Daphne was decent enough. Some mornings she was snippy, but she liked the job that Kylie did on her makeup, and she liked the skin-care regimen that Kylie had put her on, so she was happy. She still referred to Kylie as "Fat Marilyn," but Kylie was getting used to that. Apparently Daphne was bad with names and so everyone had a Daphne-anointed nickname. The costume lady was "Ginger Tramp" or just "Ginger" for short, because she was redheaded, freckled all over, and tended to wear tight clothing. One of the lighting crew was called "Hodor," the sound guy was "Hairy Dave," and Daphne called her assistant "Snoopy" because she "ran her like a dog." All in all, "Fat Marilyn" wasn't so bad of a nickname, really. She'd heard Daphne calling the dancers all kinds of insulting things, depending on if they were getting in her way or not.

"She was nicer before the drugs," Ginger told her, sewing sequins onto a dance costume for Daphne's third number. "Used to be the sweetest girl. Funny, too. Now she's just a cunt."

Kylie blinked at the harsh language. "She seems okay to me."

Ginger shrugged. "She's actually not that bad this week because her new dancer boy toy has the good drugs. Or so I've heard." She mimed snorting a line of blow, then went back to her sewing. "Until he runs out of his stash, he's her new favorite person."

Wow. Kylie licked her lips, uncomfortable. "Does, um, the label know?" Should she tell someone that Daphne was getting high before her first performance?

"They don't care," Ginger said. "Who do you think started her on the drugs? It's cheaper to keep them happy when they're well medicated. And as long as the tour sells out, no one gives a shit." Ginger stabbed a needle through the shimmery fabric, then tugged at the thread. "I've been with her for five years. She goes through this cycle repeatedly. She's clean, then someone gives her a new drug. She gets hooked, she gets nasty, she falls to pieces, then goes to rehab and she gets clean. Then someone gives her a new kind of nose candy and we start all over again."

She was so blasé about it. Kylie thought about the track

marks on Daphne's arms. "She doesn't look so good, though. Doesn't anyone worry about her health?"

"Not as much as they care about making money." Ginger bit the thread gently and then shook out the costume. "She's probably going to need you soon. You might want to surface."

Kylie grimaced and glanced at the door to Daphne's green-room, where the pop star relaxed prior to the concert. Vague crying could be heard from the other side. Her false lashes were going to be hell to stick if Daphne's eyes were puffy from crying. So with a sigh, Kylie braced herself and headed in to the greenroom to see what was going on.

Sure enough, Daphne was sitting in front of the makeup mirror, crying. She wiped her eyes with one hand and dug through all of Kylie's neatly sorted makeup with the other. Pinning a smile to her face, Kylie approached. "Hey, Daph, what are you looking for?"

Daphne continued to weep, sniffling loud. "Have you seen Marco?"

"Marco?" Kylie gave her a puzzled look.

"Marco Polo?"

At first, Kylie thought it was a joke. But Daphne kept crying and digging through Kylie's stack of eye shadows and she realized this must be another nickname for someone. "I haven't. Can I get you anything?"

This was the wrong thing to say. Daphne's eyes lit up and she turned to Kylie, a crazed look on her face. "Do you have any stuff?"

"Stuff?"

"Rock? Blow? Pills? Something? I need a pick-me-up." She rubbed a hand across her eyes again and for a moment she looked incredibly young. "I'm so tired all the time."

"I don't have drugs," she told Daphne softly. Part of her wanted to hug the pop star, and part of her wanted to give her a good shake. She settled for picking a tube of lip gloss up off of the floor and putting it back in its place. "Can I get you a water or something?"

But Daphne began to cry again. "Marco has all the good stuff and I don't know where he is and I'm so sleepy. I just want to take a nap and I go on stage in an hour and a half."

"You can't cry," Kylie told her, taking a determined tone and offering Daphne a box of Kleenex. "Your face is going to be on all kinds of magazines tomorrow and you want to look your best, don't you?"

"I don't care about magazines. I just want a nap. Why is Marco hiding from me?"

Kylie gave her a helpless look. "I suppose I could go look for him—" She stopped that train of thought when Snoopy showed up in the corner of her eye and gave her a silent shake of her head and a throat-cutting motion. Okay. So Marco was "hiding" deliberately. They probably didn't want Daphne on something when she went on stage. Poor thing. She stroked Daphne's hair, feeling sorry for her. She should be excited to start a tour, not miserable. "You know what? I think there's a coffee place up the street. I could go run and get you something to pep you up before it's time for makeup?"

Daphne's tearstained face lit up. "Really? You'd do that for me, Fat Marilyn?"

"Yup," she said. Anything to make Daphne stop crying. "How about an espresso?"

Daphne clapped her hands. "I need an extra-large iced coffee with a quad-shot of espresso. Heavy on the sugar, heavy on the cream."

"That sounds awful," Kylie said with a small laugh. "But it does sound like it'll wake you up."

"Short of them grinding the beans into the ice cubes, yup." Daphne actually looked happy. "Thank you so much. Coffee sounds awesome. I'm thinking about adding it *to my goddamn rider, not that anyone reads the fucking thing.*" She bellowed the last part and gave Snoopy a glare.

"I'll just run and get that coffee," Kylie said, grabbing her wallet and running for the door.

"Flee while you can," Snoopy told her, and it sounded like good advice to Kylie.

———————

Parked in front of the coffee shop was a hot pink Lyons road-ster that made Kylie drool with want. She was so busy admiring it and staring that she automatically reached for the door to the cafe . . . and ended up grabbing at someone's belt buckle and the fabric below.

And possibly some junk. Possibly.

"Oh!" She jerked backward, shocked. Of all the humiliating things to do. She looked up . . . and immediately felt flustered.

Kylie had to admit her instincts had great taste, though. If she had to grab anyone's junk, at least it was this guy's. Because good lord, he was gorgeous. Blond tousled hair, a gray business suit, and a pair of smiling blue eyes crinkled with amusement at her.

"Oh, my God, I am so, so sorry," Kylie told him. "I thought you were the door."

"I can safely say that's probably the first time I've heard that from a beautiful woman." He grinned at her and opened the door—the real one—for her. "After you?"

Humiliation burned her cheeks, and she ducked her head and stepped into the coffee shop, hoping that he wouldn't follow her in.

No such luck—the handsome man was two steps behind her as she went inside. She bit her lip, wondering if she needed to apologize again. *Say something clever, funny. Something. Anything.* Steeling herself, she turned around to face him. "I don't normally grab men when I head into a coffee shop," she told him. "But since I did, I feel like I should buy you a drink."

He threw back his head and laughed. "What sort of groping do I endure for a bagel?"

"Bagels are cheap," she found herself teasing back. "No more than a quick squeeze for one of those."

"Not even if I ask for lox?" His eyes were so blue, surrounded by thick lashes. He looked like an angel. A very naughty, flirty angel.

"Not even," she told him, a smile tugging at her mouth. Then she offered him her hand. "Kylie."

"Cade," he told her, shaking her hand. As he held her fingers, he leaned in. "And I can buy my own bagels, truly. I just wanted to see what was on the menu."

Was he flirting with her or just being polite? When he gestured that she should step in front of him at the counter, she decided that it was simply politeness. He was just a nice guy having a little fun at the coffee shop. She smiled awkwardly at the man behind the counter. "I need a small black coffee, regular blend, and an extra-large iced coffee with a quad-shot of espresso. Loads of sugar and cream."

Cade chuckled. "Is all that sugar for you?"

She shook her head and held out a twenty to the cashier. "Mine's the black. I can't drink all that sugar."

"Too sweet?"

She stepped aside so he could order, and wondered briefly how blunt she should be with him. Then, she supposed, it didn't matter. She wouldn't see him again. "Too many calories. I'm already fat enough."

"Small black coffee," Cade told the man behind the counter. He paid and then turned back to Kylie, waiting at the counter while their drinks were prepared.

An uncomfortable silence fell. Kylie gave him a tight expression as he studied her. Then he said, "You know, I happen to think you're gorgeous."

A pleased smile curved her mouth. He was so nice. "Aw, thank you. I bet you say that to all the girls in coffee shops."

"No, I mean it. You're really lovely. I'm not just saying that to make conversation." His grin was sincere. "If I was, I'd comment on how I had a friend that used to order a drink just like the one you did. All the espresso in the world, tons of creamer, tons of sugar. She loved it."

"It's for my friend, too." Skinny, skinny Daphne could probably be considered a friend. Theoretically.

He still wore his smile as the barista set both black coffees on the counter, and then went to work on Daphne's monstrous caffeine concoction. Cade reached for his drink and then offered Kylie hers. His smile no longer seemed friendly, though. It just seemed . . . sad, almost. And it made her wonder.

"So," she asked, since he didn't seem to be leaving, "do you live here? In Chicago?"

He shook his head. "No. I'm in town to see a friend. You?"

Kylie shook her head. "Work. We travel a lot." She avoided mentioning who she worked for. She knew from past experience that even though Cade looked nice and normal—and okay, divinely handsome—the moment she mentioned what she did, people asked for tickets. It was best to just be vague. She gestured at the street. "I was coming here to do a coffee run, actually, and I noticed that car *out front*."

"The Lyons roadster?" Cade's smile quirked and reappeared.

"That's it," she said. "It's really gorgeous." And it was. A dainty little sports car, the Lyons out front had a hot pink exterior and purple interior that made Kylie adore it despite its impracticality. She had no need for a car due to her job, but if she got one, it'd be something like that flashy little beauty out front. "Makes me wonder about who drives such a thing."

"Well, I do for the next few hours," Cade told her, sipping his coffee. At her look of surprise, he added, "Then it's going into the care of an old friend of mine."

An old friend? Judging by the utter femininity of the car, she could guess what kind of friend it was. Figured. The good ones were always taken, weren't they? Of course Cade had a romantic interest. He was gorgeous, funny, charming, dressed well, and judging from the looks of things, had a fair amount of money if he was buying a Lyons for a lady friend. "Well, your friend is quite lucky to have you in her life."

The smile he gave her was sad and troubled. He looked back at the car thoughtfully, but was silent.

And that made Kylie's heart ache. Because whoever this handsome man wanted, it was clear he was miserable over her. He didn't look like a happy man in love. He looked . . . desperate. As if he were running out of options.

Poor guy. She hated to see that.

Kylie moved in and leaned closer to him, clutching her coffee close. "Whoever your friend is," she murmured, "if she doesn't take one look at that car and drag you off to bed for the next week, she's crazy."

At that, his smile broadened, and his attention fixed on Kylie once more. "I wish my friend were more like you, then."

I wish your friend was *me*, she thought, but only gave him a friendly wink. Then her coffee order was up, and it was time to leave. She gave Cade a small wave as she left, and he returned her gesture with a nod.

As Kylie headed back down the streets toward the music hall, she was filled with longing. Why couldn't she find a great guy like Cade? Someone that cared enough about her to surprise her with a ridiculous present . . . or heck, just enough to get sad-eyed when he missed her? Why couldn't she find a guy like that to be with? Why were they always taken?

There was no denying that there'd been a connection between them. It was obvious to her; some people you just clicked with instantly, and she and Cade had clicked. She'd briefly thought about asking him for his number, but she wasn't a masochist. Work had to come first for now, because she needed the money. Nursing home care was ungodly expensive.

But one thing was clear to Kylie—whoever held Cade's heart? She didn't know what she had. And if she did, she wasn't being very careful with it. Someone like Cade only came around once in a girl's lifetime.

And someone as plain and dumpy as Kylie didn't stand a chance of stealing him away.

FOUR

⌒

Music blasted through the walls of the greenroom in the concert hall, and even though the interior walls were protected by layers and layers of padding and drywall, it still thumped loud enough to make Cade's head hurt. He drummed his fingers on his knee, holding his bourbon in his other hand, and watched another pair of strangers in schoolgirl costumes pass by, giggling as they did. He didn't know if they were Daphne's fans or part of her entourage; they all seemed to dress weird.

For the tenth time in the last hour, he wondered why the hell he was here.

Cade was backstage in Daphne's private lounge area. Except it wasn't so private. It was filled with people in varying shades of drinking and getting high, press people, and Daphne's crew. In short, what he assumed would be a private meeting with Daphne wasn't going to be private at all.

He didn't know what to make of that. But he'd suggested that he and Daphne get together and talk about things, and she'd offered for him to meet her after her first concert on the new tour. She'd promised him alone time.

And because he could never resist Daphne, he'd agreed.

Except now, looking around, he wasn't exactly sure what he'd agreed to. Another song wailed through the walls, and his drink shook from the vibrations of the speakers. The posters on the walls of the crowded room were various promotional photos of Daphne in her cutesy costumes, winking at the camera. In each one, she looked healthy and beautiful, and it made him hope that when he saw her, she'd be just as gorgeous as she was in the photos. That it wasn't just photoshop.

If happy, healthy Daphne was blowing him off, he could live with that, really. He'd just tuck his heart back into its hiding place and go about his life as he always had.

He still felt out of place, though. Here he was in a suit and tie, and everyone else seemed to be in jeans or various states of undress. In the corner, there was a girl in a dress made entirely of what looked like leather buckles, and she was doing lines off of a mirror, which made him frown. Did Daphne know her entourage had drugs? She needed to stay away from that sort of thing if she was going to get better.

Sometimes he wondered if Daphne even wanted to get better. She swore that she did, but then she surrounded herself with people who used, people who partied, people who were the worst kinds of influences to someone with weak willpower.

And maybe he wanted Daphne to be healthy and drug-free more than Daphne wanted it.

Cade took another heavy swig of his drink, disgusted by the thought. Of course Daph wanted to get better. She'd said so, and she'd said she wanted him in her life.

So here he was, ignoring an important medical conference he'd been invited to in favor of sitting backstage, waiting for a pop star and hoping she'd tell him she was eight months clean and she loved him and could they give their strange relationship another go.

And because the thought of a negative answer made him

a little queasy, Cade downed the rest of his bourbon and went to get another.

As he waited at the bar, two women wandered into the back room, arguing. One carried a bright yellow polka-dotted pyramid of cases, and the other had an armful of costumes.

"I'm not paying you," grumbled the one with the costumes. "You cheated."

"How did I cheat?" said the one with the bright yellow stack of cases. She turned and Cade admired her figure as she bent over. She wore a tight black pair of capris and wedge heels that made her shapely calves stand out. Her ass was full and lush. Maybe a bit more than was considered typically beautiful by today's standards, but he liked it. After seeing Daphne's wraith-thinness, he had a new appreciation for a healthy figure, even a thick one. If Daphne looked like this woman did, he'd be unable to keep his hands off of her.

The woman turned to face him, and Cade's eyes widened.

It was the beautiful girl that had flirted with him at the coffee shop earlier. Kylie. His cock immediately stirred and he shifted in his seat at the bar, uncomfortable. He was just looking, of course. Admiring another woman didn't mean he wasn't interested in Daph. It just meant that he enjoyed a fine-looking form. And really, Daphne had looked like that once upon a time, all lush curves and pale skin.

"Cheater," the one with the clothes said. "You knew she'd fuck up her costumes."

Kylie's full red mouth just pulled into a brilliant smile, and Cade couldn't stop staring at her. "I had a hunch, but I didn't know for sure," she told the other woman. She picked up one of the cases and set it down on a table, then opened it up and began to pull out small tubes of makeup. "If she treats her clothes anything like her makeup, you should have known better than to take the bet."

The other woman just shook her head, shoved a five into Kylie's hand, and wandered away.

Just then, the bartender handed Cade his latest drink.

Perfect timing. Cade couldn't help but head over toward Kylie, newest drink in hand. There was just something about her that was incredibly vibrant that drew him. And even though he knew his reasons weren't completely aboveboard, he couldn't stop himself from approaching to say hello again.

Her head was bent over the box of makeup, and she didn't notice his approach. It gave him a chance to get a good look at her. She was plush all right, her figure rounded, her breasts plump and straining against the fabric of her tight, low-cut shirt, as if she'd dressed to entice him specifically. He loved a fine pair of breasts, and the bigger the better.

He took another swig of his drink. Great, now he was sounding like Reese.

She was real pretty, though. Her makeup was done in a retro style that emphasized her big brown eyes, and her hair was bleached a bright yellow blond with red tips, and drawn into two ponytails that rested on her shoulders. Her bangs were big and curled, and her entire look was "plump beach bunny." And Cade loved it. She just looked so vibrant and happy. So damn alive.

Why couldn't Daphne look half as stunning as Kylie? He knew from recent pictures that Daphne was still stick thin, the only curves on her body her fake breasts. Eight months after going to rehab, she still didn't have the healthy look he remembered.

Then again, if she'd looked half as tempting as Kylie did, would he have waited eight months to see her again? Or would he have dropped everything and demanded that they get back together? It wasn't just Daphne's appearance that made him reticent, though. It was everything. It was knowing she was circling the drain and being unable to help her.

But seeing Kylie, he remembered their connection at the coffee shop. "I should have guessed you worked for Daphne when you ordered that coffee monstrosity," he told her, walking up. He wanted to lean in and whisper it, but that might have made her skittish. "Hello again."

Kylie turned around and her mouth opened in surprise, forming a perfect red O that made him think all kinds of inappropriate things. She recovered in the next moment, juggling the tubes of lipstick in her grip and sticking a hand out for him to shake. "Hi again! Oh my goodness. I didn't expect to see you here!"

He took her hand and clasped it in his own, liking that her grip was warm and firm. Her nails were a delicate, girly pink and perfectly manicured. "Pleasure's all mine."

A hint of a blush touched her cheeks and she beamed at him. "What are you doing backstage?"

"I'm here to see someone," he told her, releasing her hand reluctantly and stuffing his hands back into the pockets of his jacket, a habit of his he should really break at some point. He ended up trashing a lot of his jackets that way.

The look on her face turned to one of intense pleasure, and her eyes sparkled. "You're kidding. Really?"

"Remember? The car?"

The sparkle in her eyes died, and a bright red color streaked up her cheeks. "Right!" she said and turned and began putting down the cosmetics in her hands. "Is she on tour with Daphne?"

"She *is* Daphne," he said, still grinning. "Think she'll like the car?"

Her mouth formed that little O again, and she blinked at him. For a moment, she looked unhappy, but she hid it with a smile. "I should have guessed it was Daph. Men are crazy about her."

Men? Cade kept the smile on his face, though it was growing difficult. He wanted to ask Kylie if Daphne had a lot of men she was seeing, but that would be pointless to ask, wouldn't it? He hadn't seen her in months. If she was dating someone, so be it. Whatever it was between Daphne and Cade, it wasn't easily categorized. It wasn't a relationship. It wasn't exactly just friendship, either. It was . . . well, it was a mess. A big, uncategorizable mess.

Usually he was fine with not giving it a label. But he

supposed that had changed after that screwed up night in the cabin. Everything had pretty much changed between them.

"Daphne's going to be so happy to see you," Kylie continued, staring down at the makeup she was arranging in the case in front of her.

"I certainly hope so," Cade said, trying to keep his tone light and carefree. "So what do you do here? Are you on tour with Daph? One of her backup singers?"

Kylie shook her head. "I can't sing as much as I croak," she told him with a funny little smile. "I'm her makeup artist." She gestured at the boxes and boxes of makeup, more than any sane person could wear in a lifetime. "She usually needs refreshing after getting off stage, and tonight she's going to want to look extra-special for the press, so I'm trying to get ready in advance." She gave him a nervous smile. "It gives me something to do, at least."

She smoothed her hands down her dark capris, and he realized she was, in fact, nervous. "Want a drink? I can get you one from the bar," he asked.

Kylie tilted her head at him and then gave a small shake of her blond mane with the little flecks of color. "I'm on the job, so I shouldn't drink. But you can have one on my behalf."

"Fair enough," Cade said, and downed the rest of his bourbon. He wasn't much of a drinker himself, but tonight felt . . . off and he wanted the liquid courage. "How long until the show's over, do you think?"

She tilted her head, and he was struck again by how pretty she was. "Let's see, she's singing 'Hopeless' right now, so she has about three more songs until she's done, then there's the encore, and then she'll pop back here so I can fix her up, and then she has press. Then meet and greets. After that, she should be free."

He glanced at his watch. It was already past ten thirty at night. Not that he was going to go to bed early or anything, but it sounded as if Daphne was pretty much busy up until midnight. Why had she asked to see him?

But at least she *had* said she'd see him. Cade shook his head and took another drink of his bourbon. For the last eight months, she'd been giving him the runaround. If he got answers from her at three in the morning, he'd take them.

Kylie fiddled with the latch on one of her cases and then glanced over at him through thick lashes. "Can I ask you a question?"

"Of course."

"It's nosy."

He smiled, curious as to what she'd ask. Was she going to flirt with him more? Was it disturbing how much he liked that idea? "I don't mind—ask away."

"Is Daphne expecting you?"

That . . . wasn't what he'd expected her to ask. "She is. She asked me to come tonight. Had her assistant send me tickets."

"Ah." Kylie shook her head as if to clear it. "Right. I'm sure she'll be thrilled to see you."

But she didn't look convinced. In fact, it looked as if she were avoiding his gaze. Cade's stomach clenched and he wanted to ask Kylie if Daphne was still having problems. But he also didn't want to force Kylie to choose between her employer and him, so he simply drained his bourbon and went back to the bar for another.

And he waited for Daphne. He was already here, after all. Might as well see what shook out.

By the time the crowd roared and the lights flashed backstage to indicate that things were wrapping up outside, Cade had downed a few too many bourbons. It wasn't like him, but anything involving Daphne made him lose all common sense. He shook his head and drained his glass again, then set it on the bar. No more.

He watched Kylie instead. He could watch her all night, really. She was lively and feminine and cheery all the time. She refused all drinks and offers of drugs with a polite smile, and didn't seem bothered by the fact that they were around her and she couldn't—or wouldn't—partake.

Why couldn't Daphne be more like her? Settled, content, and fun to be around? He was drawn to Kylie repeatedly throughout the night, but had to force himself not to continue bothering her when it was clear she was one of Daphne's crew and on the job. But he liked her. Just her warm, friendly presence here soothed him, and he was definitely feeling a little rattled overall.

People began to flood through the back doors and Cade got to his feet, straightening his tie and then shoving his hands into the worn pockets of his sport jacket. He tried to catch a glimpse of Daphne amongst the crowd of sweaty people flooding into the room, dressed in wild stage costumes, but the colored wigs and towels being flung about made it hard for him to decipher who was who.

"Everyone out," an assistant bellowed. "Everyone clear the room to let Miss Petty change! Go wait in the hall. Press, that includes you."

Just like that, the crowd filed toward the door. Even the bartender got up from the bar and left. Cade moved forward to Kylie's side, because he didn't want to be shuffled out with the rest of the crew. He was a personal friend, damn it. Daphne'd invited him. He wasn't part of the riffraff.

"Is it necessary for me to go wait in the hall, too? I know Daphne's expecting me."

Kylie bit one of her plump red lips, and again, he had to fight back a surge of lust at the sight of her. Why was she so utterly perfect in his eyes? Or was it just the alcohol and the fact that he was about to see Daphne that had his dick constantly springing to attention? "I'm not sure," Kylie said. "She might not want to see you just yet."

"I've seen her in all kinds of situations," Cade told her. Hell, he'd gone skinny dipping with Daphne when they were kids, and they'd been each other's first sex partner. "I'm pretty sure I can handle her sweaty and messy."

Again, Kylie bit her lip, and then she gestured for him to sit in a nearby chair. "Wait here and I'll ask Snoopy."

"Snoopy?"

"Her assistant." Kylie gave him a dimpled smile before turning and heading off, and he tilted his head to watch her ass move as she left, which was probably terrible of him because he was here waiting for Daphne.

Had to be the bourbon. Had to.

He watched as Kylie approached another woman and talked. The other woman looked worried and wrung her hands, then shook her head. Kylie continued talking even as people moved through the room. The assistant looked nearly in tears, and she kept gesturing about something. What was going on?

Cade got his answer a few moments later. "Marco?" A familiar voice bellowed. "Where the fuck is Marco?" The double doors leading to the stage slammed open and down came Daphne, stick thin and looking wilted in her now-sweaty costume. Her black wig was askew and her makeup was smeared on her face. Her eyes looked hollow and even as she thumped down the stairs, he could tell she was unwell.

His heart sank to his feet.

She also looked pissed. "Where the fuck is Marco?" Daphne asked in that shrill voice again. "I'm done acting like the performing monkey. Now where are my fucking drugs?"

And with that, ice formed in Cade's belly.

Had he hoped that Daphne had changed? He should have known—she *never* changed. Anger, frustration, and disappointment warred for dominance in Cade's mind.

Mostly, though? He was tired of this. He was tired of Daphne's shit. Her empty promises. Her unwillingness to give up the drugs.

This wasn't what he'd signed on for, that was for damn sure.

———

The air in the room had gotten incredibly tense, or so it seemed to Kylie. She held a small fan in front of Daphne's face as the singer guzzled ice water and tried to stop sweating. She was in an odd mood—a mix of exuberance at how the performance had gone and flashes of crankiness. She was also unable to sit still, no matter how much Kylie chided her. Kylie had cleaned Daphne's face of her performance makeup, but if she wanted a fresh face of makeup for her interviews, she'd need to stop fidgeting and stop sweating.

And neither seemed to be happening anytime soon.

Even now, Daphne's foot hammered impatiently on the floor. "You said I could see Marco," she snapped at Kylie.

"Your manager said you could see Marco," Kylie corrected, blotting at the sweat on Daphne's forehead. "I need to fix your makeup first."

"Yeah, well, I need my fix. Why's it so hot in here?" She fanned her face and twitched in her chair.

This was clearly going to be a losing battle. "Let me see what I can do to get you out of the chair, at least."

The pop star was too jumpy for delicate work, so Kylie settled for foundation and some airbrushed makeup across Daphne's face, and Kylie highlighted her eyes and put on a bit of peachy gloss so the pop star looked somewhat healthy. There wasn't much she could do for Daphne's veiny, bruised arms, so she just ignored them. "Okay. Done with you."

"Great," Daphne said, sliding out of her chair. "Now we can party all night long." She winked at Kylie, her good mood returning. "You want some blow, Fat Marilyn?"

"I'll pass," Kylie said. She nodded her head at the man in the suit that sat on the couch—Cade. "Your friend's been waiting there for you for a few hours." *And he's cute. And he brought you a pink car. And you need to hit that like, yesterday.*

Daphne waved at Cade from afar. "Hey, babe!"

He got to his feet, his expression concerned. "Daph—"

"Can't talk right now," she told him, heading for the door. "I have media interviews and then I have to find Marco. I'll catch up with you in a bit!"

"Wait," he began, reaching out to her.

She gave him a little wave and then bounded out the door

of the greenroom. Immediately the crowd waiting outside began to murmur, and Kylie was left alone with Cade. His expression was stricken.

Poor guy. He was too nice to be treated like this. Too nice, and far too yummy.

"I'm sure she'll be back soon," she told him, keeping a bright smile on her face. "Hang in there."

He watched the door for a moment longer, then shoved his hands in his pockets and looked over at Kylie. "Before or after she gets her drugs, do you suppose?"

Ouch. She winced, hating that he could see the truth even through Kylie's sunny words. "I'm sorry. I don't know."

"Yeah. Me either." He rubbed his face and then gave her a faint, unhappy smile. "Join me in a drink?"

She shook her head. "I should probably stay sober, just in case she needs me."

A wry, self-deprecating look crossed his face. "Funny, I thought the same thing when I got here. Now I think I need a really tall, really strong drink."

He went back to the bar and helped himself.

FIVE

Marco must have given Daphne some good shit, Kylie decided with a yawn. It was nearly three in the morning and she was still partying hard. In the center of the green-room, she danced to music and hung off of Marco's well-muscled arm, laughing. Her other dancers were partying with her, and almost everyone had a bottle of some sort of alcohol in their hands, never mind what they were running off to the bathroom to snort. The greenroom had filled up again, and most of the behind-the-scenes staff had headed back to the hotel for some sleep before the buses left in the morning.

Cade was still seated at the bar, by himself, slowly nursing a drink. He watched Daphne, but never made a move to approach her.

Kylie had stuck around despite the late hour, because Cade was still there and she felt, well, sorry for him. Here was this great guy, waiting on Daphne, clearly insane about her, and she was blowing him off to party with Marco because Marco had good drugs. It wasn't like Marco wouldn't have drugs every night of the tour, Kylie thought grumpily. Heck, it wasn't like Marco wasn't at Daphne's side constantly since she'd hired him as one of her dancers.

But ignoring Cade, who was clearly there for Daphne and only Daphne? It bothered Kylie. Here was this perfect, nice, sexy man and Daphne was just throwing him away. Maybe she had a soft heart for good-looking guys or maybe she was just fixated on how nice he'd been to her. Either way, she didn't like it.

"I need another hit," Daphne called out, laughing and twirling around Marco. She wrapped her arms about his neck and planted a kiss on his mouth. "Come on, I'll be good to you."

Marco tilted his head, clearly pretending to consider it. "I don't know . . ."

Daphne gave another wild giggle and dropped to her knees in front of him. "I'll be *really* good—"

The crowd erupted into laughter.

Cade jerked to his feet. He snatched his keys off of the bar—the keys that had a bow on them, ready to gift Daphne with a present if she'd only paid the slightest bit of attention to him—and headed for the door.

Kylie's heart clenched and she grabbed her purse, following after him. He'd been drinking for most of the night and she couldn't let him leave. Not like this. Not without someone else driving him home to make sure he was safe.

Not without someone apologizing for Daphne's shitty behavior and letting him know that they cared that he'd been hurt.

She ran and caught up with him down the long hall leading out to the parking lot. His shoulders were slumped, but he was walking in a straight line, at least. It didn't matter—she knew he'd drank quite a bit. "Cade?" she called. "Are you okay?"

He kept walking, his hands shoved into his pockets.

"I'm sorry," she said, falling into step next to him. "I'm told she's not like this when she's clean."

He paused and looked over at her. "How long have you worked for Daphne?"

"A month now."

"Have you ever seen her clean?" There was a wealth of pain in his eyes.

Kylie bit her lip. Should she lie to make him feel better?

A faint smile tugged at his mouth. "Your hesitation tells me everything I need to know."

"I'm sorry," she said again, even as he began to walk again. She started to walk, too, unwilling to let him leave.

"Why are you sorry? You haven't touched a thing all night. I noticed that, just like I noticed her behavior."

So he'd been watching her? Kylie's skin prickled with forbidden pleasure. "I feel like someone should try and apologize for her."

He laughed and shook his head. "That someone should be Daphne, but we both know that won't happen."

Kylie said nothing, just kept walking alongside him. If anyone needed a friend tonight, it was Cade, and she wasn't leaving his side. Daphne had enough sycophants—and drugs—to keep her busy until dawn.

"Thing is," Cade said in a low voice, "I know Daphne. I know how exciting and warm and wonderful she can be when she's clean. She's brilliant. I think that's why I've always loved her." He looked over at Kylie, and there was sadness in his beautiful eyes. "But that's not the woman I saw tonight. I'm starting to wonder if she's gone for good."

"Don't give up," Kylie said. Her heart ached for him, for the pain she saw in his eyes.

"I've held on for years wondering when it's the right time to give up," Cade said, voice soft. "I'm getting tired of wondering. I think it's time to move on with my life, and let Daphne go. For good."

"She's still going to need friends," Kylie cautioned. "I imagine when she wakes up from whatever it is she's doing to herself, she's going to need people she can trust."

"If any of them are left." Cade shook his head and looked over at Kylie. "I've known her for so long. I shouldn't be surprised by anything she does and yet every time I see her . . . it still hurts."

Kylie ached for him. Impulsively, she laced her arm through his and gave his arm a little hug. She didn't know him well enough to be on hugging terms, she suspected, but she knew a person in pain when she saw one and she couldn't leave him out to dry. "You're a good man for even trying," she told him.

He gave her a sleepy smile. "Or a stubborn one."

"Or that," she said, smiling back.

The pink car was all alone in the near-empty parking lot. "That's my ride," Cade said.

Kylie frowned. "How many drinks did you have?"

"I'm fine," he told her. Then, he pulled the keys out of his pocket, fumbled, and dropped them on the ground.

"Bullshit you're fine," Kylie retorted, leaning over and scooping up the keys before he could. "How many drinks did you have again?"

His eyes narrowed at her, but she wasn't fooled. She'd thought they were bright and shiny because he was upset over Daphne—which he probably was. But it was more likely that he was just wasted and hiding it really well.

"I had several drinks," he admitted. "And normally I'd say it's irresponsible to attempt to drive back to my hotel with as much as I've had to drink, but after what I've seen tonight, I still think I'm far more responsible than anyone else I've seen."

And he gave her a dopey, gorgeous grin that told her, yup, he was plastered.

"What am I, chopped liver?" Kylie retorted, unable to keep an equally silly smile off of her face. God, he was cute.

"You are entirely too good for this motley crew tonight."

Sweet man. She held the keys away from him when he reached for them. "Well, this entirely too good woman is driving you back to your hotel, because she hates the thought of you as a smear on the pavement."

He snorted. "I can drive myself. Seriously. There's no need to babysit me."

It was on the tip of her tongue that she'd been doing a lot of babysitting tonight, and what was one more? But she suspected that it would hurt him more than make him laugh. He was putting on a brave face, but she knew that Daphne's behavior had to be bothering him more than he let on. "Just consider it a friend looking out for a friend. Now, get in." She clicked on the remote and the car's security lights flashed.

"Really, Kylie, I'm fine."

"I insist."

One corner of his mouth curved up and then he was giving her another panty-melting smile. "Who am I to resist such a beautiful woman?"

Um, an equally beautiful—if not more so—man? But she didn't say it aloud. At least he was getting into the darn car. Kylie got in on the driver's side and put the keys in the ignition, then adjusted the mirrors. Cade was several inches taller than her, so she had to pull the seat forward, too. But when she was buckled in, she looked over at him. "Ready to go?"

He was gazing at her, a thoughtful look on his face.

"Cade? Buckle up?" When he just continued to study her, she wondered if he was an "out of it" kind of drunk. He probably wouldn't remember this in the morning, any of it. So she reached across the car and pulled his seat belt over his legs. Her hands accidentally brushed over his groin, and she jerked away. "Oh, God, sorry!"

"S'okay," he told her, voice strangely husky. "I'll get it."

She waited as he fumbled with the belt, but eventually was able to get it snapped in place. That done, she nodded at him and turned the car on. "Okay. Now, what hotel are you staying at?"

"Peninsula."

Of course. It was only the most expensive hotel in Chicago. Daphne's crew was staying at a chain hotel while Daphne herself stayed someplace decidedly more upscale.

"All right," Kylie said, easing the car forward. "Let's get you home, then."

The drive to the hotel was an easy one—even the Chicago streets weren't terrible at three in the morning. She pulled up to the front of the massive hotel and the valet immediately stepped out to open her door. She grabbed her purse and then hurried over to Cade's side. He'd been quiet on the drive, and she wondered if he was half-asleep.

But he got out of the car just fine. He leaned on Kylie as they headed into the hotel, and then draped an arm over her shoulders. And since he was tipsy, she allowed it. She was sure he didn't mean anything by it. Guys like him didn't claim girls like her.

"Floor?" she asked him as they went through the big doors of the hotel.

"Eighteen."

She nodded and steered them toward the elevator. The doors shut and they were alone. She looked up at Cade, only to see him gazing down at her with that same glazed fascination. It was a little intimidating, and she wasn't quite sure what he was thinking. She patted his chest with her free hand and smiled up at him, trying to make everything seem more casual than it really was. "Hanging in there?"

"I'm great, actually," he murmured.

"Not falling asleep?"

"Not sleepy at all."

They got up to the eighteenth floor and she gazed around her in vague wonder. There . . . weren't many doors on this floor. "Which room is yours?" These looked suspiciously like the penthouse suites. Which shouldn't have been surprising, given that he was trying to gift Daphne Petty with a car on a whim. But seeing all this opulence made her a little self-conscious. Just another reminder that the guy draped over her shoulders was way out of her league.

Cade pointed at a door down the hall and she led him in that direction, noticing that he seemed to be leaning on her more and more the further they walked. They got to the door and she looked at him expectantly. "Keycard?"

"In my front pocket." He gave her an interested look. "Don't suppose I could convince you to reach in and get it for me?"

Good lord, was Cade flirting with her? The man must have been truly plastered. "That's very sweet," she told him. "But get your own card."

"Can't blame a man for trying," he murmured.

"You're drunk," she told him. "You wouldn't hit on me sober."

"Just because I'm drunk doesn't mean I don't have taste," he told her. But he fished his keycard out of one pocket, winked at her, and then slid it across the scanner.

The door chimed open and Cade pulled his arm off her shoulders, leaving her feeling oddly bereft. "Want to come in for a moment?"

She hesitated. Going into a strange man's hotel room at three in the morning? Probably a bad idea. "I really shouldn't."

"Just for a bit? I could use the company."

Kylie waited on his doorstep a moment longer. She wasn't thrilled about heading into the wilds of Chicago late at night by her lonesome, and she'd always wanted to see a penthouse. And Cade was harmless. He wouldn't attack her . . . no matter how much she might wish it, heh. "Just for a minute," she cautioned him. "And then I should get going."

"You want a drink?" he asked, stepping into the suite. "I'm sure I have a minibar around here somewhere."

She followed him in, closing the door behind her and trying not to stare at his hotel room.

It was . . . crazy. Crazy and ridiculous and utterly opulent. The beige carpet was thick underneath her shoes and the furniture shiny and new. Art—real art, not ugly hotel prints—hung on the walls, illuminated by their own personal spotlights. A pair of sliding doors led off to another "wing" of his suite, and as she stepped into the living room, she chuckled. "Is that a piano?"

"A baby grand for all of your hotel needs," he agreed, approaching with two small bottles of alcohol in hand. "I personally have never gotten to a hotel room and thought, damn it, where is a piano when you need one, but apparently someone does."

She laughed again and refused the drink he offered her. "No thanks."

"You're not driving back," he cajoled. "I insist on a cab this late. And I'd be a sad sack if I was a lonely drunk. With you here, I'm not quite so lonely."

His words warmed her a bit, and she took the tiny bottle of Patron from him, twisting the tiny cap off. He did the same, and held his bottle out to her in a toast. "Bottoms up," she told him, and then sipped it. The alcohol had a delicious burn to it. She continued to sip it, wandering around the room. "How much does a place like this cost a night?"

"You don't want to know," he told her. "Actually, I'm not even sure I know. An assistant handled it for me."

She headed through the living room—his freaking hotel room was a mess of rooms—and peered out to the balcony. "Oh, wow. This is huge."

"Shall we go out?" He opened the door and gestured.

And even though Kylie was a bit tired and she knew Cade should head to bed, she went out on the balcony anyhow, because when was she going to ever do this again? The balcony had marble tile, and elegantly maintained potted plants dotted along the railing, interspersed with heavy wooden furniture. The city looked vast from here, and she stared at the view in awe. "This is gorgeous."

"Isn't it?" Cade smiled out at the buildings, his golden hair ruffling in the night breeze. He moved to stand beside her, his presence warm. "I have to admit I ask for this room simply because of the balcony."

"I don't blame you. This place looks big enough for a party."

"Kind of sad that it's just me." His tone was melancholy, and her heart twinged again.

She lifted her tiny bottle of Patron back to her lips and drained the entire thing in one fell swoop, and her head began to buzz. "I'm sorry."

"Why do you keep saying you're sorry?" He gazed out at the Chicago night sky for a moment before turning back to look at her. "None of this was your fault."

"I know," she told him, and crossed her arms under her breasts, tucking them close to stay warm. Her thin shirt wasn't exactly made for evenings outside. "I just wish things would have turned out differently for you. You're such a good guy."

To her surprise, his mouth twisted to hear that, his expression souring. "That's the problem. No one ever seems to care how the nice guy feels, huh?" He tilted his head and studied her for so long that she began to feel self-conscious. "Except you."

Her hair was blowing into her face, and she impatiently pushed it aside, thinking. What could she possibly say to him that wouldn't sound stupid? *I noticed you all night? I can't help but be interested because you're the perfect guy and Daphne's throwing you away? I wish you'd notice me?*

None of those phrases would come out of her mouth without embarrassing her, so she stood there, mutely staring at him, this perfect, wonderful man who deserved much better.

"It's funny," Cade said, stepping closer to Kylie. His hair blew in the breeze and for a moment, he looked like a fallen angel in the shadows. "Tonight, when I saw Daphne, do you know what the first thing in my mind was? It wasn't that I was glad to see her, or worried that she was sick. Because I expected those things. It was disappointment . . . that she didn't look like you."

Kylie's brows drew together. *Huh?* "I think you're drunk, Cade."

"I'm drunk," he agreed. "Because I'd never say this otherwise. But you're utterly, insanely sexy and I've been completely attracted to you since the moment I saw you, even when I know I shouldn't be. And here I am, up on the balcony in the middle of the night after what has been a miserable experience, and all I can think is that I'm not all that miserable, because I like watching you." His fingers reached out and brushed a lock of hair off her forehead, tucked it gently behind her ear. "And it makes me wish I was one of those guys that didn't give a shit about anyone but themselves, because I'd ask you to stay the night with me."

Her eyes widened. His fingers traced the curve of her ear, sending shivers down her spine. He wasn't moving away. His speech wasn't slurred. He . . . couldn't be that drunk, could he? To be propositioning Kylie? "W-what do you mean, stay the night with you?"

"It's late and you're gorgeous," he said bluntly, cupping her rounded cheek in his hand. "And I'm wondering if we should both live a little. Have an incredibly intense one-night stand and not think about it in the morning. What do you say?"

She stared up at his handsome face. His fingers were warm on her skin, his touch making her every nerve ending sit up and pay attention. She wanted to say yes. It had been at least two years since she'd dated someone. The last man she'd cared for was Jerred. And Jerred had done a really great job of hiding just how much of a dick he was until the last minute. He'd known just what to say and how to act to shatter Kylie's fragile self-confidence, to the point that she hadn't wanted to date again after him. Going on tour made it easy to skip personal relationships. It meant her schedule wasn't her own, and it meant being away from home for long periods of time. And while on tour, she was surrounded by so many fit, lean, sexy dancers (or pop stars) that no one paid attention to curvy Kylie. Normally it didn't bother her, and she was content to blend in with the wallpaper.

But tonight . . . wouldn't it be nice to have a torrid fling with a man who wanted her for her? Scratch the itch for sex that desperately needed scratching?

Especially with the handsome Cade, who seemed to embody everything she liked in a man?

But Kylie wasn't that kind of girl. Not really. Even though

she might dream of being reckless and wild for a night, she was responsible. She'd be needed back at the tour HQ by noon so they could roll out to the next city. The smart thing would be to go back to her own hotel, get a few hours of shut-eye, and try to forget about tonight. Forget about Cade's sad eyes, his wind-blown curls, the way he'd flirted with her in the coffee shop before the night turned into a bad dream.

Because she knew how things would turn out. He'd wake up in the morning, find himself next to her fat ass, be embarrassed, make excuses, and then they'd both feel awkward until Kylie disappeared.

So she shook her head and patted the front of his jacket. "Cade," she said softly. "You're hurting. That's why you're propositioning me—"

"It's true," Cade said. His arm—strong and firm—went to her waist and he pulled her against him, close enough that her breasts pushed up against his chest. "I'm hurting. I'm fucking wrecked over how Daphne's acting. I'm so disappointed in her I can hardly stand it, and I think, for the first time in ten years, I'm really truly done with her. But that doesn't mean that I'm not attracted to you. It's the opposite, really. I couldn't stop looking at you at the coffee shop, and I told myself it was okay to look, because I'd never see you again. Except I did. And I stared at you all night in the greenroom. Every time you laughed, every time you smiled, it turned me on. I hate that it all seems to be happening tonight, but I'm not going to think too hard about it. I want you." He leaned in and gently kissed her mouth.

She gasped, surprised at the feel of his mouth against hers. She . . . hadn't expected that. And yet, she was filled with the desire for more. The kiss had been way too brief.

His thumb grazed her lower lip, his gaze on her face. "I want you so much I can hardly stand it. It's not just because you happen to be here and I'm horny. It's because it's Kylie here, Kylie pressed up against my chest, and Kylie that makes my dick hard every time she smiles. Will you stay the night with me?"

She gazed up at him, considering. Part of her was screaming that this was stupid. That he was hurting and rebounding
from Daphne's antics. That if he was playing her just to get
back at Daphne, he was the most sincere-seeming man ever.
Because everything he did made it seem like he truly wanted
her. From the way he watched her mouth as she licked her lips,
to the way he pulled her body against his, it truly did seem as
if Cade was attracted to her.

To *her*. Kylie Daniels. AKA, Fat Marilyn.

And really . . . what would it hurt to stay the night with
Cade? He'd made it clear that this would be a fling. A one and
done. A gorgeous guy wanted her for just one night of hot sex?
No strings attached, no worries, no relationships, no nothing?

How was there possibly a downside to this?

There probably was, Kylie's conscience told her. Daphne
was her boss, and she was playing with fire to even think
about hooking up with Cade.

Even so . . . hadn't Daphne tossed him away earlier
tonight? Hadn't she made it quite clear that she was more
interested in partying and getting stoned than spending time
with Cade?

And Cade was gorgeous and Kylie was basking in his
attention and that oh-so-brief kiss and the Patron was mud-
dying her head and it was late and she possibly wasn't thinking too clearly herself.

Because she wanted this man, and he wanted her.

What could possibly go wrong with that?

So she bit her lip, leaned forward, and pressed her mouth
to his in a silent answer to his question.

SIX

Kissing Cade Archer was better than ice cream. Sweet, creamy chocolate ice cream with hot fudge dripping down the sides? Tasty, but not nearly as appealing to her senses as the warm breath of the man kissing her. Of his tongue slicking against her own in response to her kiss. Of his mouth opening wider to accept her tongue. Of the groan he made when their mouths locked, and the way his hand stole down to her ass and clenched her against him as if she were beautiful and sexy and he wanted her like he wanted no other woman.

And when her mouth parted from his, a small, dreamy sigh escaped her.

"Want to go inside?" Cade murmured, and cupped her face with his long fingers.

"I shouldn't."

"The question wasn't whether or not you should, but if you wanted to," he said, and one of his fingers traced her full lips again.

She took that fingertip between her teeth and licked the tip. "More than anything."

"Then let's not overthink it. Let's just feel for a night."

That sounded kind of wonderful. She nodded and he gave her another quick kiss, then took her by the hand and led her back into the hotel room. He flicked off lights as he went, leading her through the maze of rooms.

And then they were in the opulent bedroom. The walls were a soft warm wood, the drapes a pale cream color. The bed was a sumptuous king with a quilted white headboard and dozens of pillows tossed onto it. It looked like something out of a dream. "This is like no hotel room I've ever stayed in before."

"It's nice, isn't it? You should see the bathroom."

"Can I?"

He gestured at a door off of the bedroom. "Be my guest."

She wandered in and gasped at the sight. It was beyond luxury—a rain shower; a sunken, jetted tub; thick, plush carpets—it had everything. She peeked at a door off to one side and laughed to see exercise equipment. "My goodness. This place is bigger than my last apartment."

"Mmm. Then I'm glad you're here to enjoy it."

He pulled her against him, pressing her back against his front. His arms went around her waist and he nuzzled at her neck, brushing her hair aside and kissing her nape.

Kylie shivered. Her instinct was to draw Cade's hands away from her waist so he wouldn't figure out how fat she was—but that was stupid, of course. He knew just how big she was. She wasn't a slim girl. Her breasts were big, her hips were big, and there was no hiding that. So she forced herself to relax in his arms. If he hated the way she looked, well, she'd never see him again, would she?

So she turned around, wrapped her arms around his neck, and pulled him in for a long, scorching kiss. Her tongue played against his, then flicked against his lips. "I've seen enough in here. I think we should go back to the bedroom."

Cade groaned and gripped her ass in his hands. "I couldn't agree more." But he didn't stop kissing her. Instead, he walked backward in small, slow steps, heading back toward the bedroom. And she giggled against his mouth, still kissing him in return.

Mouths locked the entire time, they staggered back to the bedroom. She accidentally stepped on his foot and he winced. "Sorry," she breathed.

"I can carry you the rest of the way," he told her between kisses. His blue eyes were heavily lidded with passion and fringed by dark blond lashes, and she couldn't stop staring at that sultry gaze. He was gorgeous, right down to his sinfully pouty mouth. No man should have a mouth that pretty, Kylie decided. It was just darn wrong.

And then she realized what that pretty mouth was saying. "Carry? Me?"

He nodded and moved to put a hand behind her legs, and she quickly stumbled out of his grip. "Wait, no!"

"What's wrong?"

"You must be really drunk if you think you can carry me," she told him. She was a nice, solid size eighteen, and there was no fudging that number. "I don't look like Daphne."

"Thank fucking Christ for that," he said, and put his hands at the sides of her neck and drew her in for another searing kiss. "I love the way you look," he murmured against her mouth. "I love your lush body. It's one of the reasons I'm attracted to you." His hands slid to her shoulders, and then down her arms, and he studied her with pleasure. "Your breasts. Your hips. Your curves. Your softness. Fuck, you're pretty."

All right, this one-night stand was going to be more fun than she thought. Her hands went to the buttons of his shirt, undoing them. "I want to see *your* body."

"Only if I get to see yours," he told her, a cocky smile curving his mouth. "One piece of clothing for one piece of clothing."

"That seems fair," she teased. A game took the tension out of undressing in front of a stranger. "But I get to pick your item of clothing."

"As long as I get to pick yours."

"All right. Can I go first?"

"Always." His eyes gleamed. "Ladies first."

She tapped her lip, pretending to consider things. "Well, let's start with the basics before we get to the good stuff. Off with your jacket."

Cade made a big show of removing his jacket, humming a bawdy song under his breath and pretending to strip it off for an imaginary crowd. He swung it over his head and then tossed it to the ground, while Kylie laughed and clapped her hands.

How much of this was the real Cade and how much was alcoholic silliness, she wondered? Either way, she loved it. She was having a blast. She usually wasn't ultra-playful in bed, being too self-conscious to really let her hair down. But how could she possibly be worried about how she looked when this drunk, heavenly man was pretending to strip for her, complete with burbled music?

It was freaking adorable.

"Your turn," Cade said, wiggling his eyebrows at her. He tapped his mouth with one long finger, pretending to consider her clothing, and Kylie raised her arms above her head and gave a little wiggle of her own, modeling her clothing. "How about . . . your bra?"

"You can't ask for my bra yet," she told him. "It's under my other clothes."

"I don't remember us establishing rules, my pretty." He pretended to twirl a mustache like an evil villain, and she couldn't help but laugh again. "Now. Bra."

With a faked sigh, she pulled her arms through her sleeves and began to wriggle around inside the cocoon her shirt made, unhooking the six industrial-strength clasps at the back of her bra. A bra for larger boobs wasn't an ultra-feminine, delicate thing—not if it wanted to get the job done. Kylie's bra was big and strong and sufficient. Eventually, she worked it off and held it out of her shirt with one arm, hoping he wouldn't notice that it was a plain beige and not something wild or sexy.

She bet Daphne wore wild and sexy. Which made her worry.

But Cade just wiped his lips, his gaze on her now-loose breasts in her shirt. "I think my mouth just watered."

And suddenly everything was okay again. She grinned and tossed her bra down on his jacket and then slid her arms back through the sleeves of her tight black shirt, not minding that her big breasts were bouncing with every move she made. "My turn, is it?"

"Might I suggest a lovely sock? I have two of them." His voice was teasing, but she noticed his gaze was glued to her loose breasts in her shirt, and it made her nipples harden with excitement to see his need so blatantly. Heat pulsed between her thighs and she fought the urge to press them tighter together.

She considered his clothing, instead. He wore his button-up shirt, the collar open and loose, and a pair of slacks, socks, and shoes. Underneath, she assumed, he wore boxers. Or briefs? She wasn't entirely sure, but she didn't want to spoil the anticipation by going straight for the payday. Even now, she could see the bulge in the front of his trousers increasing and she licked her lips with anticipation.

And to her surprise, he groaned, his gaze hazy with lust again. "Can I just say I love that mouth of yours? God almighty."

Kylie licked her lips again, teasing him, and then gestured at his shirt. "Off with that. I want to see your chest."

He removed it quickly, less playful than before, and now she could see the firm outline of his cock against his pants, thick and erect. And oh, rather stunning if she was a judge of these sorts of things. He was definitely well equipped.

Yep, tonight was a good call after all.

Cade stripped off his shirt, then quickly removed his undershirt and Kylie sucked in a breath at the sight of his bared chest. "Oh wow," she told him, unable to stop herself from moving forward and running her hands over his sculpted body. "You're gorgeous." Daphne, she decided, was an utter fool for passing up this delicious man. Cade's body was long and lean, his chest lightly brushed with tawny hairs across his etched pectorals and down his belly. There was an ugly black tattoo of skulls and such on his left bicep, but she ignored it in favor of running her hands down his chest. She was actually touching a man with a six-pack. She, Kylie Daniels of the wide butt and even wider hips, was getting to put her hands—and soon, her mouth—on male six-pack. "I have to say, this is a fun game," she breathed, dipping the tip of one finger against his belly button.

He groaned, closing his eyes at her touch. "Fun . . . and torture all at once."

She knew what he meant. Now *her* mouth was watering. "Your turn, I believe."

His heavy-lidded eyes considered her. "Can I touch?"

"Not yet," she murmured, even though she was running her hands up and down his gorgeous chest. But seriously, how could she possibly stop caressing a chest as perfect as his? That would just be masochism.

"All right, then," he murmured. "I think I know what I want to come off of you next."

"What's that?" she asked, breathless from touching his skin. He was so warm and smelled so good.

He leaned in and his lips brushed against her ear. "Your panties."

And Kylie moaned. This man did not play fair. "But they're under my pants."

"That's not my problem, is it?" His voice was like silk, caressing her skin.

She shivered, her mind racing as she tried to see a way to prolong the tease, to remove her panties without giving up all the goods. But she couldn't think of anything. It didn't help that her mind was mush thanks to Cade's nearness and the Patron she'd drank.

And then, because she couldn't think of any way to save herself, she sighed and stepped out of her shoes, then undid the button on her pants. "I'm thinking this is a two-for-one that you're getting here," she told him, turning her back to draw the tease out a little. Kylie unzipped her pants and then, bracing herself, tugged them down over her hips and let them fall to the floor. Now she stood in nothing but her panties and her shirt, and her panties were a cheeky design with lace at the seams, so they exposed more of her pale ass than covered it. Which . . . hadn't mattered this morning when she'd dressed. She'd liked the panties due to the fact that they left no visible line under her clothing.

Now? Well, her butt cheeks were exposed in all their pale, fleshy glory.

Cade groaned again and moved toward her. "You have a gorgeous ass. I'm dying to touch it."

"Hey now," she told him, teasing. Then she wiggled out of his grip, and then out of her panties, too. "No one said anything about touching, did they?" She could play hardball, too.

"At some point, I'm going to want to touch," he murmured. "And kiss. And caress. And lick." His voice dropped to a near whisper, and he dragged out each word as he leaned in, close but not touching. "And suck . . ."

And now she trembled with want. Her mind was on fire with the potential of skin being licked and kissed and nibbled and sucked. She turned to face Cade. "Your turn. I need your underwear, too."

He was standing so close to her that she was a little surprised she couldn't feel his cock pressing against her skin. She longed to press her body against his, to feel his warmth and his hardness against her. This game was going on far too long, and she was aching and needy and wet between her thighs with sheer anticipation.

Cade's gaze was on her face, and she kept her eyes locked on his. It was like a titillating dance between them. They didn't break eye contact even as she heard his zipper, heard the rustle of fabric as they fell to the floor, and watched his mouth curve into a sexy smile as he tugged his boxers off. Since he was down to nothing, it was only fair that she finish undressing, so, eyes still locked to his, she tugged her shirt off.

And then she was naked in front of him, and he was naked except for his socks, and the time for playing was past. As if on the same wavelength, Kylie reached for him at the same time as he reached for her, and then they were kissing fiercely, mouths locked together. Her breasts pressed against his bare chest and now she could feel the length of him, hot, hard and erect against her belly.

She kissed him again and he tasted like alcohol and man and all the delicious things she'd been longing for. "Cade," she moaned against him.

"Fuck, I love the feel of your breasts pressed up against me," he murmured against her mouth. "Screw the whole 'no touching' thing. I want to touch all of you."

And before she could come up with a teasing protest, his hands cupped her ass and he pinned her hips against his in a blatant show of just what he intended.

All the breath escaped her lungs, and Kylie could do little more than moan a response.

Cade took charge. He continued kissing her, but began to steer them toward the large bed. When the backs of her knees hit the mattress, he gave her a little push of encouragement and she went onto her back, only to have his body press against hers a moment later. The kissing continued as he moved over her, and then his knees were between her thighs and he tugged one of her calves around his hip.

She moaned, clinging to his shoulders.

"You're beautiful," he murmured between kisses, his mouth pressing on her neck. "So many perfect things about your body. Look at these breasts." His thumb rolled her nipple, enticing a gasp of pleasure from her throat. "Look at how big and luscious they are, with beautiful pink nipples."

His hand on her was the best thing she'd ever felt. She arched against his touch, pressing her breast into his hand, eager for more. She wanted to cry out in pleasure, to demand that he lick and bite and suck like a wild animal, but shyness took over.

"That feels really good," she told him in a soft voice, and

then winced at herself and the dumb words. *Gee, really good, Kylie! Way to encourage him.* Her hand crept to the curls of his golden hair, and she couldn't help but drag her fingers through them, adding to her sensory pleasure.

"Are your breasts sensitive, Kylie?"

She nodded in response, and whimpered when he leaned down and took one aching nipple into his mouth.

"Then that makes teasing them even more fun," he murmured against her skin, then licked one tip sensuously.

Kylie cried out, digging her nails into his shoulder. "Oh, Jesus, do that again."

"I plan on it," he murmured, nuzzling the other breast. His fingers teased the peak of one while his mouth worked the other to a tight peak. And just when Kylie thought she'd come out of her skin with need, his hand left her breast and slipped between her legs and brushed through the curls of her pussy. "Goddamn, you're wet, aren't you?"

"Cade," she moaned, unable to articulate anything but his name. She was existing in a pool of delicious need, and her body was desperate for release.

"I can't wait any longer," he murmured as he kissed his way back up to her mouth. His lips were urgent on her own, and when his tongue speared into her mouth, she licked it in encouragement.

She didn't want to wait any longer, either. "Yes, please."

And even though she'd been encouraging him, she was still shocked when he pushed her legs apart a little further and sank into her in one swift stroke. It was on the tip of her tongue to ask about a condom, but then he put a hand under her hip, raising her at an angle, and stuffed a pillow underneath her bottom. He stroked in again.

And her entire body came alive.

Oh God, that must have been her G-spot. When he sank into her, he pressed against something that made her crazy with need, and her skin prickled at the surge of pleasure. A hoarse little gasp escaped her.

"Is that the spot?" he murmured, his breathing as rapid and harsh as her own.

Full of wonder, Kylie could do nothing but nod.

He clasped her hips tight and began to pound into her with sure, deep thrusts. Every single one felt better than the last, and before she knew it, her toes were curling and she was clenching him tight with her legs, and moaning like a wild woman. Her hips rose to meet his thrusts, and oh mercy, that felt even better.

"Close?" he asked, pumping into her again. He gave his hips a little swivel that made her entire body clench up in response, and she clutched at the blankets, trying to brace herself.

And oh, sweet Jesus, she *was* close. He was thrusting into her like a jackhammer, moving so hard that the bed shook and her breasts bounced with every motion. And it felt incredible. She'd never felt so good.

If this was impulsive, drunk sex, she was all for it.

His hand left her hip and began to tease one of her bouncing breasts, toying with the nipple and pinching the tip between his fingers. "So sexy," he murmured. "God, so sexy."

Her head went back and a tremor rocked through her body, and then she was coming, hard. A cry escaped her and her body tensed in the throes of an orgasm—the best one of her life—and she seemed to come for what felt like forever and ever and ever, each thrust of his cock into her body just ratcheting the delicious friction higher and higher.

Then, Cade groaned and his movements became jerky, uneven. She felt a pulse of warmth flooding inside her as he came, and he continued to pump slowly into her, each throb of her body sending another wave of pleasure through her.

And then she was slippery-wet between her legs, more so than before. He slid out of her, leaned down, gave her a quick, hard kiss on the mouth, and then collapsed next to her on the bed, breathing hard.

Kylie stared up at the ceiling of the hotel room, replete. Man, she felt incredible. That was her first time for G-spot sex, and clearly she'd been missing out. With a lazy yawn, she stretched an arm over her head and sighed contentedly. So she was a bit slick between the legs and needed some clean-up. She'd get to that soon. Right now, she was just feeling good. "I don't think I've ever had sex bareback before," she murmured to Cade drowsily.

He made a soft noise in his throat.

"I'm on the pill, though, so no worries about kids. I take it you're clean?"

A soft snore met her question.

Surprised, she looked over at Cade and saw him asleep, mouth slack. His angelic curls were sticking to his damp forehead, and she propped up on her elbows to regard him, amused. Well, it *was* late. Her gaze trailed down his gorgeous body, pausing at his cock, still half-erect and gleaming wet from their mutual arousal. She looked farther down . . .

He was still wearing socks. Kylie stifled her giggle.

She got up from the bed and turned off a few lights, then padded to the bathroom and cleaned herself up a bit. Then, yawning, she headed back to the bedroom and pulled her phone out of her purse. She set her alarm for seven in the morning and put her phone on vibrate. She was a light sleeper, so she'd feel the vibrations if she left it in bed next to her. With that, she put the phone on a pillow, laid back down, snuggled next to Cade, and promptly fell asleep.

SEVEN

⌒

Cade Archer was never going to drink again.

Ever, *ever* again.

He squinted at the broad daylight streaming in through the windows of the hotel suite, and raised a hand to shield his eyes. Ugh. Why was the sun so damn bright? He yawned and then put a hand to his forehead as it protested even that small movement. Rolling over, he buried his face in the pillow.

And immediately smelled sex.

Oh . . . fuck.

He bolted upright in the bed, ignoring the throb of his head. Confused, drunk memories swam through his head, offering no answers. Had he had sex last night? The blankets were rumpled but he didn't see another person in the bed with him. He was alone. "Hello?"

No response.

Maybe it was just his imagination. He put his head to the pillow and sniffed again. Nope, definitely smelled like sex.

God, just how drunk had he been last night? His brain was still fuzzy this morning, which told him pretty damn drunk.

But Cade wasn't the type to have a one-night stand. The last one he'd had was Daphne, and he hadn't wanted to think of that as a one-night stand. He'd been hopeful that it was the start of something else, something brighter.

Until she'd OD'd, crushing all of his dreams again.

He scanned the room, trying to remember. Bits and pieces of alcohol-laden memory filtered through his mind. He vaguely recalled a rather arousing striptease, and a pair of large, gorgeous breasts, and flame-tipped hair . . .

Kylie!

Oh God, he'd drunk-fucked Kylie? You were supposed to drunk-fuck people you *didn't* like, people you never wanted to see again. But he liked Kylie. Maybe he liked her too much. She was nice, and beautiful, and she laughed a lot, and she didn't belong in his fucked-up life.

Ugh. He moved to the side of the bed and rubbed a hand over his aching brow. As he did, he noticed a tiny note written on hotel stationary, propped up against the phone. He picked it up and admired her neat cursive handwriting.

Cade,

Thanks for last night. Hope you find what you're look-ing for.

XO,
Kylie

PS—I slept in the wet spot. You're welcome. ☺

That was it. No phone number, no *call me*. Nothing. It was absolutely a one-night stand. She wasn't asking for more.

And damn it, that just sat all wrong with him. Cade wasn't the kind of guy to drag a girl into his bed with empty promises and deliver nothing. He'd done that with Kylie, and she deserved better than that. She deserved someone to give her all the attention in the world, to treat her like a princess and make love to her for hours, not a drunk that stabbed at her with whiskey dick and then passed out.

He should call her and apologize.

He searched through the nightstand and his phone wasn't there. Okay, it was in his jacket somewhere. Or still in his trousers. He got up and headed across the room to where his clothing was thrown, and noticed with grim amusement that his socks were still on his feet. He was naked . . . except for his socks. What must Kylie think of his smooth moves? He snorted and scooped up his pants. His phone was still in one pocket.

So was his wallet, where he kept an emergency condom.

His mouth went dry. Cade ran a hand over his chin and pulled out his wallet, half afraid of opening it. What if he hadn't used a condom last night? Jesus, what if he'd gotten Kylie pregnant on a drunken hookup? She'd hate him forever. Wincing, he cracked open his wallet . . . and recoiled at the sight of the condom still sitting there in its bright purple packaging.

"Fuuuuuuck me."

That did it. He needed to talk to Kylie. If nothing else, to apologize. To explain. To see if she was clean, to see if she was pregnant. To see if she hated him.

Hell, all of the above.

Cade's phone didn't have Kylie's phone number, though. This was just getting worse and worse. Nor did he recall a last name. He closed his eyes and tried to concentrate, but the only image he had was of her pretty, smiling face, the way her hair danced on her shoulders as she moved, the way her breasts heaved and bounced as his cock pounded into her—

He scrubbed a hand down his face and willed his morning wood to go away. Thinking about naked, moaning Kylie wasn't helping his control.

He couldn't call Daphne, though. What on earth could he possibly say to her? *Hey, are you busy? Remember how last night I showed up to give you a car and talk with you and you ignored me? What's the full name of your cute makeup assistant? I drunk-fucked her bareback and I'd really like to make sure everything's cool. Hope you don't mind.*

Because he knew Daphne, and he knew she'd mind. Daphne was many things, but open-minded wasn't one of them. She was a jealous sort, and that extended to her friends. If everyone wasn't dancing to her tune, it'd upset her.

And he didn't need to unbalance her more than she already was.

Cade threw his phone down and stormed off to the bathroom to take a shower.

By the time he emerged, he had a game plan. He called his personal assistant, Jerome. Unlike his friends, he wasn't keen on using an assistant to do basic things that he could do himself, like take his clothes to the cleaners or return a DVD rental. As it was, Jerome tended to have it easier than most, and Reese's wife, Audrey, had laughingly told Cade several times that he needed to hand off more things.

Well, now was his chance.

"What's up, boss?" Jerome said, answering immediately.

"I hate to bother you—"

"No bother. You pay my mortgage." Jerome sounded amused at Cade's apology. "Least I can do is answer when you call."

"I need a favor."

"Name it."

He looked at the clock. One in the afternoon—Daphne's tour would already be on its way to the next city. "Can you tell me where Daphne Petty's next tour stop is?"

A pause. "I can, but there is this neat little thing called 'the Internet.'"

"Just pretend I'm a helpless man with tons of money and an inability to do things for myself."

"Pretending real hard right now," Jerome teased, but Cade could hear him typing on the other side of the line. "Looks like her next stop is tomorrow night in Des Moines."

"Okay. Get me tickets. And backstage passes."

"I'm probably being presumptuous, but can't Daphne get those for you?" Jerome had worked for Cade for a long time and knew about his mixed-up relationship with the pop star.

"It's . . . complicated."

"Try me."

So he told Jerome about his night, and how it was part wonderful and part awful. And how he wanted to contact Kylie now without getting Daphne involved.

Jerome was silent when Cade finished.

"So . . . tickets?" Cade asked to break the silence.

"You want to know what I think, boss?"

"Probably not, but hit me with it anyhow."

"I think you need to stay far away from anything even remotely related to Daphne Petty."

He wasn't the only one thinking that. The more Cade was around her, the more he felt mired in quicksand.

"I also think you need to let Reese's wife know about her sister."

Cade rubbed his forehead, his headache pounding. He headed toward the minibar for some hair of the dog. "Noted."

"And I think you should get tested to make sure you're clean of any diseases."

He closed his eyes. God, what a nightmare this was turning out to be. The one bright spot in everything was Kylie. Sweet, laughing Kylie with her gorgeous body and her lovely smile. An image of her with her head thrown back as she came flashed through his mind. "I'm pretty sure she's clean."

"You were pretty sure Daphne was stable eight months ago, too."

Ouch. "Point taken. All right, then. What do I need to do?"

"You sit tight. I'll get you tickets and passes for the upcoming show. And I'll contact your personal doctor and see if he can fly out to Chicago."

"You want to call Reese and Audrey for me?"

"Hell, no," Jerome said. "I'll do the easy stuff. You get the hard work."

Cade smiled grimly as he hung up the phone, uncapped a tiny bottle of tequila, and swigged it. Hair of the dog—tasted as awful as it smelled. Still, maybe it would help settle him. Telling a six-month pregnant Audrey that her sister was back off the wagon again? Yeah, that wasn't going to go over well.

Then again, he was starting to have a feeling that the rest of this week was going to be a mess. Putting down the tequila, he moved to the bed and looked at Kylie's note again. So simple, so brief. It was so completely noncommittal that it was driving him insane.

At least he knew where he'd find her. Wherever Daphne was, Kylie would be there trying to make her look good. He supposed that made things easier, in a way.

It also made things a lot, lot harder in so many other ways.

———

After a nap in her hotel room, a shower, and breakfast, Kylie was feeling rather pleased with herself as she climbed onto the tour bus. She was alone in her bus seat, doing a sudoku puzzle and sipping her coffee while everyone around her chatted and laughed—or nursed hangovers. Daphne had gotten a decent write-up in the local newspaper, the show had sold out, and everyone was riding high.

Especially Kylie.

She'd just had a one-night stand with a gorgeous man. She'd done something completely out of character, and she was feeling pretty darn good about it, actually. Instead of worrying that he was just hooking up with her as a rebound, she'd controlled the situation. She'd gotten her rocks off (so to speak), had come so hard her brain felt like mush, and then she'd left before the situation had a chance to get awkward.

No phone numbers exchanged. No excuses, nothing. Just one night of fun and then done. She couldn't even regret things—what was there to regret? That she'd had meaningless sex with a sexy man?

Maybe she should have felt bad that he'd shown up for Daphne, but Daphne had made it quite clear that she wasn't interested in Cade. That made him fair game. Even Cade had said there was nothing between them.

So she did her puzzle and enjoyed the pleasant soreness between her thighs, and her daydreams were full of blue-eyed men with blond curls and sad smiles.

Blue-eyed men with big packages that they knew how to use really, really well. She couldn't forget that part.

She was lost in pleasurable daydreams somewhere outside of Cedar Rapids when a familiar figure flopped down in the empty seat next to her.

"Hey, Fat Marilyn," Daphne said, plucking at the hem of her designer T-shirt. She licked her lips and then rubbed her hollow eyes. "You got any sleeping pills?"

Kylie sat up and frowned, putting down the sudoku. "Why would you think I have sleeping pills?"

"Because I can't sleep and I've tried everyone else?" Her eyes were red and she was twitchy, a sure sign that she was on something. Daphne leaned her head back against the bus seat and to Kylie's horror, her lower lip trembled. "I think someone gave me some bad shit last night."

"That sucks," Kylie said sympathetically. "I have some Advil and Midol, but nothing else."

"Can I have those?"

"Which ones?"

"Both."

Seriously? "You can have some Advil, I guess. Unless you're cramping?" When Daphne shook her head, Kylie got out her purse and carefully doled out two pills.

"That's all?"

"That's all I feel comfortable giving you," Kylie told her.

Daphne snorted and shook her head, but took the pills. She swallowed them dry, and Kylie made a mental note to hide her purse in the future, just in case Daphne came snooping for more. And when her boss didn't leave, Kylie supposed she should continue talking to her, even though she was feeling a lot of uncharitable things for Daphne at the moment. The way she'd treated Cade last night was deplorable, but it wasn't her problem. She couldn't get involved. She had to remain neutral, because Daphne was her employer. So she said, "Sorry you're feeling bad. How late were you up last night?"

"I haven't slept," Daphne said, rubbing her eyes again. For a moment, she looked childishly young. "I think. Last night's pretty much a blur. But the papers said the concert was good, so that's something at least."

"Do you remember . . . anything?" Kylie edged.

"Drugs," Daphne said with an unhappy sound. "I remember bad drugs." And she rubbed at her eyes again.

Kylie frowned and dug through her purse, then pulled out some eyedrops and offered it to her. "Do you remember . . . an old friend showing up to visit you?"

"Thanks," Daphne said with a grateful smile. She tilted her head back and put the drops in her eyes, then handed it back to Kylie. "And nope. I was pretty wasted, and not in a good way." She wiped at the corners of her eyes, smearing black liner that was probably a leftover from last night.

And like a mother hen, Kylie pulled out a package of makeup wipes and offered them to Daphne, as well.

Daphne giggled as she took them. "Jesus, what don't you have in that enormous purse of yours?"

Dignity and self-respect, she wanted to retort, but she was feeling wounded on Cade's behalf, and that was a dangerous road to go down. She had to work for Daphne, after all, and she'd likely never see Cade again. "I just try to be prepared," Kylie said in a neutral voice. "So you don't remember Cade visiting you?"

Daphne's overbright eyes popped open and she sat up straight in her chair. *"What?"*

Oh, hell. "Cade Archer? Good-looking guy? Blond hair? He showed up last night and you blew him off." She tried to keep the judging out of her tone. Really, she did. Tried and failed, but hey.

To her surprise, Daphne immediately burst into noisy tears.

Shit. Kylie awkwardly patted her on the shoulder while everyone in the bus stared at them. As Daphne continued to sob, she hunted down a packet of Kleenex in her purse and handed it to her. "You okay?"

"No," Daphne wailed. "Cade was here and I ignored him?"

And you almost went down on some guy in front of him, Kylie wanted to tell her, but she didn't. Across the aisle, Ginger was giving them both odd looks. Kylie just shook her head. "Let's just say you were partying pretty hard."

"Oh my God," Daphne sobbed. "He's going to hate me." She buried her face against Kylie's shoulder.

Kylie stroked her hair, wincing. "I'm sure he doesn't hate you. He's a nice guy. I bet he doesn't hate anyone." God, why was she trying to make Daphne feel better about the fact that she'd thrown him away last night? Especially after Kylie had scooped him up?

This was bad. If Daphne found out that Kylie had slept with him she'd be fired for sure. She'd have to make sure Daphne *never* found out. She needed this job. Needed the money it brought in, otherwise she wouldn't be able to afford Nana Sloane's nursing care.

"Cade's my oldest friend," Daphne said, continuing to cry huge tears. "God, those drugs were so awful. I can't believe I didn't realize he was here. I'm never doing drugs again. Never. *Never.*"

A few feet away, Ginger rolled her eyes and went back to her knitting.

"Where's my phone?" Daphne yelled out. "Snoopy?

Where the fuck's my phone? Get Cade on the line. I need to talk to him ASAP." She staggered out of the bus seat and into the aisle.

Kylie breathed a tiny sigh of relief as Daphne left. The whole situation was terribly awkward. It was clear that she couldn't say a thing about her own hookup with Cade last night. Not if she valued her job. To make matters worse, it didn't sound like Daphne was resolved about things after all.

And didn't that just make everything even more awkward now that Kylie had slept with her man?

She sucked in a breath as Daphne leaned back over her chair. "Thank you, Fat Marilyn. You're the best." She reached out and pinched Kylie's cheek and winked at her. Then she turned and bellowed at Snoopy again. "Why do I not have my goddamn phone already?"

Kylie shrank down in her seat. The urge to hide her face underneath the newspaper was overwhelming.

"Cade, huh?" Ginger said from across the aisle. "Old friend of Daphne's?"

"Sounds like it," Kylie said, trying to keep her voice nonchalant.

"Someone in lighting told me you headed out last night with a blond guy in a suit."

She could feel her cheeks burning. "Ginger, please don't—"

"I won't," Ginger said, looping her yarn over her needles and letting them clack again. "But if you value your job, don't say anything to the boss. She's very possessive of her toys . . . even the ones she throws away. Understand?"

"I got it," Kylie said, and turned toward the window to stare out at the highway. Talk about a messy situation getting worse.

But she tried to look at the bright side. It had only been a one-night stand. Nothing would happen again. And hey, if Daphne was going to swear off drugs now, that would be a good thing, right?

Cade put off calling Audrey Durham for as long as humanly possible. And when he could delay no longer, he picked up his phone . . . and called Reese, Audrey's husband, instead. It wasn't that he didn't want to talk to Audrey. Audrey was efficient, practical, and nothing like her twin.

But, she was also six months pregnant and prone to tearful outbursts due to hormones. When in doubt, test the waters with the husband first.

"Hey, my man," Reese said as he picked up. "You have perfect timing. I just got out of a meeting with a few of the CFOs. We're about to go public with Celebrity Cruises."

"That's great. Congrats." He stared out the window of his hotel room at the Chicago skyline. "You have a moment to talk about nonbusiness things?"

"Oh shit," Reese teased. "Did you get someone pregnant?"

Cade flinched. That was hitting a little too close to home at the moment, considering he had an unused condom in his wallet. "It's not about me. It's about Audrey."

Reese got quiet. "What about Audrey?"

He could just picture his friend's shoulders locking straight, his defensive side rising to the forefront when it came to his wife. Reese was a flirt and a player, but when it came to Audrey, he was all business, and he was extremely protective of her. "It's Daphne," Cade told him. "There are . . . problems."

"Fuck," Reese swore. "How bad is she this time?"

"I saw her last night and she was blitzed. And she looks worse than before." Mentally, he pictured her skinny arms and hollow eyes. "Probably worse than before she went to rehab."

"Goddamn it, she just got out not four months ago. What's wrong with that girl?"

Everything, Cade wanted to say.

"So it's not just alcohol?"

"When I left last night, she was begging someone for another hit of the good stuff."

Reese swore again.

"I need to tell Audrey," Cade said. "So she can step in if she needs to. I just wanted to let you know first so you could be there to support her."

"Hang on," Reese said. "You're not telling Audrey anything."

Cade frowned into the phone. "What do you mean?"

"I mean my wife is six months pregnant and under pressure over both her baby and preparing Logan's office for her impending maternity leave." Audrey was Logan's long-time assistant and invaluable to their friend. She refused to quit her job, despite being married to an extremely wealthy man herself. "We both know Daphne's toxic," Reese continued. "I don't want her stressing out Audrey any more than she already is. You know she's been sick constantly with the baby, right? It hasn't been an easy pregnancy for her."

He knew that. "But Daphne—"

"Daphne's a mess, I know that. Here's the thing, though. Daphne's always a mess," Reese said. His voice was cold and unforgiving. "I'm not going to have my wife losing her mind wondering if her sister's out of control again. Go talk to Daph's people, if you have to. Talk to Daphne yourself—we both know if she listens to anyone, she listens to you. But don't involve Audrey, all right?"

Cade was silent. He knew Reese was being protective, but it didn't feel right to him. "What if something happens?"

"Then I'll take full responsibility," Reese said, voice heavy. "She can't handle more stress right now, all right? She's barely sleeping as it is. Her headaches are crazy and she vomits at the drop of a hat. Her doctor's worried she's going to develop preeclampsia and so he's got her on this crazy diet that makes her stomach even more upset and she can't take prenatal vitamins because they make her puke so she has to go and get shots and she cries all the damn time and . . ." He sighed. "Just. Please, Cade. For me, all right? I know Audrey's Little Miss Capable but for a few months, can we take one thing off her plate?"

Cade suddenly felt guilty. He had no idea Audrey was under so much duress. She was always so in control when he saw her. She and Reese looked so happy. "I didn't know."

"Audrey doesn't like sharing her problems. We both know that."

They did. "You do realize I didn't understand half of that pregnancy jargon you threw at me?" Cade made his voice light, because now Reese was sounding strained, too.

On the other end of the phone, Reese chuckled. "I wish to God I didn't know about it, either. Let me tell you, I have learned way more about babies and childbirth than I ever cared to. Don't even get me started on mucus plugs."

"Jesus, I don't even want to know," Cade said quickly.

"You don't. Trust me."

He rubbed his still-aching forehead. "Okay. I won't say anything to Audrey, then. But if something changes or gets worse—"

"I know, I know," Reese said. "Just call me and let me know and I can break the news to Audrey gently, okay? In the meantime, can you talk to Daphne's people? She's got to have fucking people looking out for her, doesn't she?"

"You would think." He had his suspicions they were the ones providing her the drugs, but what could he say? "All right, man. Will keep you posted."

"Thanks, Cade," Reese told him.

"No sweat." He hung up and headed out onto the balcony. He crossed his arms and closed his eyes, lifting his face to the breeze. Reese had one thing right—Daphne always seemed to carry trouble with her.

And for once, he was really and truly tired of it.

It surprised him to realize that. Cade headed to the edge

of the balcony and leaned over the railing, gazing down at the trickle of cars on the streets below. Kylie had loved this balcony last night, he remembered. His memory was full of holes, but he did recall that part, the way her face had lit up at the sight of it.

She still appreciated things in her life. She was still full of joy.

He couldn't say the same for Daphne anymore. The teen-age spitfire he'd loved so long ago, who charmed with her witty comments and her wry attitude? Cade didn't even know if that girl existed anymore. Maybe he'd been holding on to an image, a dream, for the last ten years.

And Cade was finally ready to move on. Last night with Kylie had been eye-opening. Not only because she'd been sexy and beautiful, but because she'd been kind and gener-ous, and thoughtful of his feelings.

He'd forgotten what that was like—to be interested in someone that gave a damn how you felt.

And he realized he was truly mentally done with Daphne. The door had closed. The girl he'd wanted for so long had turned into someone else, and she wasn't the person he loved anymore. It was refreshing to realize it. As he stood on the balcony, the breeze ruffled his hair and he felt light and clean and whole again.

He felt like a new person.

Strange how holding on to an image of who Daphne used to be had made him feel so weighted down. He should be sad that he was finally giving up on her, but instead, he felt . . . good. He felt free. Maybe he'd never loved her after all. Maybe he'd just been focused on how he thought things should go instead of letting them take their natural course.

Either way, he was done.

Now, he just needed to see Daphne to firmly close the door on things . . . and he needed to see Kylie again.

His phone buzzed with an incoming text.

Cade pulled it out of his pocket, hoping that maybe Kylie had decided to contact him after all.

Hey!! Heard u were here 2 see me! Sorry I missed u. Call me back????

Daphne.
That sour feeling immediately returned to his stomach. Cade stared at the text for a long moment, and then deleted it.

He was done with her. Done with her games, done with her mood swings, her drug use, everything. He tucked his phone back into his pocket, gazed out at the balcony, and smiled.

EIGHT

W hy on earth had she taken this job again, Kylie wondered as she hauled her makeup case into the greenroom backstage. Daphne had been like Jekyll and Hyde for the last twenty-four hours, alternately raging at everyone and then acting clingy. She had decided that Kylie was her new best friend, and spent half the day in her makeup chair, just chatting and then alternately weeping.

Marco, he of the "good drugs," was in the doghouse it seemed, and all of the dancers were giving Daphne a wide berth, unsure of her mood. She didn't seem to be partying, but Kylie wasn't sure if that was due to being between shows, or if she was really and truly trying to clean up.

Kylie was just glad the next concert had begun and Daphne was finally on stage and occupied with something. At least for a few hours, there would be a reprieve from her mood swings. She hauled her four makeup cases, each one stacked on top of the next.

"Let me help you with that," a familiar, warm voice said, and someone lifted the cases out of Kylie's hands.

Oh, sweet baby Jesus. Her face turned bright red and she stared in a mix of surprise and horror at Cade Archer as he took the stack from her and set them down on the lit makeup table.

He turned to give her a gorgeous smile. "Hello again."

God, he was so good looking. It was unfair. He wore a dark button-down shirt, slightly open at the collar, with a white undershirt underneath. The sleeves were rolled up to his elbows, and an expensive watch decorated one wrist. And he wore slacks again. No jacket this time, but he still managed to look delectable and wealthy all at once.

Kylie blinked repeatedly, but he didn't disappear, wasn't a figment of her imagination. Well, shit. So much for her one-night stand thing. "What are you doing here?"

"I had to see you again," he told her, those blue eyes focusing on her face.

"You did?" Her initial bubble of pleasure popped as she realized there could be another reason why he was here to visit her. He *had* to? There were only a few reasons why a man would have to see his one-night stand again . . . and none of them were good. "Oh God, you're not clean, are you? What do you have?"

His eyes widened and then he laughed, a smile crinkling the corners of his eyes. "I don't have an STD, Kylie." He grimaced. "Though I really do need to apologize." He leaned in. "I'm normally the kind that wears a sock."

"I'm not normally the kind that goes for a one-night stand," she murmured, still in a daze.

"Me either," he confessed. "Which is why I had to see you again."

"But why?" Her brows furrowed. "I thought it was supposed to be wham-bam-thank-you-ma'am. I wasn't expecting anything—"

"I know," he told her, his beautiful mouth quirked with amusement. "I think that's one of the things I like about you. But maybe I wanted to see you again for myself? I thought we could talk. Maybe over dinner?" He gave her an inquisitive look.

Her initial shock at seeing him gave way to horror. "You what?"

"I just asked you out," he told her, a sheepish look on his face. "I'm sorry, are you already seeing someone?"

"I, what? No!" She shook her head. "I'm not seeing anyone." She looked around the greenroom, and was chagrined to see that Ginger and Snoopy were both watching her talk to Cade. It was going to get back to Daphne for sure. She grabbed his arm and dragged him toward one of the couches set up for Daphne's guests. "Daph's on stage right now," she said loudly. "But when she's done, I'm sure she'll be glad to see you."

"I'm not here to see Daphne," he said, taking her hand in his.

Oh boy. Kylie closed her eyes, willing herself not to panic. "Cade, you can't imagine what trouble this is going to cause."

"Trouble?" His blond brows furrowed and he glanced around, as if just now noticing that several people were watching them. He leaned in. "Can you not talk here?"

"Understatement," she told him with a faintly apologetic look.

"Then come to dinner with me," he said. "We'll talk there."

"I can't," Kylie said automatically. "That would be very, very bad."

"Worse than talking here?"

He had a point. She looked around, biting her lip anxiously. The crowd began to roar, a sign that Daphne's show had just started.

"I'll have you back before curtain call," he promised.

God, she was so weak. "Come on, I'll show you out," she said loudly. If she left her purse here, no one would notice she was gone, right?

Cade grinned, and her heart skipped a little beat of happiness at the sight of that. "Thank you."

When they got to the front of the concert venue, he raised

a hand and a limo driver at the curb nodded at him and moved to open a door. "After you," Cade said.

A limo? "Why is there a limo out front?"

"Because everyone thinks that a limo belongs at the front of a concert instead of waiting in the parking lot," he said with a devilish grin. "Hop in."

This seemed like a spectacularly bad idea, but she seemed to be running low on spectacularly *good* ones.

So she got into the limo, because it was either that or have a messy confrontation back in the greenroom, right?

Cade got in after her. "Closest restaurant, please," he told the limo driver. Then he turned and looked at Kylie for a long moment. "I have the most intense urge to kiss you hello right now."

Oh. She clamped her thighs together, willing her pulse to stop beating in her girl parts. "You can't kiss me," she told him desperately. "We shouldn't even be seeing each other. Daphne—"

"I'm not interested in what Daphne's doing or saying," he said, his voice curiously flat.

"No, you don't understand," Kylie said. "She was on some bad drugs the other night. She didn't even remember you were there. When I told her, she got really upset and started crying. She still wants you and I know you want her, right? She said she was going to give up the drugs."

"Kylie," Cade told her softly and leaned in closer. "I've known Daphne for years. Ask me how many times she's promised to give up the drugs."

"How many times?" she asked, fascinated by the tanned skin of his jawline, his firm mouth so close to her own. They really, really should have been sitting further apart.

"Dozens," he told her. "Now ask me how many times she's actually given them up for good?"

"How many?"

"Never." He shook his head. "It's always promises with

Daphne, but she never follows up on them. Never. And I'm tired of waiting for a day that will never come."

"How do you know it's not different this time?" Daphne had seemed sincere to Kylie. In fact, she'd cried for hours and had been so miserable that Kylie couldn't help but feel sorry for her.

"Because I know Daphne," he told her. "And I'm not interested in seeing her tonight. I wanted to talk to you." He looked down at her hand on the seat of the limo, and took it in his own. "And about what happened between us."

A warm flush crept up her cheeks. "You mean our evening of spectacularly bad decisions?"

Cade grimaced, but he didn't let go of her hand. "That bad? How drunk was I?"

He didn't know? She tilted her head, considering him. "You don't remember?"

"Only bits and pieces."

"So you don't remember dressing up in my clothes and letting me put makeup on you?"

His eyes got round. "What?"

"Or the part where you cried like a baby and sucked your thumb?"

Cade threw back his head and laughed. To hear his pleasure at her joke made Kylie smile, and she relaxed a little. He shook his head and chuckled at her, then wagged a finger. "For a moment, I thought you were serious."

"So you really don't remember? You seemed pretty sober."

"I've heard that before," Cade murmured. "In college, it used to drive my friends crazy because I'd never really seem that drunk until I fell over and couldn't get back up again. But I'm pretty sure I was loaded."

"You must have been if you took me home," she agreed.

Cade's brows furrowed and he looked over at her. He squeezed the hand in his. "I'm not saying I don't regret things—"

And her heart felt like it was about to shatter into a million pieces of hurt.

"But I regret that I was loaded and I can't remember. Not that I spent the evening with you. And I really, really regret not using a condom. It seems very unsafe." He grimaced. "I'm not normally one to take risks."

"Me either," she admitted. "But you were drunk and then things felt too good for me to protest. I'm on the pill, by the way."

Relief crossed his face. "I saw my physician yesterday. I'm clean."

"I am, too. I haven't had sex in two years, and the last check I had was squeaky clean. That's one question out of the way," she told him, and couldn't seem to stop smiling. "So you really don't remember all that much?"

"I remember this," he said, and with his free hand, reached out and touched a lock of her red-tipped hair. "I remember that it looked like bits of flame against your pale shoulders. And I remember the way you looked when you came, and the way your breasts bounced when I fucked you." The look in his eyes was scorching. "So I remember the important things."

Her breath caught in her throat. Okay, now she was picturing all that, and getting all aroused, too. My goodness.

"And I think I'd really like to see you again," he told her, and lifted their clasped hands to his mouth. He pressed a kiss to the back of her hand. "Sober, this time."

"I'd like that, Cade," she began. "But we really can't. Daphne—"

"Doesn't interest me any longer," he said with a small shake of his head. "Last night just reinforced that she's become someone I no longer know or care to know."

He might have felt that way, but she was pretty sure Daphne had different opinions on the subject. "Daphne's still my boss."

"And she's an old family friend of mine," he said lightly. "So when she finds out I intend on dating you, she's just going to have to get over it."

Warmth flooded through her, and she bit her lip, considering. Could it really be that simple? "I don't know."

"Then let me entice you with dinner," he said, and pointed out the tinted window of the limo. "I sincerely hope you are in the mood for pancakes."

She peered out the window and had to smother a giggle. The limo had pulled up to a roadside waffle joint. "I could go for some coffee at least."

"Great." He released her hand, opened the door, and then waited for her to exit the limo.

Kylie patted her pockets. "I left my wallet back at the concert hall."

"I insist on paying. I'm sure they take credit cards." He eyed the sketchy establishment. "Hopefully."

And she giggled again. "Do you not eat at places like this often?"

"I can honestly say I don't think I've been in one since college." The grin he flashed her was so boyish, so charming, that she felt her heart do a funny little flip in her chest. "But I'm looking forward to the experience."

"Because you've missed out on greasy sausage and stacks of pancakes?"

"Because of the company," he said simply.

And just like that, her heart melted a little more. How was it that he always knew the right thing to say?

They entered the diner and sat down at a booth. The waitress brought them both coffee mugs and two plastic menus, and Kylie's lips twitched as Cade considered the meal offerings very studiously, as if he were at the finest restaurant. "What do you recommend?" he asked the waitress.

"That you eat somewhere else," she said, bringing a coffeepot and filling up both of their mugs.

And Kylie got the giggles again.

"But if you're eating here, the waffles aren't bad," the waitress said with a wink at Kylie.

"Two plates of waffles, please," Cade told her.

"Oh no," Kylie protested. "I already had dinner." And the last thing she wanted to do was be the fat girl stuffing her face on an impromptu date with a gorgeous man.

"I insist," Cade said, and the waitress disappeared. He leaned in and added, "I figure if I come down with something toxic, I'll have company in the emergency room."

And she couldn't help the laugh that erupted from her. She shook her head at him and picked up her coffee mug. "You're incorrigible."

"So I hear."

Still smiling, Kylie gazed around the restaurant. It was nearly empty, the only other person a trucker sitting in a booth at the far end of the diner. For some reason, this felt cozy. She glanced at her date and decided to go for the typical "getting to know you" first date questions. Why not, right? "What is it you do, Cade? I'm curious." She took a sip of her coffee.

"I'm a billionaire."

She choked on the mouthful of coffee. Hot, scalding liquid went down the wrong pipe and she grabbed a paper napkin and coughed into it.

"You all right?" Cade asked, leaning in. "Should I fly in a team of doctors to see you?"

Kylie gave the most undignified snort-giggle. "You're horrible."

"I really am a billionaire, though." He gave her a rueful smile.

"Of course you are," she murmured. Because why not? He was already perfect in every other way. Buttloads of cash instead of a working man? It didn't surprise her. "Have you always been incredibly wealthy?"

"Not in the slightest. I grew up in a trailer." He grinned at her surprised expression. "It's true. But I went to college on a scholarship, and met the right people. Graduated summa cum laude, started working at a hospital in the finance department, and met a friend who wanted to patent some new medical equipment. I'd been making the right investments, and so

I backed him as an investor partner. He sold his patent for seven hundred million two years later. From there, I supported a few upstart companies and the next thing you know, I have my hands in a dozen other related patents. And medical technology patents are worth a fortune." He gave her a crooked grin. "I try not to let it get to my head."

"Of course not," she murmured, taking a more careful sip of her coffee.

"In all seriousness, I do try to stay a bit humble."

"Uh-huh. How many cars do you have?"

The grin he gave her was perfectly boyish. "Twelve, but I have a friend who is an automaker. So that's an unfair question."

"Uh-huh," she teased, but she was smiling.

"So, what about you? Why makeup?"

Kylie grew silent. How did she explain to a beautiful man who had scads of money that, growing up, she'd never felt attractive or valued, and so she'd learned to make her outside pretty? That makeup had power and it was her way of claiming some of that power? She wasn't sure he'd understand. So she shrugged. "I've always liked makeup."

The look he gave her was shrewd, but he didn't press. "So where do you live when you're not on tour?"

"Malibu." She gave a small shrug. "It's expensive and hot and I'm not overly fond of it, but that's where a lot of the work starts out, so that's where I am. I live with a friend when I'm not on tour."

"And no boyfriend, right?"

"The last one was enough for me, thanks." She grimaced.

He raised an eyebrow. "You're not going to leave me hanging at that, are you?"

She sighed, her cheeks flushing at having to go into detail. "It's a really stupid incident. One I'm not sure you'd be interested in hearing about."

"Well, now I'm extremely interested."

Kylie squirmed in her seat. "There's not too much to tell,

really." God, she'd been so messed up when she was with Jerred. How to make their fucked-up, ugly relationship sound decent? "I had a boyfriend two years ago, and we were pretty serious." *At least, I was, but he mostly just liked fucking.* "We spent a lot of time together and we decided that it would be a good time to move in and test the waters." *Jerred thought he would be getting free maid service and a blow job every night if we lived together so he thought it was a good idea.* "So I let my apartment go, sold all of my extra stuff, and moved in with him. Unfortunately, I lost my job at a department store as soon as I did. Just bad timing." She shrugged and stared at her coffee.

Bad timing. More like Jerred was constantly trying to get her to skip work. To be late, because it wasn't as important as spending time with him. Then, when she lost her job, it was suddenly her fault.

Cade made a noise indicating she should go on.

Right. "About two weeks after I lost my job, he said I wasn't helping him with the rent." That she was a *burden*, but she couldn't say that word. It stuck in her throat. "We had a pretty big fight. And a week after that, I came home to find that he'd thrown all my stuff to the curb and changed the locks. I couldn't do anything because I wasn't on the rental paperwork just yet, so I had to pack up my boxes and figure out what to do with myself."

Cade's eyes were wide. "What *did* you do with yourself?"

"Cried a lot," Kylie said with a smile.

Cade didn't laugh.

She shrugged. "It wasn't so bad. It just . . . taught me a lot about people." *That you could never, ever ever be a burden to someone if you wanted to keep their love.* "I spent a few days sleeping under a bridge—"

"Under a bridge?" Cade exploded. "What?"

"And I got back on my feet soon enough. It's fine," she soothed. "Like I said, it was a good learning experience."

"How can you call that a learning experience? He sounds like a nightmare."

"Looking back, I'm glad things didn't work out between us. Hence the learning." Her smile was rueful. "And it taught me something about myself, that there's nothing I hate worse than being an obligation to someone."

His jaw set and he looked unhappy. "Is there a remote chance that I'm ever going to meet this man?"

"I doubt it very much."

"Good," Cade said. He looked ready to spit nails, which surprised her. They barely knew each other. Why so defensive of her? She . . . didn't know what to make of it.

An uncomfortable silence fell. "Why don't we go back to talking about jobs?" Kylie asked. "Please?"

"All right." He shrugged. "Do you travel a lot?"

"I do. One of the perks, I suppose."

"Do you enjoy traveling?"

"For the most part, yes. You never stay someplace long enough for it to get old. But sometimes you get tired of hotels." She shook her head. "And you get really tired of having no roots. Like, I can't even have a pet because I'm gone so much. My address is basically just a place to send bills." She gave him a wry look. "You? Where are you from?"

"New York City," he told her. "It's expensive, not as hot, and has this strange smell in the summer. But I still like it a lot. There's always something going on."

"I like New York," she said. "Every time I've gone through there, it seems like a vibrant place to live."

The waitress set their plates down and left again. Cade eyed his waffle, and then hers. He lifted up his coffee mug in a toast. "To intestinal fortitude?"

She laughed and clinked her mug against his.

The waffle was surprisingly delicious, and Kylie cleaned her plate without even really thinking about it. Cade ate heartily, too, and the conversation flowed between them as they ate. They kept it on simple things, like weather, and places to eat in New York, and other places he'd traveled for business. She teased him about how many houses he had (six) and how many corporations he owned (nine) and he took her teasing with good-natured rejoinders of his own, like asking how many lipsticks she owned (dozens).

Then their plates were cleared away and all the coffee was drunk, and the bill was produced. Kylie found herself strangely reluctant to leave. It was nice being here with Cade. Kind of wonderful, really. He was smart, good looking, successful, and utterly focused on her. He laughed at her lame jokes, found her conversations interesting, and okay, he was pretty amazing in bed. Every time he smiled at her, she got a little weak in the knees.

"I should take you back," he said, glancing at his watch. "I don't want you to get in trouble."

"All right," she said, because really, she shouldn't have been gone this long anyhow.

"So when can I see you again? Tomorrow?"

"Tomorrow we're heading to Indianapolis," she told him. "Another concert."

"Then the night after that?"

"More travel."

"Then tell me what night you have off so we can meet up."

Kylie hesitated. It wasn't that she didn't like Cade—she liked him too much, really. It was that the whole situation with Daphne was sticky. "I don't know," she admitted. "I feel like you need to talk to Daphne first."

She expected him to protest, but he nodded. "I do need to talk to her." An impish twinkle lit his eyes. "So, Friday then?"

And she couldn't help but laugh. "I'm not committing to anything."

As the limo drove back to the concert hall, they exchanged phone numbers. Kylie programmed him into her phone with a silent ringtone, because she was wary about more people finding out about them. Then the car pulled up in front of the hall and there was no longer any reason to stay in it.

But when she put her hand on the door handle, he stopped her. "Before you leave, I've been waiting all night to do this."

Cade leaned in and very gently kissed her. His mouth landed on her upper lip, and he softly, sensuously pressed his own lips to hers. Then, over and over, he continued to kiss her as she sat there, utterly shocked and completely and totally aroused. His tongue brushed against her parted mouth, and she swallowed the whimper that wanted to escape. She didn't dare make a sound, because she wanted this to go on forever. He was making love to her with each sweet, delicious, light kiss. She'd never been touched like this in her life, and she savored it.

"You have the most incredible mouth, Kylie," he murmured between kisses. "So full and pink and plump. I've wanted to put my lips on it for hours now. And you taste even better than I remember."

This time, she couldn't help the whimper that escaped.

He chuckled, as if he knew just what he was doing to her. "I feel the same way," he murmured, and his lips moved against hers in a tickling motion. It was as if he didn't want to pull away, not even to talk. And when she opened her eyes, she saw his were heavy, wicked slits of desire.

And that made her panties wet to see.

"I shouldn't be kissing you," she murmured, but she didn't pull away. That was the last thing she wanted.

"Why not?"

"Because it's . . . complicated." Because her job depended on it. Because she wasn't sure if he was still mixed up with Daphne. Because she worried that if Daphne got clean, he'd dump her like a hot potato if the pop star came calling again.

"Well, maybe we'll take it slow, then," he told her. And he leaned in and gently brushed his lips over her mouth one more lingering time. "I'll save the rest of my kisses for the next time we meet."

Dazed, she could do nothing but nod. His scent was in her nostrils, his body pressing against hers, and it took everything she had to open the door and get out of the limo. This time, though, he didn't stop her. They headed into the venue once more, Cade at her side, and took the long walk back to the greenroom backstage.

There, things were in a flurry. Crowds were everywhere, and it was clear the show had just ended. Kylie felt a twinge of alarm. She should have been back already. If Daphne was waiting for her, well, things were going to get ugly, and they were going to get ugly fast. The greenroom had filled up with people, and both press and fans were waiting outside. They glared at Kylie as she took Cade by the hand and dragged him inside with her. In the room, it was quieter, but there were still too many people around, which meant that they were late.

"Looks like the show is over," Kylie told Cade. "Are you sticking around to see Daphne?"

"I'm not sure," he said. "I didn't really intend to see anyone but you tonight."

Hearing that made her body flush with pleasure. She turned to smile at him . . . and noticed that a fair amount of her lip gloss was on his mouth. Oh lord. With an alarmed gasp, she leaned forward and smoothed her thumbs over his mouth, trying to wipe away the evidence even as he chuckled.

"Cade?" a voice shrieked. "Oh my God, you're here!"

A sweaty Daphne pushed past Kylie and flung her arms around Cade. Kylie watched as his eyes went wide, and then he reluctantly patted her on the back. "Hey, Daph."

Daphne wrapped her arms around his neck, crawling all over him, and then began to press quick kisses on his cheeks. Cade looked embarrassed at the show, and his gaze flicked to Kylie.

Yeah, well, Kylie should have seen this coming. Squashing down her feelings of irritation, she headed toward the makeup chair and started unpacking her things. Daphne would want her face refreshed before she went out to face the media. But she couldn't help but peer over at Cade and Daphne as they hugged.

Okay, so she was being a little prying and a lot jealous. So what? She could be a little possessive of a guy if she'd had a one-night stand with him, right? It didn't mean anything, but she also wasn't able to just turn things off just like that.

She watched as Daphne bounced, still in her shiny leotard with the black tutu, and grabbed Cade's hands. "I'm so excited you're here!"

His smile was warm. "I'm glad."

"You didn't answer my texts!"

"I was busy. You never answer mine," he chided.

"I'm busy, too," Daphne said coyly. "So what made you stop by?"

He glanced up and his gaze met Kylie's. "Kylie, actually—"

"Oh?" Now Daphne turned, and she beamed at Kylie. "You got him for me, Fat Marilyn? You're so sweet!"

"I—" Kylie began, then clamped her mouth shut. What could she possibly say?

"Fat Marilyn?" Cade asked, a frown on his face.

"Well, come sit with me," Daphne said, grabbing Cade's hand and ignoring his question. "We can catch up."

"You have press duties," Snoopy reminded Daphne.

"Don't fucking snap at me," Daphne snarled, and Snoopy's eyes went wide. So did Kylie's. Daphne had been volatile for the last few days but her reaction to Snoopy's mild comment was alarming.

The room got quiet. "Maybe I should go," Cade said.

"No!" Daphne cried, and she clung to Cade's chest. To Kylie's horror, Daphne began to cry. "I need you here with me, Cade. I don't have anyone to lean on. Please don't go." Big, racking sobs shook her thin frame. "You don't know how hard it's been for me—"

"Shhh," Cade said, voice soothing. "Let's sit down. You need to relax, Daphne. You're under a lot of stress." He gently steered her toward one of the comfortable sofas and set her down. She didn't let him go, instead clinging so that he had no choice but to sit next to her. As he did, she buried her face in his shirt and huddled against him like a sad puppy.

"Please don't leave me, Cade," she repeated.

"I'm here," he said, glancing over at Kylie. The look in his eyes was a mixture of sadness and resignation, and she gave him a smile to try and encourage him, to let him know it was all right. Daphne needed him tonight, and if it hurt Kylie to see Daphne crawling all over him, well, it wasn't like Kylie owned him, was it?

"I'm so glad you're here," Daphne murmured against Cade's chest, not raising her head.

He stroked her hair. "Why don't we get you some water to drink and then we'll see about getting you ready for the press meet and greet, okay?"

"But you'll stay?"

"I'll stay," he said softly.

After that, things fell into a blur of activity. Daphne eventually calmed down enough for Kylie to wipe off her old makeup and set her up with fresh new makeup. Daphne was twitching and kept scratching at her skin, so Kylie had to do the best she could.

Cade remained nearby, and when Daphne did her press interviews, she insisted that he stay. So he did, and late into the night, the fans left and only the hard-partying types remained. The backup dancers broke out the alcohol, and a few people in the crew started to pass around drugs.

Kylie packed up her things and glanced over at Cade and Daphne again. Daphne wasn't shooting up in the bathrooms, so that was progress. Instead, she had splashed herself across Cade's lap and was sipping on a beer while talking to someone else.

And instead of Cade looking content at having Daphne's attention, he kept looking over at Kylie.

She should have guessed this would happen.

It didn't matter how wonderful he was, or how they'd connected over dinner. Of course Cade was great. And of course Daphne wanted him.

Kylie was just a momentary distraction. A drunken hookup, just like she'd suspected.

And really, that was okay. At least Cade wasn't being an ass about it. He wanted Daphne, and his one-night stand was staring at him with big moony eyes. He probably felt awkward that both Daphne and Kylie were in the room together. Heck, he probably felt bad for Kylie because she was clearly second fiddle.

"I'm heading out," Ginger said. "You coming?"

"Coming," Kylie said. Leaving was the best thing she could do for all parties involved. She grabbed her purse and slung it over her shoulder, heading out with the rest of the staff.

———

Cade watched Kylie leave with the crew, and tried to squash his annoyance at Daphne as she clung to his chest and seated herself in his lap. She'd done that a million times in the past and he knew it didn't mean anything.

But Kylie didn't know that.

And now that his interest had moved squarely to Kylie? It felt wrong for Daphne to drape herself all over him.

Funny how his mind had changed so quickly. A week ago, he would have been beside himself with joy if Daphne had paid half the attention she was giving him tonight. But a week ago, he hadn't realized Daphne still hadn't changed. That she was still the same messed-up girl she ever was. A week ago, he'd still had hope that she was clean after her latest round of rehab.

And a week ago, he hadn't met Kylie. Hadn't realized how pure and good and right just having someone normal in your life could be.

"Get me another beer, Cade," Daphne said in her coy, flirty voice. "I'm so thirsty after all that sexy performing I did." She fluttered her lashes at him, trying to be cute.

But instead, all he could think about was how hard Kylie had worked to make Daphne look good, the thoughtful look on her face as she had carefully pressed the fake lashes onto

Daphne's eyelids, the way she'd leaned in to blow gently on Daphne's eyeliner.

Makeup had never been so erotic.

He couldn't think about that now, though. Not with Daphne being a stage-five clinger. The last thing he wanted was an erection right now. So he pushed Daphne off his lap as gently as possible. "Don't you think you've had enough beer?"

"No such thing," laughed the girl sitting on the couch next to them. One of Daphne's dancers, maybe. He'd seen her disappearing into the bathroom repeatedly tonight, which could only mean food poisoning or lines of coke. He'd bet his money on the latter.

"She's had plenty of beer for someone that's trying to get clean," Cade chided in his mildest voice, even though he secretly wanted to give the girl a verbal dressing down for encouraging Daphne's bad behavior.

Daphne pouted. "Water, then. If my man wants me to drink water, I will." And she put her hand on Cade's chest possessively.

He removed it just as quickly again. "We're not together, Daphne."

Her eyes—so enormous in her lean face—looked hurt. "What do you mean?"

The dancer chose that moment to get up from the couch and head for the bathroom again, and it was just him all alone with Daphne.

"I mean that I was here two nights ago to see you after we'd talked about it, remember? You told me to come to your concert. We'd spend time together and catch up. Instead, I spent all night nursing a drink on the sofa while you threw yourself on anyone moving."

"Jealous?"

Surprisingly, no. "Disappointed. You were more interested in getting drugs than seeing me. And you were out of your mind on something all night. I want nothing to do with that woman I saw. Not friendship, not anything."

"Someone gave me some bad stuff that night. I shouldn't have been acting like that—"

"No, you shouldn't have."

"But sometimes I need something to keep me going because I'm tired." She blinked repeatedly, as if she was going to cry. "I'm trying to stay clean, but it's hard."

He really didn't think she was trying to stay clean. But he didn't want to punch her while she was down. "I know, Daph. But for your sake, you've got to stop with the drugs. They're not good for you."

"I know." Her lower lip trembled. "I haven't had anything in two days. Not since they told me you were here and I didn't even realize it."

"That's good," he told her. "That's a start." Mentally, he wanted to wring her neck. Two whole days and she was acting like it was something impressive? "Keep going in that direction."

"And you'll help me?"

"As a friend? Of course."

She laughed as if he'd said something funny. "Oh, Cade. We've always been more than friends."

Maybe once. Not anymore. So he simply gave her a faint smile and repeated himself. "As a *friend*."

NINE

Thursday

Cade: I feel like we should talk about last night.

Kylie: What's there to talk about?

Cade: Daphne confessed to me that she's been clean for two days now. Two days . . . isn't much. Can you keep an eye on her? Let me know if she starts making lots of emergency trips to the bathroom or hiding out in corners with the wrong kind of people?

Kylie: Of course.

Cade: She's a really old friend and I'm worried about her.

Kylie: You don't have to explain anything to me.

Cade: Don't I? I'm pretty sure you weren't happy with me when you left.

Kylie: Why would you say that? I am neither happy nor unhappy with you. I don't have a claim on you.

Cade: Don't you?

Kylie: Not in the slightest. You're free to do as you choose.

Cade: I thought it was pretty obvious who I choose. ☺ Someone with a warm smile, a great laugh, and the softest skin I've ever experienced.

Kylie: Are you flirting with me?

Cade: Possibly? Is it working?

Kylie: Cade . . . I really like you. Really really like you. But I can't fight with Daphne over you.

Cade: No one's fighting. We're just talking, right? Friends talk. We can be friends, right?

Kylie: . . . I suppose so. Do you tell all your friends they have soft skin?

Cade: Only the ones I've slept with.

Kylie: Why am I laughing at that?

Cade: I don't know, but it's clear I'll have to make you laugh more so you don't avoid my texts. ☺

Kylie: I have to go. ☺

Friday

Cade: So how was the concert tonight?

Kylie: Good! Daph got a standing ovation. Little surprised to come into the greenroom and not see you here.

Cade: Couldn't make it today. Will try to be at the next one, promise. Will you be there if I am?

Kylie: Duh.

Cade: Duh? Ouch.

Kylie: But not because of you. Because I, yanno, work for Daphne.

Cade: Double ouch. How is Daph?

Kylie: I think she's clean. But it's hard to say. Sometimes she's in a great mood, and sometimes she's . . . not.

Cade: Well, I'm glad.

Kylie: I'm glad for you two also.

Cade: What about us?

Kylie: There is no us.

Cade: I think there should be.

Kylie: I think I should be a size four, but we don't always get what we want.

Cade: I don't know why you'd want to be a size four. I think you're gorgeous.

Kylie: You're just blinded by my soft skin and enormous tracts of land.

Cade: God, yes I am. Now I'm picturing you in my mind and it's getting a little hard to concentrate.

Kylie: You're welcome.

Cade: You're flirting with me. I'm breaking down your barriers.

Kylie: Good night, Cade. ☺

Cade: It is now.

Kylie: It is what?

Cade: A good night.

Saturday 1 A.M.

Daphne: Hey Cade!! Missed u tonight, bb. U coming to see me? Will save u spot in greenroom 4 my favorite man. Xoxoxo

Cade: Can't tonight, Daph. Busy. We'll talk soon ok?

Daphne: K

Cade: Stay clean for me?

Daphne: Fine fine. Quit acting like my mom.

Saturday night

Cade: Hey.

Kylie: Hi there.

Cade: Where are you at tonight?

Kylie: Concert in Louisville, KY. You coming in to say hello?

Cade: Wish I was. I am currently in Botswana.

Kylie: I . . . don't even know where that is? Why are you in Botswana?

Cade: It's north of South Africa. Very pretty country. One of my organizations is opening a new HIV clinic and I wanted to be here. It's a good cause.

Kylie: Wow . . . that's noble of you.

Cade: Eh. I just like to help out where I can. I don't like to sit on all my money like Scrooge McDuck.

Kylie: Did you just compare yourself to a cartoon duck?

Cade: Depends. Are you laughing?

Kylie: Yes!

Cade: Then yes, yes I did. ☺

Kylie: You're so noble. Seriously, a clinic. Wow. I don't even know what to say.

Cade: I'm not all that noble. I keep thinking about kissing you again. How your lips felt against mine. How the . . . rest of you felt against me. I'm obsessing.

Kylie: You shouldn't. ☹

Cade: Why not? You're an adult and I'm an adult. Do you want me to leave you alone?

Kylie: Not really . . . but the whole Daphne thing. It makes it awkward. You know she wants you. And I want my job.

Cade: But I don't want her.

Kylie: Really? Didn't seem that way the other night when she was sitting in your lap.

Cade: First of all, she dropped herself there, and second of all, is that jealousy I hear in your sweet voice?

Kylie: Text. The correct term you are looking for is "sweet text."

Cade: Don't avoid the question.

Kylie: I'm not.

Cade: You just did again. And as for Daphne, I'm just trying to be a friend to her. She desperately needs a few that aren't ready to push drugs her way.

Kylie: . . . which is why we shouldn't get together. It's hard for me to be her friend when I want to pull her hair out for sitting in your lap. ☺

Cade: So it was jealousy.

Kylie: I shall plead the fifth. ☺

Cade: I miss you. I wish you were here in Botswana with me.

Kylie: Why, do you know someone there in need of a makeup artist?

Cade: Me! But not for obvious reasons. I just need to make a certain one scream with pleasure again.

Kylie: Oh my lord, why are you texting me dirty things??

Cade: Because it makes me smile and I've been stuck traveling for the last eighteen hours. And because I'm picturing how pink your cheeks are right now. When did you say I could see you again?

Kylie: I didn't. Busy busy busy.

Cade: I'm looking at Daphne's schedule online and she doesn't have a concert scheduled for this upcoming Wednesday. Tuesday in Vegas but Wednesday is free. I can fly in and see you.

Kylie: Cade, we shouldn't.

Cade: Just a meeting between friends. She doesn't have to know.

Kylie: I'll . . . think about it.

Sunday

Daphne: U coming 2 visit me tonight?

Cade: Overseas on business, sorry.

Daphne: Fine. Fuck u. I thought we were friends.

Cade: You know I have to work, Daph. You work, too. Doesn't have anything to do with our friendship.

Cade: Hello?

Cade: Sigh. Daph, I hope you're staying clean. Not for my sake, but for yours.

Monday

Cade: Still thinking about it?

Kylie: It's a long, involved thought process. Truly.

Cade: What can I do to persuade you?

Kylie: Promise me that Daphne will not lose her shit if she finds out about it? Actually, just promise me she won't find out at all?

Cade: She won't find out.

Kylie: Uh-huh.

Cade: But we're still discussing it, which must mean that you want to go with me after all.

Kylie: It's not a question of want. It's a question of practicality. Like, is it practical for me to date the man that my rich and famous boss wants? Risk my job? I consulted my Magic 8 Ball this morning and all signs point to no.

Cade: Those things are liars. Mine told me that you would say yes.

Kylie: They ARE full of lies!

Cade: What if I offered to buy an orphanage in some third world country?

Kylie: Now you're not playing fair.

Cade: I don't have to. I have money.

Kylie: Fine, fine, we'll go out. If we must. ☺

Cade: Excellent. I will see you Wednesday night.

Kylie: Just . . . I'll send you my hotel info, okay? Let's keep this out of Daphne's eye. I don't want her to even know you're in town.

Cade: That makes two of us. I won't say a thing. Looking forward to seeing you, then.

Kylie: Just FYI we're not sleeping together.

Cade: I'm fine with that. I just want to see you. Maybe kiss you.

Kylie: Maybe?

Cade: Well, I thought it might frighten you if I said that I intend to kiss every inch of you at least twice.

Kylie: Not frightened here. ☺

Tuesday

Daphne: U coming 2 the show tonight?

Cade: Can't. Busy schedule. How goes keeping clean?

Cade: Hello?

———————

Kylie was humming to herself as she mixed the foundation colors for Daphne's skin. It was ridiculous to be in such a good mood, but she was. She was going to see Cade tomorrow night, and they were going to talk for hours and have a wonderful time.

She wasn't even going to sleep with him. Just to prove to herself that she didn't have to. But she was definitely looking forward to those kisses.

And she might wear some sexy lingerie because, well, just because.

She checked her phone for the millionth time that day, but Cade must have been busy. He'd only sent her a few small texts, like the occasional smiley face or 'thinking of you.' They'd been text flirting for the last week. While it was just as easy to pick up the phone and have a phone call, there was something fun and relaxed about texting. She found herself having to hold back on responding, just in case he thought she was sitting by her phone for hours on end, waiting for him to text back.

Which . . . she was. But he didn't have to know that, of course.

She was still humming when Daphne threw herself in the director's chair in front of Kylie and gestured at her face. "Let's put this on, shall we? I have plebs to entertain tonight."

Kylie eyed the pop star. Was this Pleasant Attitude Daphne or Nasty Daphne? It was hard to tell sometimes. Lately it had been Nasty Daphne. "Sounds good," Kylie said, keeping her voice reasonable and mild. "Any particular requests tonight?"

"I liked that glitter and rhinestone shit you did at my temples for the last show," Daphne said, pressing her fingertips on her forehead. "They stayed in place really well. But can we skip the fake lashes? I fucking hate that crap and one always starts to fall down midshow, and then I think there's a spider attacking me."

Kylie chuckled. "We can always go a little wilder with the eyeliner to hide the fact that you're not wearing fake lashes. Totally doable."

"Thanks, Fat Marilyn." Daphne beamed at her. "I don't know if anyone's told you, but you're all right."

"Wow, thanks." She was actually touched by Daphne's compliment. Celebrities were hard to please, so this was a rare treat. She was even going to ignore the Fat Marilyn stuff. This must have been Nice Daphne today. "How are you feeling?" she asked tentatively, since she was supposed to be watching Daphne for Cade. "You look great."

"Really?"

"Sure," Kylie lied. Daphne pretty much looked the same— skinny and pale—but her attitude was nice today, so she'd go with that. "Still clean?"

Daphne's eyes narrowed, and Kylie wondered if she'd pushed too far.

She plugged in her airbrush and acted as if nothing was amiss. "You mentioned to me the other day that you were trying to go clean again. Only reason I asked."

"Well, it's going great. I feel awesome."

"That's really wonderful," Kylie said, and meant it. She pulled out a bottle of primer and a makeup sponge and began to dab Daphne's face. "I'm happy for you."

"I've been clean a week now," Daphne told her, obediently closing her eyes and tilting her head back so Kylie could prime her entire face and neck. "Cade's going to be so proud of me."

"I bet he will."

"I'm doing it for him, you know. He told me he couldn't have a relationship with someone on drugs."

Kylie paused. Daphne's eyes were still closed, so Kylie dabbed at the primer again and then continued to cover Daphne's face. "So you two are in a relationship?"

"Yup," Daphne said, and she smiled. "He's a great guy, isn't he?"

"The best," Kylie said softly. She cleared her throat, blinking back angry tears. "Now, hold still. We have to do foundation once the primer dries."

It took a little over an hour to get Daphne's stage makeup just right. To hide the track marks on her arms, they were airbrushed with foundation and then decorated with glitter, too. Kylie contoured Daphne's face to make it seem rounded with health, then worked on sweeping glitter outward from her eyes. She made her black liner into an exaggerated cat's-eye so the lack of lashes wouldn't seem so odd, and added tiny rhinestones along the corners of her brows to draw the attention there. When she was done, she presented Daphne with a mirror. "All good?"

"All good," Daphne said triumphantly. "Thanks again. Off to wardrobe." She winked at Kylie as if they were best buds, and then hopped out of her chair. As she sauntered to Ginger's changing room, Kylie started to put away the stage makeup. Her hands trembled as she considered Daphne's words.

Was Daphne in a relationship with Cade? Was Kylie being played?

Either way, things were messy. Her mind whirled with unhappy thoughts as she packed up her things, and then to keep her hands busy, she refreshed her own makeup. Not that there would be anyone to see it, but she felt more confident when she looked good.

Daphne headed up to the stage area a short time later in her opening number costume, and Ginger emerged with a spare tutu from the night before. "I swear, that girl goes through more costumes than anyone I've ever worked for," she said with an eye roll. "And when she's not stepping on the hems, I have to take them in." She paused near Kylie and peered. "What's wrong, honey?"

God, was she that obvious? Kylie blinked rapidly. "I-I'm okay."

"Bullshit. I'm a mom. My youngest is twenty-three now but I can still recognize when someone's unhappy." She nodded her head at the door. "Come on. Come out on a smoke break with me."

"I don't smoke," Kylie said.

"Just come out on a smoke break with me," Ginger repeated, staring pointedly at Kylie.

"Okay." Because clearly there was something that needed to be said that shouldn't be said inside.

Ginger just smiled thinly at her, snagged her purse, and headed out the fire escape. Kylie followed her, and they both showed their badges to the security guard, then strolled out along the back wall of the building, heading toward the Dumpster. Ginger leaned up against it, fished a cigarette out of her purse, and lit it. "Sure you don't want one? Menthol. I tried that vapor shit but couldn't get past the taste."

"No, I'm good," Kylie said. She crossed her arms and gazed out at the far side of the building where crowds were forming near a barricade to get in to the concert. They'd be letting them in very soon and then the opening act would go on.

"Daph sure seems to be in a good mood lately, doesn't she?"

"I guess so."

"She told me all about the new guy she was dating." Ginger gave Kylie a pointed look. "New guy with blond hair and an old friend of hers."

Kylie winced and looked away again. "Mmmhmm."

"Which is funny, I think to myself, because I could have sworn I saw Kylie go home with some guy the first night of the tour. Some guy that showed up to see Daphne. Some guy with blond hair."

Kylie said nothing. What could she possibly say?

"And I thought I should show you this," Ginger said. She dug in her purse and pulled out a folded copy of *Celebrity!* Magazine and handed it to Kylie.

She took it from Ginger and gazed at the cover. There was a starlet with a new baby on the front page, someone else's cheating drama in a sidebar, and in a tiny corner picture, it read: DAPHNE PETTY: NEW TOUR, NEW LOVE! SEE P. 12. And because she was a sucker, Kylie flipped over to page twelve and skimmed it. There was a picture of Daphne on stage, surrounded by her dancers, her microphone held in the air. The caption box stated:

New beginnings for troubled heartthrob? Everyone's favorite pop princess, Daphne Petty, is starting her first North American tour since hitting rehab last year, and rumor has it that she has a new flame as well! Though we're told that Petty is very committed to making her show the best possible, a source has leaked to us that Petty has been seen multiple times in the company of billionaire philanthropist Cade Archer, 30. The source says that they're keeping things on the down-low for now, but seem "very cozy" when together. "They're childhood friends," our source says. "Cade understands Daphne better than anyone else, and he's completely supportive of her. He's been interested in Daphne for years, and has waited for the right time to make his move." Sounds like someone's right time is now!

Ugh.

Kylie closed the magazine and handed it back over to Ginger.

"Revolting magazine, isn't it?" Ginger said, then took another drag on her cigarette. "Fucking puff pieces galore, and you know they're planted by publicists who are looking to get attention for their clients."

"Do you think that was a puff piece?" Kylie asked, trying to keep the hopeful note out of her voice.

"I have no clue," Ginger admitted. "But he has been around a lot, they are childhood friends, and now Daphne's blabbing about dating him. Let's face it, kid. When it comes down to things, you and I are the hired help, and she's the star of the show. If it comes down to you or her . . ."

"He's going to pick her," Kylie said softly. Of course he would. He'd try to let Kylie down in the nicest way possible, but he'd still pick Daphne. How could Kylie possibly compete against someone Cade had wanted for years on end? "Thanks for the warning, Ginger."

"You bet, honey. I just don't want you to get hurt, you know?"

It was a little late for that, Kylie thought. She might have been okay with having a one-night stand if Cade hadn't shown up again. If he hadn't kissed her in the limo and romanced her over dinner and sent her funny little texts all week.

Because now? Now her heart was committed. Now her heart wanted more, and if things went south from here? She was going to be really, really hurt. Best to just detangle while she could, without getting her heart broken.

She pulled out her phone and flipped open her messages.

"Whatcha doing?" Ginger asked, fishing out another cigarette to smoke.

"Just checking the weather," Kylie lied.
"Uh-huh," Ginger said.

Kylie: Something's come up. Can't meet you
tomorrow night.

Cade: That's too bad. Anything I can help
with?

Cade: Or did you want to meet after the show on
Thursday?

Cade: Kylie?

Kylie: Busy. Can't talk.

Cade: Can you talk later?

Kylie: Nope, gotta go!

———————

All right, what the hell had happened? Cade stared down at
his phone, frowning.

Kylie—sweet, laughing Kylie—had given him the brush-
off. Had he said something? Done something? Heck, he
hadn't even been around for the last week or so. Was something new going on with Daphne?

Instead of texting, he tried calling Kylie. She didn't pick
up. Frustrated, he stared down at his phone, and then texted
someone who knew a few things about women.

Cade: What would you think if you ask a woman
out, she accepts, and then a day later, she
declines?

Reese: Who is this?

Cade: Very funny. I'm being serious.

Reese: Man, you must be serious if you can't even laugh at my joke. This isn't a Daphne question, is it? Please tell me it's not.

Cade: Not Daphne. Done w/her. Daph's makeup artist.

Reese: That's bad news, too. I would keep my dick far away from anyone or anything involved with her.

Cade: Kylie's different. Trust me.

Reese: Okay.

Cade: And help me. We already slept together. Flirted all week. Agreed to go out tomorrow night, and she just texted me 5 minutes ago and said she's busy.

Reese: Ouch.

Cade: You're not helping.

Reese: It's clear one of her friends got to her.

Cade: It is?

Reese: Yep. Unless you gave her something?

Cade: Gave her something?

Reese: You know, the kind of gift that keeps on giving and requires a doctor visit and medication?

Cade: Jesus. I didn't give her an STD! Why do I even ask you?

Reese: Because you know I'm right. If it's not that, then one of her friends convinced her you are a bad deal.

Cade: So how do I change her mind?

Reese: Convince her otherwise.

Cade: How? She won't talk to me.

Reese: Do things that don't involve talking.

Cade: I'm sorry I asked.

Reese: I don't mean that in a filthy way (though that works, too). I mean if she won't see you, send her presents. Or get her to come to the presents. She probably wants proof that you're into her.

Cade: Such as?

Reese: Jewelry?

Cade: I don't know if she's the type.

Reese: Audrey isn't. Jewelry types are much easier to buy for. So what does she like?

Cade: Makeup?

Reese: Jesus, I'm no help there.

Cade: All right, I'll think of something. So basically flush her out and shower her with presents?

Reese: Bingo. And then, you know, fuck her silly. Make it impossible for her to brush you off again. Fuck the senses out of her.

Cade: I'm going now.

TEN

"Delivery for Daphne Petty's makeup artist," the girl at the hotel front desk told Kylie over the phone. "That's all it says on the box. I called a few of the other people in the show and they said I should call you. Do I have the wrong person?"

"No," Kylie said, frowning at the walls in her small room. "Does it say who it's from?"

"Nope. Maybe a vendor of some kind? It looks like a shipment or a delivery of supplies or something."

"Huh. I'll be right down." Kylie slipped on a pair of flip-flops, turned off the TV, and headed down to the elevator on her floor. She wasn't expecting a package, but makeup samples from big-name companies sometimes found their way to Daphne's people. And, hey, she never turned down free goods, because she was broke and cheap. As long as it wasn't a shipment of drugs that Daphne wanted her to hide, she was cool with whatever it was.

Part of her wondered if it was Cade, and her heart gave a traitorous little thump of excitement that she squashed.

Yawning, Kylie got out of the elevator and headed toward the lobby desk. Since it was Vegas, it was still fairly busy in the lobby despite the late hour. She went to the counter and waited her turn. When the clerk smiled at her, she pulled out her tour badge and showed it. "I'm Daphne's makeup artist. You have something for me?"

"Yes, actually." The clerk smiled at Kylie and retrieved a large box from behind the counter. "It's rather light." The look the attendant gave her was interested, and so Kylie examined the box there at the desk. The return address was one she didn't recognize, and it had been sent airmail. Huh. "Got scissors?"

The attendant handed a pair to her and peered over the counter. "From a secret admirer?"

"God, I hope not," Kylie said, but there went that traitorous thump in her heart again. She took the scissors, slit the packing tape, and peeled the flaps of the box back to peer inside.

A pink balloon rose and bounced against her face. Surprised, Kylie pushed it aside, and it floated up another foot before bouncing again and stopping. The balloon's ribbon was tied to a note and what looked like . . . breakfast.

"Um . . . is that a waffle?" the girl asked as Kylie tugged the note free. "Attached to a balloon?"

Kylie didn't answer. She was too busy scanning the note.

Dearest Kylie,

I know you called off our date, but I can't stop thinking about you. You say you're busy, but I'll only take five minutes of your time. Truly. Meet me outside the hotel so we can talk.

Cade

PS—If you don't come outside in five minutes, I have a marching band out here ready to start playing, and

fireworks that will spell out KYLIE GO OUT WITH
CADE. Just FYI.
   PPS—Wasn't kidding about the five minutes.

Eyes wide, she crumpled the note in her hand.

"Why's someone sending you a waffle, if you don't mind me asking?" the girl at the front desk asked again.

"Because he's insane," Kylie replied. "Just flat-out insane." She reached over the counter, grabbed the scissors, popped the balloon viciously, and then stormed out to see why Cade was outside. He thought he could strong-arm her? She'd let him have a piece of her mind.

But all of that outrage disappeared when she went outside and saw the limo pulled up in front of the hotel. Cade leaned against the door, a flowerpot tucked under one arm. She looked around but she didn't see a marching band anywhere. In fact, there was no one outside except for Kylie . . . and Cade.

He grinned at the sight of her, uncrossing his legs and standing a bit straighter. "I take it you got my waffle?"

"Where's the marching band?" she asked, hands on her hips as she strode out to confront him. "Where's the fireworks?"

"Marching band got the sniffles," Cade said. "And I lied about the fireworks." He held the potted plant out to her. "For you."

She paused and took the plant from him, baffled. "What's this for?"

"I wanted to give you a present," he said. "I thought about a pet, since you'd mentioned that you wanted one and couldn't have one, but I couldn't think of anything that would travel well and didn't require walks. Except maybe Sea-Monkeys."

Kylie bit back her smile.

"So I thought maybe a nice violet would do. I'm told they're very hard to kill. And I wanted you to have company. It was either this or a Chia Pet." His mouth quirked in a lopsided grin. "And you will not believe how many stores are out of Chia Pets at the moment."

She gazed down at the violet and then sighed at him. "I'm trying to be mad at you."

His smile widened, flashing a dimple at her. "I know, and I'm not sure what I did to encourage it, so I'm doing my best to be appealing."

"You're far too good at it," she grumbled. "But, really Cade, you should go."

"Go? Why?" He reached forward and brushed a lock of hair off of her shoulder. "I just got here and I've barely had a chance to look at you."

"Someone will see you here," she told him. "You need to leave."

"Not before you tell me what I did wrong." Cade's eyes were so somber as he gazed at her. "Tell me what I did to mess things up and I won't bother you any longer."

Kylie hugged the potted plant close. Part of her wanted to storm off in a fury. To declare *you know what you did* and let him stew. But that would be childish. Adults had conversations, and she was an adult, darn it. "You should have told me you were dating Daphne."

He tilted his head, studying her. "That's a fair point. And I would have told you . . . if I was actually dating her. But I'm not. Where did you get that idea?"

"From the magazines? The tabloids? And every other word out of Daphne's mouth about how she's staying clean because you want her that way?"

His brows drew together, and for a moment he looked really, really confused. "But where are they getting that information? I'm not dating Daphne. I haven't even seen her since last week. She's texted me a few times, but I've spent all of my time talking to you." He raised his brows. "You probably see her more than I do."

"She texted you, huh?" Kylie asked, then wanted to bite back the words. They sounded jealous as hell.

"We've texted in the past," Cade said. "But the only one filling up my phone with love notes this last week was you."

Kylie snorted, feeling defensive. "Mine weren't love notes."

"A guy can dream, can't he?" He pulled out his phone, tapped the screen, and began to thumb through a few things. Then he offered it to her. "Here. Take a look."

She knew she shouldn't be as suspicious as that. She knew she should just turn it down and say she trusted him and let it go. But because she was small and petty and couldn't really believe that a guy like Cade preferred her to megastar Daphne, she took the phone and peeked through his text history. He wasn't lying; everything was from her. There were a few short messages to Daphne, but nothing out of the ordinary. Nothing that screamed "we're dating." And because she was nosy, she swiped over to his phone records. Daphne's number wasn't in the last couple of weeks.

"Find anything good?" Cade asked, grinning.

She handed the phone back to him. "No. I'm sorry if I got all suspicious. But, Cade, you know that we shouldn't go out."

"Actually, I don't know anything of the sort," he told her, moving a little closer. Heavens, he was standing so close she could smell his aftershave, and he smelled amazing. He leaned in and murmured, "Why not go out with me? Just tonight. We'll go to dinner, have a glass of wine, see if we still click. If we do, great. If we don't, I'll leave you alone."

He made it sound so simple. Kylie hesitated, then glanced down at her feet. She wiggled her toes in her green flip-flops. She could use her clothes as an excuse to get out of this. "I'm not really dressed to go out."

"Then we'll keep it someplace casual," he said, turning and opening the limo door.

"I should go upstairs and change," Kylie hedged.

"Absolutely not. You're not getting out of my sight again until we have a date," he said, and gestured at the open-and-waiting limo door.

It was like he could read her mind. Instead of being

annoyed, though, she was amused. She paused for only a moment longer.

"Someone might see you out here with me," Cade teased. "It's safer in the car."

"Damn it," Kylie said with a laugh. Then, clutching her potted flower, she crawled into the limo.

No sooner had she sat down than Cade got in behind her. The look he gave her was an intense one, and he gazed at her up and down. "You look great."

Like a silly girl, she put a hand to her hair and tried to finger-comb it. She was wearing old jeans, a faded T-shirt, and her hair was a mess. Her roots were even starting to show. It wasn't like she'd planned on going out, of course. Jesus, she was even wearing granny panties. But now that she was here with him, it seemed silly to put up a fight. "Thanks. You look pretty good, too. I'm sorry I canceled on you."

"I'm sorry you canceled on me, too," he said, grinning to take the sting out of his words. "Any place in particular you want to go tonight?"

"You pick," she told him. She didn't care where they went as long as it was private and she could spend time talking to him. Heck, she didn't mind if he did all the talking and she just got to stare at him. He was so gorgeous she didn't even care.

"Well, this is Vegas," he said. "There's bound to be someplace open." He was smiling at her, and her heart pitter-patted at the sight.

"Let's go someplace quiet and low-key," she told him. She knew Daphne's crew was hitting the town and the last thing she wanted was to run into them at one of the better-known nightspots.

"All right. Do you like . . . seafood? I know a great place that has an amazing wine list."

An "amazing wine list" sounded fancy. In jeans and flip-flops, she wasn't prepared for that. "Think more casual."

"Do you like . . ." He thought for a minute. "Fondue?"

"Never had it," she told him.

"Then that's what we'll have. Fondue."

"And what exactly is fondue?"

"Cheese and little pots?" He shrugged. "I don't know. It was the first thing that came up in my list of the area's restaurants . . . after the seafood place."

She laughed. "You googled the area? Don't you know Vegas?"

"Not as well as you'd think. My friend Reese knows it better than me. I'm afraid that I know more about the area hospitals and medical companies than the night life."

"Sounds . . . exciting."

"Oh, there's nothing more exciting than talking about the materials of a particularly revolutionary colostomy bag, let me tell you."

She giggled again. "You make yourself sound so boring."

His smile was easy, gorgeous. "I *am* boring, Kylie. That's what I'm trying to tell you. I'm not exciting. I spend ninety percent of my time working. I don't hit the town. I don't date much. I don't even know what fondue is."

Her mouth was twitching with the need to burst into another round of laughter. "So you *googled*?"

"What else can I do? A guy needs to be prepared when he goes out on a date."

"But . . . you're a billionaire." She giggled.

"So?"

That threw her for a loop. Billionaires didn't do things that normal people did. "So I find it weird that you're googling things for yourself. Don't you have an assistant?"

"Yes, but I also have two hands and I'm perfectly capable of using the Internet on my own." He wiggled his fingers at her. "Can't I be a normal guy and do things without having to ask for assistance?"

"I guess so?" She thought of Daphne with her poor browbeaten personal assistant and her entourage. Hell, Kylie's only job was to put makeup on Daphne before performances and press interviews. But to have money at Cade's level was just inconceivable, so to see him acting like a normal guy . . . ?

It was nice. Surprising, maybe, but nice.

He pressed a button on the door of the limo and the partition glass separating them from the driver went down. "Fondue House," Cade told the driver, then raised it again so he and Kylie were alone once more.

She studied him. "So what if we both eat fondue and we hate it?"

"Partners in intestinal fortitude once more?" he said with a wicked grin. "If we're sharing a bowl, we'll share any food poisoning as well. And like I said, I know every hospital in the area very well."

"That's a rather terrible way to view dinner."

"Yes, but if it gets us in adjoining beds in a hospital room, I'll take my chances," he said, taking her hand in his and tracing the veins on it.

"You shouldn't be thinking about hospitalizing a girl post-date," Kylie said, amused. "It puts a pall on things."

His fingers played against her skin, sending shivers through her body. "I thought about you all week, you know. It nearly drove me insane that you canceled on me and I couldn't figure out the reason why."

Well, now she felt guilty. "Don't you read *Celebrity!* or any of those magazines?"

"Not if I can help it. I don't have a very positive view of that sort of lifestyle."

No, she supposed he wouldn't if he was friends with Daphne. Kylie knew her own experiences with megastars had soured her on them as well. "It's got an article about you and Daphne being together."

"Might be publicity from her team," he said, still tracing the veins on her hand. "It'll probably quell some of the rumors about her actions if she seems like she's in a stable relationship. Do you want me to get my people to issue a statement on the situation?"

It was hard for Kylie to concentrate with those featherlight touches on her arms. It took her a moment to process, and then she shook her head. Making a statement would just make things worse, she imagined. Daphne would get upset if Cade publicly declared they weren't dating. It would draw more attention back to things, and somehow Kylie suspected that would be the last thing anyone wanted. "Nah."

He rubbed his thumb over her knuckles. "Just . . . if you hear anything crazy come out of Daphne's mouth, check with me first, okay? I will always be honest with you."

Kylie nodded. "I'm sorry I didn't trust you."

"We don't know each other well enough yet," Cade said. "It's understandable." He glanced over at her. "But make no mistake, I intend on getting to know you extremely well."

She shivered at the pulse of heat that flared through her body. "Are you always so forward with women?"

"Just you," he admitted. "Normally I'm content to let things fall by the wayside, but the more you try to get away from me, the closer I want to pull you."

"I suppose I should be flattered." Her voice had a light, fluttery note to it that she wished would go away. She blamed his light caresses of her hand. His fingers were making it so hard for her to concentrate.

"I don't want you to be flattered," he murmured, and then lifted her hand to his mouth. "I just want you to say yes." And he kissed her fingertips.

"Y-yes to what?"

The look in his vivid blue eyes was sultry. "Whatever I ask."

Oh, mercy. She needed a fan right about now. "So . . . what are you asking me?"

"Nothing yet. But the night's still young."

Definitely needing that fan.

The fondue place was just around the corner, and as they got into the restaurant, Kylie was relieved to see that it was extremely dark inside, and not all that crowded. Perfect. They could hide in here and still enjoy themselves tonight. A surge of guilt rose at the thought of lying about where she was to Daphne, but this was just a date to catch up. It wasn't going to be anything serious. They'd talk, get whatever they had out of their systems, and then they'd move on with their lives. He'd go back to Daphne and she'd go back to . . . well, her makeup brushes. Still, she got a little melty when she thought of the potted flower he'd brought her so she wouldn't be so lonely on the road. It was so thoughtful. He was the only one that had bothered to ask if she was lonely while on the road. No one else ever cared.

But she couldn't get sidetracked. She had duties. She had burdens that could only be made worse by flirting with a man her boss thought was her property.

Cade's thoughtfulness kept distracting her, though. He was asking all the questions that she had to keep buried or she'd snap. He kept poking at her worries, her fears, her insecurities— and making her feel good about them. That she was doing a good job somehow.

And that was what kept throwing her off guard. What kept making her vulnerable.

Cade talked to the hostess for a few minutes while Kylie waited nearby. She saw him point at the seating chart a few times, and he kept using that megawatt smile that made Kylie's panties melt, so she could only imagine how dazzled the restaurant hostess was. Cade seemed pleased when the woman eventually nodded and grabbed two menus. "Right this way."

As Kylie walked forward, Cade put his hand on her back in a move that felt a little possessive and a lot right. She was blushing as they moved to a booth in the back of the restaurant. The booth was tucked in between four others that were all empty, and as the hostess led them, she lit a candle on the table and then set it inside a lamp. "You two enjoy."

Cade gestured that Kylie should sit first, and so she picked a side of the booth, sliding in.

To her surprise, Cade slid in right next to her. His arm brushed hers, and he grinned. "Hello again."

She was suddenly thankful for the dim lighting, because her blush had returned fiercely. "You don't want to sit on the other side?"

"Not if it means missing out on being next to you."

She raised an eyebrow at him. "What if I'm right-handed and you're left-handed?"

"Then we're just going to end up hitting each other a lot as we go for the cheese pot," Cade said easily. "But it'll give me an excuse to reach for your hand." And he brushed his fingers over hers.

And Kylie knew she should pull away, but she couldn't bring herself to do it. When his fingers laced with hers, she ran her thumb along his, enjoying the feel of his hand in hers. "I guess it's a sacrifice we'll have to make."

"Guess so," he murmured.

The waitress appeared a few moments later. "Hi! Welcome to Fondue House." She handed Cade a menu card. "This is tonight's wine list, if you're interested."

He looked over at Kylie. "Like wine?"

She shrugged. "As long as I'm not driving, I like a glass. But I'm fine with drinking water, really."

"Don't even try it," he said, and handed the card back to the waitress. "The white at the top, please. Bring the bottle."

The waitress beamed. "Be right back with your drinks."

Cade gave Kylie a small, mock-disappointed shake of his head. "Water? Really?"

"Water goes with everything," she retorted. Plus, water was cheap, and Kylie tended to eat cheap lately. Nana Sloane's care was the best that she could buy, but it was also tearing through Kylie's savings. "Besides, you never know when you have to drive a drunk billionaire home."

Instead of being wounded at her needling, he just smiled

that slow, gorgeous smile of his. "I'll have you know that was the best night I can remember in a long damn time."

It was for her, too. She stared down at their joined hands and then carefully pulled hers from his. Maybe that was what made this so hard. "Cade. I really only came out because I wanted to tell you that we can't date. We really, really can't. I need my job, and you know Daphne's going to be furious if she finds out we're dating. It's just not smart for me to be out with you." *Even though everything in me wants this to go on forever.*

"And I told you, I'll handle Daphne."

Thing was, Kylie wasn't sure Daphne could be handled. But she didn't disagree again. The waitress arrived with the wine and a silver bucket full of ice, and made a big show of uncorking while chattering about the menu and tonight's specials. They were both quiet as wine was poured. Then they took their glasses, gave a tiny, awkward toast, and sipped.

It was utterly delicious: rich and full-bodied and just a hint of sweet. She took another sip just because it was so good. "This is lovely."

They ordered surf and turf since neither one of them was familiar with fondue, and the waitress eventually set down a pot on a burner in front of them, filled it with cheese, and gave them an assortment of breads and vegetables to dip, and several skewers for them to use.

Kylie tried to skewer a baby carrot and failed. "I . . . don't think I'm very good at this."

Cade chuckled and speared a piece of bread, dipping it into the sauce. "How about I just feed you instead?"

She squirmed uncomfortably in her chair. The hot guy feeding the fat chick? How was that going to look? Ugh. She glanced around and for the first time noticed that this entire side of the restaurant was deserted. "Boy, they're not very busy tonight, are they?"

"I offered to pay a premium if they left these tables empty," Cade said, dipping the bread into the cheese and then lifting the entire thing toward Kylie's mouth. "Now, open up."

"Cade," she protested, "really—"

"If you don't, I won't fund an orphanage in China."

She began to laugh despite herself. "Do you use that line every time?"

"Yes. Now open up."

Obediently she did, and to her surprise, he plucked the bread off the skewer and placed it gently between her lips, his fingers brushing against her mouth. Okay, that was sexy. Just like that, she felt another charge of desire ricochet through her. She swallowed and then quickly reached for her wine again. She shouldn't be doing this. Really, really shouldn't. When he attempted to feed her another piece, she waved him off and pretended to focus on her wine . . . which wasn't so difficult, since it was rather yummy. "This wine is incredible."

"I'd hope so at five hundred a bottle."

Kylie choked, just a little. "Did you say . . . five hundred?" Jesus. No wonder it was so heavenly. She eyed the bottle. Cade's glass was still nearly full and he wasn't drinking much. She'd feel like an ass if they didn't drink all of it, so she picked up the bottle and refilled both of their glasses. "You have to drink with me, then."

He lifted his glass to her. "Bottoms up?"

"Sounds good." She clinked her glass to his and took another healthy sip.

"So," he said, after taking a drink. "How is the tour going?"

"Onstage or offstage?"

"The fact that you have to qualify that makes me worried." Cade's handsome face drew into a frown. "Has she been sick a lot, then?"

"Sick?" Kylie took another healthy sip of the wine. It really was delicious. "I don't recall her being sick."

"She smoking a lot?"

Funny . . . she didn't recall that, either. "Not sure. Why?"

"She likes to smoke when she's trying to wean herself off the drugs. Has her personal doctor been in to check on her?"

Kylie shrugged. "I'd have to ask Snoopy."

"Snoopy?" Cade's lips twitched. "Is that really her name?"

"Not exactly," she said. "Do you not know about Daphne's nicknames for everyone?"

"What nicknames?"

"She has a hard time remembering names so she gives us new ones." Kylie picked at a piece of bread absently. "I think Snoopy got her name because Daphne jokes that she treats her like a dog."

"That's . . . terrible." He looked rather shocked.

"I kind of thought so, too, but everyone seems to just accept it, so what can you do? Whatever Daphne does, everyone turns a blind eye to it." She was a little surprised he didn't know about some of Daphne's bad behavior. If they were as close as she'd thought, wouldn't he know more about how she acted on tour? The tantrums she threw on a daily basis?

But he was still frowning and looked uncomfortable. "She has nicknames for . . . everyone?"

Kylie nodded, dipping a piece of bread.

"So what does she call you?"

She suddenly felt awkward, staring at the cheese-dipped bread in her hand. "Uh . . . so she calls me Fat Marilyn."

"She what?"

Kylie dropped the bread on her plate, embarrassed. "Fat Marilyn. I guess because I was dressed retro so she thought I looked like Marilyn Monroe? And *fat* for obvious reasons."

His jaw clenched. "She called you that the other day. I thought I misheard. And it doesn't bother you?"

Oh, it bothered her. But no one went against Daphne. Not when she was the headliner. "It's not a big deal, really."

"It is a big deal." He ran a hand over his chin. "I'm going

to talk with her. She has no right to rename you based on what she perceives as a flaw."

"Oh no, please don't." The last thing she wanted was to get more of Daphne's attention. But when his nostrils flared, she realized he was actually really furious. Wow. "Cade. Please." She put her hand back on his. "For me, all right?"

She watched as his jaw worked, as if he were trying to swallow the concept of not speaking up. Eventually, he gave a terse nod. "Fine."

Now her stomach was all clenched in knots. She took another swig of wine, feeling the pleasant burn move through her body.

"The more I learn about her, the more I'm horrified," Cade said in a low voice. He shook his head. "She's really not the girl I thought she was. I don't know how it took me so long to see it."

"It's . . . not an easy situation. She's in a fragile state of mind, and I think a lot of people let her get away with things simply because it's easier than arguing with her. And if you make her upset? The repercussions go on for days." Heck, Marco was still in the doghouse because Daphne was convinced he'd given her bad drugs. He'd been her favorite boy toy up until that point. It wasn't hard to fall from Daphne's favor lately. Things changed in the blink of an eye, and the entire tour felt a little uneasy around the star.

"Perhaps I should step in, then," Cade said, his look grimly determined. "If she won't listen to me, she won't listen to anyone."

"I think"—Kylie poured more wine into both of their glasses—"that we need to drink up and stop talking about Daphne while we're together."

"I'll drink to that," he said, and his foot nudged hers.

She took another sip of wine and then gave him a teasing look. "Was that your foot? Are you playing footsies with me under the table, sir?"

"I'm not."

"Pity," she said, and eased off one of her flip-flops. She rubbed her bare foot against his leg, curious to see how he'd react. Maybe it was the wine—okay, it was *probably* the wine—but she suddenly wanted to flirt.

He closed his eyes and groaned low. "You know I want more than just your foot on me."

"Yes," she teased. "But my foot's all you get. Now drink your wine."

He clinked his glass to hers again.

ELEVEN

Next door, a maid started a vacuum, and Kylie's head throbbed in crescendo with the sound. She groaned and pressed a hand to one aching temple. Even the pillow against her face felt too hard. Wasn't it too early for noise like a vacuum? Surely that was against the rules somewhere.

God, her head hurt. Too much wine. Nothing got her toasted quite like wine did. Smacking her dry mouth, Kylie pulled the pillow over her head.

Something on her hand caught on the pillowcase at the same time a warm arm wrapped around her waist.

And slowly, these things didn't add up. Through the pulsing of her head, Kylie forced herself to roll over in bed, which was harder than she'd anticipated.

It put her nose to nose with a sleeping Cade Archer.

Kylie jerked backward in shock. Oh, shit. Shit, shit shit.

Cade kept sleeping, though. He apparently was a heavy sleeper. Thank God for some things. He was also gorgeous, his full mouth slightly slack, tanned skin—tanned *naked* skin—peeking out from under the white sheets. While sleeping, she got a great view of his sinfully long blond lashes and the perfection of his nose. What on earth was he doing with a girl like her?

Then again, what was she doing in bed with a guy she was supposed to be avoiding? She carefully slid off the side of the mattress, tugging a sheet around her. She was naked. Oh, sweet Jesus, this was what she got for not wanting to waste a five hundred dollar bottle of wine. She should have sipped one glass, said thank you, and left it at that. Instead, she had vague memories of licking melted chocolate off of Cade's fingers, staggering back to the limo drunk, and . . .

All right, she was pretty much a foggy blank after that. A big, slutty, foggy blank.

Seriously, though, had she walked under a ladder recently? Broken a mirror? Why on earth was she so damn unlucky? She padded to the bathroom. Maybe it wasn't so bad, she told herself. Maybe they both got really damn drunk and naked, but no one had sex. Sure, that was entirely plausible . . . if you were twelve. Still, she clung to the hope, heading into the bathroom.

When she got there, though, the hickeys on her skin told a different tale. Kylie put a hand between her legs and groaned. Damp and sore. Definitely not the trademarks of someone that hadn't had sex. There was a bruise on one of her breasts, too, and she reached up to touch it, wincing . . .

And noticed the huge honking ring on her hand.

She nearly passed out at the sight of it.

Dear sweet lord, what the hell was *that*?

Kylie stared at her hand. Just stared. There was a huge double-ring on her ring finger, big enough to cover her entire knuckle. The stone was a bright red square surrounded by dozens of tiny sparkly yellow stones that she sincerely hoped were fakes. The band was silvery with more of the yellow stones, etched designs swirling over the thick band. It looked . . . really expensive and not fake.

Oh God. Oh God. Her breathing sped up.

Bad enough that she'd slept with Cade again after vowing

to leave him alone. Bad enough that she'd apparently gotten drunk and climbed him like a tree despite knowing that he was putting her job in jeopardy.

But seriously—how fucking drunk was she that she'd *married* him?

Clutching the sheet close to her body, she headed back out to the bedroom, noticing for first time that this wasn't her hotel room. It was too big, too opulent. Where was she? She ran to the nightstand and read the label on the phone—the Belaggio. Okay. Okay. Okay. The clock read eleven thirty, so she had time to get back to her own hotel, check out, and head to work as if nothing had happened. She just needed a shower, something to cure her pounding headache, and to get rid of the ring and the husband she'd magically acquired overnight in a drunken bender.

First things first, she told herself, and tried to pull off the ring.

It wouldn't come off.

Horrified, Kylie twisted at the enormous rock, trying to drag the band over her knuckle. It didn't move. How had she gotten this thing on? Frantic, she pulled at it for a moment more, then ran to the restroom and squirted hand soap all over it, rubbing wildly. As she did, she noticed a dent in the back of the ring— the soft metal had hit something last night, and that was why it wasn't coming off. A jeweler might be able to snip it, but no amount of twisting and silent praying on Kylie's behalf budged the damn thing. Now, with all the attacking she'd been doing to her hand, the skin was red and chafed and beginning to swell. There was no shot in hell of getting the bands off now.

A sob broke from her throat, and she rushed back to the hotel room. "Cade! Wake up!"

He bolted awake, his soft blond curls sticking straight up. The sheets fell to his waist, revealing a chest covered in scratches and hickeys of his own. "What is it? What's wrong?"

"This," she cried out, holding up her hand with the huge ring. "This is what's wrong! Did we get married last night?"

Cade scrubbed a hand over his eyes wearily. "You don't remember? Really?"

"Exactly how much wine did I freaking drink?" She didn't remember anything beyond fondue, which was fun to dip food in but not so great for soaking up copious amounts of alcohol.

He rubbed his head, which only caused his hair to stick up even further. It might have been gorgeously adorable if she hadn't been so panicked. "You liked the wine so much we ordered a second bottle." His lips twitched with amusement. "You insisted, actually."

Oh God. "Why did you let me insist?"

His mouth curled into one of those panty-melting smiles. "Because I can't resist when you ask for anything."

She stared down at the vivid ring on her finger. "Did I . . . did I ask for this?"

"If I recall—and my memory is pretty hazy, too—we passed by a jewelry store, and I suggested it, and then you threw your arms around my neck and started kissing me." He was grinning now, the bastard. "Do you like the ring? We thought it matched your hair. Rubies and yellow diamonds."

So those weren't fakes. They were expensive and real. "And the band?" she asked faintly.

"Platinum." He held up his hand. "Mine, too."

"I bent it," she told him, moving toward the bed. Her voice sounded as weak and tremulous as she felt. "Look at the back of the ring. I bent it."

He patted the bed and because her knees probably wouldn't hold out much longer, she went and sat next to him, tugging her sheet-dress close as she showed him her hand.

"It won't come off," she said, and had to sniff to hold back tears. She didn't want to cry in front of him, but her stupid brain wasn't listening all that well. "I thought platinum was supposed to be a hard metal."

"Shh," he said, taking her hand in his. "Let me look at it." Kylie sniffed quietly as he examined her hand, pulling her fingers apart and gazing at the ornate band. He was taking this well, all things considered.

Cade shook his head. "Look at your poor fingers," he murmured, and leaned in to kiss one. "You've rubbed them raw, Kylie."

"But the band—"

"Will stay put for a bit longer," he murmured. He looked up at her with hooded eyes and kissed the tip of her finger again. "I can't say I'm sad to see you still in my bed this morning."

His mouth on her fingers was making her shiver. God, this was such a bad idea. She really should pull away.

He kissed her palm.

Any moment now, she was going to pull away.

His tongue flicked over the soft center of her palm.

Any moment.

But then he nipped at the fleshy part of her hand and she had to bite back a moan. "Can you please concentrate?" She sounded out of breath and incredibly horny . . . which she was. But now wasn't the time. "We need to figure out what we're going to do."

"Do?" He arched an eyebrow at her and kept nibbling at her sensitive hand.

"About these rings. About us."

"Well, I know what I'd like to do."

She braced herself. "What's that?"

He nipped again, sending a shiver through her body. "Pull that sheet off of those plump breasts and get my mouth on them again. Lick you between your legs for hours until you're quivering and begging me to fuck you again. Push my cock so deep inside you that when you come, I feel every bit of your body tensing around mine." He flicked his tongue over her palm. "Again."

Her nipples responded by tightening into traitorous little buds.

"But . . . marriage—"

"Married people have great sex, or so I am told." He

kissed the soft flesh at the inside of her wrist and began to move up her arm.

"But we're not supposed to be married!" Why was he not listening to her? Didn't he care? This was the worst possible thing that could have happened to them. To him for sure. The last thing he needed was to be saddled with a fat, insecure, broke makeup artist. She yanked her arm out of his grip as the implications of everything began to roll through her mind. "Oh God. Did we sign a prenup last night?"

"I'm pretty sure both of us were too drunk to sign anything," he said with a chuckle. He slid closer to her on the bed and brushed a lock of her hair off her shoulder, then leaned in and kissed her skin. "But don't worry, I won't go after your money."

Was he trying to be funny? She couldn't be funny right now. Not when he was kissing her and her nipples were aching with the need to be teased and her sex was aching with a memory that Kylie's brain didn't have. Not when her head was pounding and her conscience was screaming for her to get out of bed right now, *right now.*

"Cade," she said, pushing him away. "Listen to me. Please. Just listen."

"Listening," he murmured, tugging at the sheet she was holding to her breasts. "Be assured that you have my utmost attention."

"We can't be married," she protested, trying to keep the sheet over her body even as he exposed one nipple and began to tease it with his fingers. A hot flush of need slammed through her body and she had to bite back a moan as he rubbed the underside of her nipple in the way that drove her craziest. "We weren't even supposed to go out last night. You and me . . . it was only supposed to be one night. Nothing else. No strings, nothing. We weren't supposed to see each other ever again."

"But we did see each other again," he murmured, flicking her aching nipple with a practiced thumb even as he continued to kiss her shoulder. "Also? You are so fucking pretty naked. My cock is aching just looking at you."

This time, the moan did escape her throat. "Cade, we shouldn't."

"Oh, we should. We definitely should." His fingers coaxed her nipple to a stiff little point, and his other hand eased the rest of the sheet down, until Kylie was topless and covered only by the pooling fabric in her lap. He took her hand again, kissed the palm, and laid it on his cock, thick and hard and aching.

And she sucked in a breath, fascinated by that intimate touch. Her fingers grazed the head of his cock and she was surprised to find it wet with pre-come already. "You're that turned on?"

"Are you kidding me?" He took her big, heavy breast in his hand and lifted it until her nipple was pointing toward his mouth, and he gave it a long, lascivious lick. "Just seeing you makes me so hard I can barely stand it."

She moaned again. Her fingers tightened around his cock and she gave him a squeeze as his mouth nipped at her breast. "We need to talk about this marriage—"

"Talk later. Breasts now."

"But you're not listening to me," she said, torn between frustration and desire. "We shouldn't be married."

"I see nothing preventing us from the fact," he murmured. "I want you." His hand covered hers on his cock. "See how much I want you?" Then, his hand slipped between her rounded thighs and pushed to rest against her pussy. "And I can feel how wet you are for me." His fingers slid along the damp seam of her. "So tell me that you don't want me, Kylie? Because I have proof." He lifted his hand and showed it to her, gleaming with her fluids.

She shook her head, still dazed. "We-we can't. Cade—"

"Shhh," he murmured, pressing those damp fingers against her lips. The taste of her own salt hit her tongue, and it was strangely erotic. A gasp escaped her.

"That looks delicious," he murmured, and leaned in, capturing her mouth with his and then lightly sucking on her lips, cleaning them of her taste. "Mmm."

"Cade," she moaned. Oh God, he was driving her to distraction. She couldn't think when he was kissing her own juices off of her mouth. All she could think about was his hand on her pussy again, or her hand on his cock. And even though it was wrong and she shouldn't want him to touch her, she positively ached deep inside for him.

"Condoms," he murmured, kissing her jaw, her neck, and then pulling away reluctantly. "We need condoms." He leaned over the bed, giving her a gorgeous view of his long, lean, tanned body, and her hand gripping his length as if she were holding on for dear life. He pulled a drawer open on the bedside table and then cursed. "I know I have more condoms around here somewhere." He sat up and kissed her quickly. "Be right back."

Then, extracting himself from her grip, he hopped up and headed across the suite to the bathroom, tight ass flexing as he moved.

The moment he left the room, reality set in. What on earth was she doing? They needed to annul this thing and forget it ever happened. The last thing she needed was to have sex with him again. It was supposed to be one freaking night, damn it. She was never going to keep things from Daphne at this rate. She was going to lose her job at this rate.

And . . . then what? Mooch off of Cade? Let him think she was a gold digger? Become his *burden*?

Her stomach clenched hard at that.

She heard him rummaging in the bathroom. "Just a moment," he called out. "I know it's here somewhere."

Her jeans were pooled by the bed and she grabbed them and slid them on, shoving her feet into her flip-flops. She grabbed her shirt, hauled it overhead, snagged her purse, and ran for the door, closing it quietly behind her.

So she was a chicken and was going to run away. So what? She told herself Cade was a nice guy. That he'd understand why she needed to get away. Why she needed to get away so fast that she'd abandon him in a petting session and leave behind bra and panties. She frantically hammered at the button on the elevator, glancing back at the hotel door. *Come on, come on.*

It dinged an endless moment later just as she heard her name shouted. *"Kylie?"*

Fuck. The doors opened and an elderly couple stood there, blinking at her. She must look like a sight, breasts jiggling from a lack of a bra, shirt stained, hair a bedhead nest. Cheeks burning, she quickly punched the Door Close button over and over again.

As they began to slide shut, Cade's door opened and he sprinted out into the hall, holding an unbuttoned pair of slacks at his waist. Her eyes met his as the doors closed, and she mouthed a quick *Sorry.*

But they didn't close fast enough for her not to see the flare of anger in his eyes.

Then, it was shut and the elevator was heading down. She punched the lobby button and took a deep, shuddering breath, determined not to cry.

Cade would eventually figure out this was better for both of them. He really would. Right now he was just dazzled by easy sex. He'd come to his senses and then they could talk sensibly about an annulment and no one would be the wiser.

Once the elevator hit the lobby, Kylie sprinted for the doors. She was terrified at the thought of seeing a half-dressed Cade coming down the stairs and got into the first cab she saw out front. "Drive," she bellowed. "Please, just drive."

Click went the meter, and then she'd escaped. She was home free. With a sigh, Kylie looked in the rearview window, but there was no Cade waiting on the sidewalk, watching her leave. That was good, she told herself. She gave the driver the address to her hotel and tried to fix her appearance with a comb and a bit of makeup during the ride back.

Then she was at her hotel. She paid the driver, headed in, and went up to her floor. She kept her head ducked, avoiding eye contact in case she saw someone she knew.

She'd almost made it inside and was at the door to her room, fumbling for her key in her oversized purse when the door next to hers opened. Ginger stepped out, wheeling her small carry-on suitcase behind her.

They stared at each other for a moment, and then Ginger slowly shook her head. "Walk of shame, Kylie?"

"Of course not," Kylie lied, hoping that her lip gloss covered her swollen mouth and her hair would hide the worst of the hickeys.

"Then where's your bra?"

Kylie had no immediate response for that. She remained silent, and Ginger shook her head. "You are playing with fire, girl. Your ass is going to get canned if you're not careful."

"I'll be careful," Kylie said.

But Ginger just snorted, clearly not believing Kylie's protest, and wheeled her suitcase down the hall.

———

Just when Kylie couldn't get any lower, her phone rang that afternoon. She winced at the caller ID, but answered it anyhow. "Hi, Nana."

"Kylie Daniels," the old woman's shaky voice sounded pissy, even over the line. "Where are you?"

Her head ached and she rubbed her temples. "Busy."

"Don't you sass me, young woman. Do you know where I am right now?"

Uh-oh. "The nursing home?" Please? She desperately hoped her grandmother hadn't escaped again.

"That's right! I hate this place. I told you that already. But you keep shoving me here because you're mad at me. Isn't that right?"

Old, familiar pangs of hurt rippled through Kylie. "I don't have you there because I'm angry, Nana. You're there because they can give you the best care possible. You need someone to look after you 24/7."

"Lies. You come get me right now."

"I can't, Nana. I'm on tour right now."

"Touring? Why?"

Her grandmother always forgot what Kylie did for a living. "I do makeup for singers on tour, Nana. Remember? It pays the bills."

"Don't you remind me about paying bills, young woman. I've worked two jobs for the past ten years to keep you fed. And are you grateful? No! You just keep eating. I swear you're fatter than a little pig. It's a wonder I can keep a roof over our heads. Your grandfather would roll over in his grave if he knew what a burden you were." The elderly woman's voice shook. "Don't you try and lecture me about responsibility. I know all about it."

There was that word: *burden*. Her grandmother always tossed it in Kylie's face. It hurt worse than any other insult. "Well, now I'm working and taking care of you, Nana. Just like I should. How are you feeling?"

"I hate this place." Her voice wobbled. "Come and get me. Right now."

"I can't, Nana. I wish I could. I have to work."

"Then put your mother on the phone, Kylie. I know she'll come get me. She's not ungrateful. Not like you. You get that from your father's side."

Kylie's head throbbed. She hated these conversations. If she told her grandmother that her daughter was dead, she'd just get confused—or worse, cry. "She's in the bathroom, Nana. I'll have her call you back."

"You do that. I have to go to work now."

"All right, Nana. Talk to you later." Kylie's throat felt like a dry knot when she hung up. A call from her nana always made her feel like dirt. Unloved, ungrateful dirt.

Count on the burden of family to kick you while you were down.

TWELVE

B y the time Daphne went on stage for her second Vegas show, Kylie had mostly relaxed.

Mostly.

She'd showered and fixed her hair into an elaborate set of sausage-curls and clips that would show off her newly redyed bright red ends. She'd taken care of her roots, and her makeup was carefully done as well. All of this was to hide the fact that she had rings under her eyes and a hangover pallor to her skin. If she looked put together, no one would ask questions. She wore a cute swishy navy dress with a striped top and fluffy skirt hemmed with red, and wore red and navy sandals with it. Today, she supposed she'd look the part of Fat Marilyn. And if the rest of her was a bit glammed up, maybe no one would ask why she was wearing rings on every finger, or why the one on her ring-finger was turned inward, the stones hidden unless she opened her palm.

But no one asked, and as Kylie prepped Daphne, she began to feel better about things. Cade would understand once he had a few hours to digest things, she told herself. He'd come to his senses and they'd talk things through like normal consenting adults that just needed to step away from the alcohol for a bit. Lots of people made mistakes in Vegas, she told herself as she packed away the stage makeup kit and began to take out the palettes she used for Daphne's postshow interview makeup.

And as Daphne began to perform and the music swelled through the backstage area, Kylie sat in her chair and rubbed her aching forehead. She could almost believe that things were normal. Almost. Except when she rubbed her head, it provided her with a good look at the huge red-and-yellow wedding ring she had turned inward. The ring that wouldn't come off no matter how hard she tried.

That, and her phone was missing. She'd left it in her mad dash to get away from Cade. That was okay, though. She'd get a replacement phone when she got her next check.

Ginger wasn't speaking to her, either. Every time she saw Kylie, she pursed her lips in a disapproving look and left the room. She took Snoopy on smoke breaks with her instead of Kylie, and Kylie tensed every time she saw Ginger talk to Daphne. But Daphne never freaked out and her mood was rather mellow, so Kylie had to assume that Ginger wasn't saying anything.

So. Almost normal.

She twisted the wedding ring absently, staring in the mirror, and wondered what Cade was doing tonight. Heading back out to Botswana? More medical conferences? Or had he gone back home to New York? Maybe he was at a law office requesting an annulment even now. She ignored the guilty feeling that gave her, and the vague unhappiness.

It wasn't meant to be. She needed to remember her priorities. She should call her nana, see if she was lucid again. Check with her caretakers to make sure Kylie's account was up to date and everything was going well. See if Nana was screaming at everyone still. See if she still considered Kylie her "burden."

But of course she didn't have her phone. Cade did.

As if her thoughts had conjured him, the door to the greenroom opened and Cade Archer stepped in, looking inhumanly gorgeous and supremely pissed. Kylie froze in the director's chair at the makeup stand, and she cringed in place as his furious gaze scanned the room and then locked squarely onto her.

———————

Kylie didn't want to play fair?

He'd fucking show her how dirty he could play, then.

For the first time in a very long time, Cade was so angry he could hardly think straight. He didn't get mad when a business copied one of his patents illegally, selling poorly made equipment to customers who thought they were getting legitimate products. He simply sent his lawyers after them. He didn't get mad when a massive donation of medical supplies to a war-torn country was stolen by local insurgents. He resent the supplies and had his organization send along trained guards to protect the goods and make sure they got to the people that needed them. He didn't even get mad when he found out Daphne was using again. He was just disappointed.

But with Kylie?

He was livid.

Why couldn't she accept that they were married? Sure, it had happened when they were drunk, but he was starting to think that these drunken interludes were some of the best things that had happened to him. The first night had brought him Kylie. The second had given him Kylie in marriage. Neither one he saw as a problem. He didn't understand Kylie's panic, either. Was she worried that Daphne would fire her? He'd handle Daphne. Was she worried that he would be upset with her? She couldn't be, not the way she'd touched him and devoured him with soft, needy eyes that morning.

So he didn't fucking get her. And when she'd run away like a coward? He *really* fucking didn't get her. Running out midsex with both of them aching with need? Her taste still on his lips? Just so she could avoid having to lose an argument with him?

It was beyond frustrating.

He'd called Jerome again that afternoon. "I need more tickets to Daphne's Vegas show tonight. Backstage passes, too."

"Uh, everything okay, boss?" Jerome had asked. "You need to talk about it?"

Even though he and Jerome were more friends than employer-and-employee, he didn't want to talk about it, no. "Just get the tickets for me. I'll explain when I'm in a better mood."

"All right, but I'm probably going to have to butter up some scalpers with some huge money. That concert's been sold out for weeks."

"I don't care how much it takes," Cade told him. "Just call me back when you've got the will-call details."

"Got it."

Jerome had called back a half hour later, told him the exorbitant amount the tickets had cost, and given him the details. And Cade showered, tried to get rid of his anger doing some remote work, failed, dressed for the show, found Kylie's phone, got pissed all over again, and then eventually headed to the enormous music hall that was housing Daphne Petty's big concert. Fans were everywhere, and the limo had to crawl its way to the entrance, which only irritated Cade even more. By the time he got his tickets and slung his backstage pass around his neck, he was in a foul mood, which was pretty unusual for him as he was considered the level-headed peacemaker of his group of friends.

But Kylie had pushed him past the limits of his patience. If she wouldn't listen to what he wanted, then he was going to make her listen, damn it.

He stalked his way backstage, his hands shoved into the pockets of his dark blue sports jacket. His own ring was still on his finger, and it was going to stay there, damn it. Kylie would see that it could be a good thing to be married to him, damn it. He was already enjoying the thought of being married to her. Waking up next to her every morning? Getting to fuck that sweet, gorgeous body of hers every night? Hearing her laugh whenever and wherever? He liked the thought of that more than he should.

When he got to the greenroom, he scanned it for two faces in particular—Daphne, so he could avoid her, and Kylie, so he could pounce on her. Music reverberated in the room and when he heard the strains of Daphne's voice, he realized it wouldn't be necessary to avoid her just yet. Well, there was one obstacle down. His gaze moved to the cosmetics table normally set up in a corner of the room, and then he saw her.

Kylie.

She looked good, her makeup perfection on her face. Her buxom figure was shown off in a tight striped white-and-navy shirt that seemed to accentuate her generous breasts and the taper of her waist, and her skirt was a full blue circle that went to her knees. She wore bright sandals and a lot of jewelry and looked stunning and not nearly as wrecked as he felt . . . which made him just as frustrated and angry as before.

Wasn't she affected the way he was? Or was she somehow able to just shake off this insane need they felt for each other and go on about her day? He sure as shit couldn't.

Her eyes widened at the sight of him and she grabbed one of her shabby makeup cases and clutched it to her chest, then put her head down and began to walk away, through one of the doors marked STAFF ONLY.

Oh no, she was *not* about to get away from him.

He hurried after her, grabbing her arm just as she opened the door to slip away.

"Leave me alone," she hissed, shooting him a furious look. "Seriously, Cade!"

Leave her alone? She was his goddamn wife, whether she wanted to be or not. And he was not about to leave her alone. He released her arm, but when she pushed through the door, he followed her. A pair of security guards were guarding a door nearby, obviously to Daphne's private room apart from the lounge area. They eyed him as he followed Kylie.

That could be trouble. Time to be ruthless. "Kylie," he said in a low voice. "You need to find someplace quiet for us to talk—"

"No, I don't!"

"Because if you don't, I'm going into that next room and telling everyone that we got drunk together and ended up married. And then I'll leave and let you sort through the fallout."

Her jaw dropped. She cast another furtive look around, then tucked the makeup case under her arm and grabbed his sleeve with her free hand. "Come with me."

Fine with him. As long as he got some answers.

Kylie smiled nervously at the guards and pulled her hand from his sleeve long enough to flash her badge, and then continued dragging him down the empty hall. She walked a hundred feet or so, not saying a thing, and then moved to an unlabeled door to their right. She turned the knob and opened it, and then flicked the light on and gestured for him to follow her in.

He did, and as they stepped inside, he realized it was a janitorial closet. Mops and brooms leaned in one corner, and there was a shelving unit full of different types of cleaners. Buckets were stacked neatly on the bottom shelf.

She shut the door behind them and clicked the lock, then turned back to glare at him, the makeup case still clutched against her chest like a shield. "What are you doing here, Cade?" The look on her face was guilty. "Daphne won't be off-stage for at least an hour."

He clamped down his frustration. "We both know I'm here to see you, not Daphne."

"Well, I don't want to see you! I want you to leave me alone."

"Is that why you left in the middle of sex, then? Because I seem to recall rubbing my fingers between your legs and finding you soaked with need for me."

Her cheeks colored and she averted her gaze. "That wasn't desire."

Oh *really*? "What was it then?"

She lifted her chin. "It was a mistake."

Cade's tenuous control broke. "A mistake," he repeated flatly. "Is that so?"

Her eyes went wide and she nodded.

He took a dangerous step forward, and he noticed she pressed her back against the wall. His eyes narrowed at that. What did she think he was going to do? Then again, her color was high in her cheeks . . . what did she *want* him to do? "A mistake," he said again, just to emphasize it. And he took the case of makeup from her hands and set it on top of a nearby shelf. He wanted her hands free. Cade turned back to her, and he gave her a cold, dangerous smile. Did she want him to prove her wrong? Because he would.

So he moved forward, moving so close to her that her breasts—God, those big, beautiful breasts—brushed up against the buttons of his shirt. Her eyes were wide as he cornered her against the wall, and he leaned in.

"This mistake," he murmured. "You were wet for me, and it was a mistake?"

He watched her tongue dart out and she nervously licked her lips. She didn't speak. He wondered if she could, or if her senses were as overwhelmed as his felt.

"Your pussy was dripping with juice," he murmured in a husky voice, leaning in so close that his nose rubbed lightly against her own, as if he were about to kiss her. "Clenching deep inside with the need for my cock, I bet."

Her lips parted, and he could feel her breathing speed up. Her nipples pushed against his shirt as she panted, and he was overcome with the urge to touch her. Cade's hand went to her knee and he began to hike up that fluffy, flirty skirt of hers.

"Because," he murmured, and his lips grazed against her own, "I seem to remember how you reached for my cock, as if you couldn't stand not to touch me."

A soft whimper escaped her throat.

"Your fingers wrapped around the head and slicked in my cum. Do you remember that, Kylie? Did you taste me on your fingers when you ran away?"

Her gaze was rapt on his face, and his hand went higher under her skirt. His other hand braced against the wall over her shoulder, effectively trapping her between him and the wall itself.

Not that she couldn't leave, of course. One of her hands still rested on the door handle, and all she had to do was open it and step out. The fact that she didn't told him volumes. The fact that she wasn't telling him to stop? The fact that her breathing got more excited the higher his hand went under her skirt? It told him that perhaps the lady doth protest too much, as the saying went.

And he wanted to prove it to her. If that meant giving her a wet, raunchy orgasm in a janitor's closet? So be it.

"So, Kylie," he murmured, and then sucked on that juicy lower lip, since it was so invitingly close. He could feel the whimper she bit back, and it encouraged him to be a bit bolder. His hand now moved to her inner thigh, and she was silky smooth and soft. His fingers grazed her skin and he continued to tease upward. "If I touch your panties, am I going to find them wet for me?"

Her eyes closed, her breathing shallow.

"Are you going to tell me to stop?" he asked, rubbing his nose along hers again. "Tell me not to touch this sweet pussy of yours that's just begging to be petted?"

Her lips moved, formed a small circle as if she were dying to say no, but only a soft breath came out.

"Then," he murmured, "I'm going to touch you and find out for myself if you're wet."

His fingers teased along the edge of her panties, where the hem met the inside of her thigh. Even from here, he could tell she was soaked. "Oh, sweetheart," he murmured. "You like this, don't you?"

She bit her lip but said nothing, her gaze focused on his mouth.

She didn't have to say anything. They didn't even have to speak. Just as long as he could touch her, they'd both know the truth. That when she touched him, he grew wild with need, and when he touched her, she lost all control. Slowly, his fingers pushed aside the damp fabric of her panties, and he felt the curls of her sex. She was wet, all right—she was positively soaked. His fingers eased between the lips of her pussy, and then he began to rub back and forth, teasing her.

Kylie's head fell back and she moaned.

"That's right, sweetheart," he murmured, his own cock like a heavy brick in his trousers. "Show me what you like. Show me how you want to be touched."

Her hand went to his chest, her eyelashes fluttering. He was half-afraid she'd push him away, tell him no, but instead, she rubbed his chest. "Touch me, Cade," she murmured, breathless and so fucking sweet it made him ache anew.

"You want me to touch your clit?" he murmured, his fingers gliding through her slippery folds until he found the little sensitive nub. She arched against his fingers and nodded, then began to flex her hips, trying to move into a rhythm with him.

And he wanted to give her what she needed. So when she moved her hips into a circular motion, he followed, circling the hood of her clit with the pads of his fingertips, and enjoying the way she arched against him, her mouth opening wide in a silent plea. Christ, she was pretty. He wanted to palm those big, heavy breasts of hers and tease her nipples. Hell, he wanted to touch her all over and intensify what she was feeling, but he knew if he lifted his hand from the wall, she might slip away.

Which made him rub her a little harder, with a little more intensity, more speed.

And she moaned again.

"Spread your legs wider for me, Kylie," he murmured, rubbing up and down her sweet cleft. She was so slick that when his fingers moved, he could hear the sounds of her flesh parting for his touch. He wanted to fuck her with his fingers, to bend her over, push that plump ass out, and ram his cock into her hot, snug warmth.

But this was about proving a point, he reminded himself. This was about proving to Kylie that she wanted him as badly as he wanted her. So he continued to stroke and slick his fingers against her pussy, circling her clit and rubbing against the entrance to her cunt, where her nerve endings were the most sensitive.

Her hands went around his neck, and she suddenly gripped the collar of his jacket and shirt tight. "Oh God, Cade, I need . . . need you inside me."

Sweet words, but this had to be about her and her orgasm, not about him sticking his cock inside her. But he could give her a little something, at least. He paired his fingers together, gave her clit one last teasing rub, and then sank his fingers deep into her warmth.

He groaned at the same time she did.

"Ride my hand, Kylie," he murmured, thrusting his fingers deep. "Spread your legs for me and ride my hand, sweetheart."

"Yes," she moaned, clinging to him. "Push into me. Fuck me."

Ah, fuck. She was turning this around on him. Trying to make him lose control. He pressed his face against her soft neck and thrust harder into her sweet warmth, attuned to every quiver of her legs. And every time he sank deep, he ground his palm against her clit, trying to make her as wild as she made him.

"Need more," she said breathlessly. One of her legs went up and she propped her foot on a nearby shelf, spreading herself wide for him. "Oh, God, please. I'm so close."

"You want me to bury my face there, Kylie?"

She shuddered in response, her eyes tightly closed.

"You want me to put my lips on your aching little clit and suck on it until you come?"

She trembled and nodded.

"Then beg me to, sweetheart. Tell me what you need."

"I need to ride your face," she told him, arching her back and pushing against his hand.

He swallowed back his groan of pleasure. The visual of his face between Kylie's legs as she rocked her hips, feeding him her pussy? It was the hottest thing he could imagine. "You want me to lick you out?"

She shuddered again and nodded once more. "Please, Cade. I need you."

His hand left the wall and he cupped her chin. "Look at me. Kylie, look at me."

Slowly, those gorgeous eyes fluttered open. Her pupils were dilated with need, eyelids heavy. Sexy. Beautiful.

His.

"You need to watch me," he murmured, and then leaned in to kiss her, stroking his tongue along the seam of her mouth like he was about to do to her pussy. "You're going to watch me as I make you come, aren't you?"

Her head jerked in a nod.

Cade slid down to his knees, kneeling in front of her spread legs. He pulled his hand from her slick warmth, hating to do so, and then with both hands, carefully tucked her skirt into her belt until her entire front was exposed to him. Then, he put his hands on her silky little panties—wet with her need—and tugged them down her rounded hips. When they fell to the ground, he put them in a pocket, claiming them for himself. Kylie was beyond noticing, though. Her eyes were closed again, and her breathing was rapid, her body tense with anticipation.

So he leaned close, the scent of her arousal in his nostrils, in his lungs, and she smelled incredible. His mouth watered with anticipation. "Are you watching, Kylie?"

She moaned again, but he didn't move. Her eyes fluttered open and then she looked down at him.

His gaze locked onto hers and then he leaned in, pushing his tongue between her folds and flicking it against her clit.

Her breath hissed out of her, and he felt her thighs quiver.

"Keep watching me," he told her, not lifting his mouth from her slick, delicious pussy. "I'll keep doing this if you keep watching me."

He saw her bite her lip, felt the whimper echoing through her, but her gaze remained locked on his. She was going to watch. Good. His hands bracketed her soft thighs and he buried his face between her legs, licking and sucking. With one hand, he pulled her pussy lips apart, forcing her clit to poke out further, and he took the little protruding nub and rolled it against his tongue.

Her whimper grew louder.

He kept her spread for his mouth, enjoying the sight of her pink, gleaming wet flesh pulled open for him to explore. And he sank two fingers into her core and began to thrust again, licking and sucking at her clit as she watched.

He felt her thighs tremble moments before another burst of wetness hit his lips, and then her breath caught on a sob as she came. And damn, she was sexy as she did. Her gaze remained on him even as he continued to thrust his fingers into her, his mouth full of her juices and his tongue on her clit.

When she finally came down, she sagged against the wall and drew in a deep breath.

Cade gave her one last swipe of his tongue and then he,

too, reluctantly pulled away. He could have stayed there for hours, pleasuring her, but his point was made.

"That . . . wasn't . . . fair," she panted.

"I'm no longer interested in fair," Cade told her, getting to his feet. His cock ached and throbbed, reminding him that he hadn't had a chance to sate himself, but that wasn't why he'd pleasured her. He'd done it because he wanted her to acknowledge that she wanted him.

Still, it was going to be awfully difficult for him to walk out of the janitorial closet with a massive erection. He leaned back against the door—blocking her from leaving—and closed his eyes, trying to regain his control. The scent of Kylie's pleasure was still on his lips and in his mouth, though, and it was damn hard for him to focus.

To his surprise, a warm hand slid across the front of his trousers, cupping his length. "You might not be interested in fair," she murmured, leaning in to him. Her breasts pushed against his chest for a moment before she slid down his front. "But I'm a firm believer in it."

And she knelt in front of him and began to undo his belt.

And holy fuck, that was like something out of one of his nighttime fantasies, to see Kylie's red mouth hovering near his aching cock, her kneeling in front of him to service him.

At the same time . . . he didn't want her to put her mouth on him simply out of obligation. He shook his head. "I didn't touch you so you would be forced to touch me."

"Don't you think I know that?" Her full mouth tugged into a seductive smile. "Don't you think I can tell when a man wants to eat a pussy and when a man's trying to get reciprocation only? It's all about enthusiasm, and you are a very enthusiastic man." She smiled up at him. "It makes a girl want to reciprocate for a variety of reasons."

"Is that what this is? Reciprocation?"

"Mmm. That, and I don't like holding grudges. And I think something like that orgasm I just had should be rewarded."

"If you're sure—"

"I'm sure. Now hush." Her fingers tugged at his zipper, and then she was pushing the fabric of his slacks down, followed by his boxers. Then, his cock was exposed to her, erect and inches away from her mouth, the head beaded with pre-come and purple with need. As he watched, she took him in her hand, gripping his length, and rolled the head of him along that red, red mouth. "Are you going to watch me?" she said, her voice low and practically purring.

"As if I could look away," he said hoarsely. He'd be dreaming about the sight before him for years to come.

She painted her lips with his moisture, and then licked them in a wholly sinful fashion. His own mouth parted as she took the head of his cock into her mouth and her tongue began to swirl around the crown, tickling and teasing. His balls tightened and his hands clenched against the wall, determined not to shoot his load immediately. Not when she was pleasuring him so prettily.

Kylie popped the head out of her mouth and rolled it along her lips. "Keep watching me," she murmured, then took his length into her mouth again. Her cheeks hollowed and he felt the suction increase as she tugged him deeper into her mouth, her glorious tongue gliding along the underside of his cock. Fuck, she was good at that.

Then, she began to work him with her mouth, keeping the suction tight as he shuttled in and out, her hand gripping the base of his cock and her mouth working him so hot and wet that it was almost as good as being buried balls deep inside her. Almost.

"Kylie," he murmured, wanting to run his fingers along her jaw, wanting to wrap his hands in her hair and fuck her face so badly that his hands shook with the need of it. "Pull away, sweetheart. I'm going to come."

Her eyes lit with satisfaction, and she released him from her mouth. But instead of pulling away, she began to roll the head of his cock along her full, red lips, teasing him with only the tip of her tongue.

What she was offering him was clear—and it was the most obscene, most incredible thing he could imagine. He took his cock in hand, stroking himself toward completion while she let her lips toy with the head of him.

Then, he came, spurting, on the tip of her tongue and her lips. His semen painted milky ropes on her chin and her lewd red mouth and her tongue slipped out and licked and licked even as he groaned and came for what felt like forever.

Panting, he watched as her fingers moved over the streams of cum he'd left on her face, delicately wiping them away. Then she licked her fingers clean. And . . . God. He'd never seen a woman do that.

The image would be burned into his mind forever. Her savoring him. Savoring his spend that he'd spread all over her gorgeous mouth and tongue and chin.

"Jesus," he murmured.

There was no fucking way he was divorcing her now.

THIRTEEN

~~~~~~~~~~

Okay, janitor closet was going to officially go down as
the weirdest place Kylie had ever had sex. She shouldn't
have done that. Shouldn't have gone down on Cade, because
it was going to send him mixed signals. And yet . . . she was
feeling pretty damn good at the moment. Her mouth tasted
of Cade and sex, and her pussy was damp and she was feeling replete down to her bones.

Feeling like the queen of bad decisions? Absolutely. But
replete? Definitely.

Kylie dragged her skirt out of her belt and straightened
it again. She glanced around the floor but couldn't find her
panties. "Do you know where my underwear went?"

"I think we need to talk," Cade told her in a low voice,
tucking his cock back into his pants and then adjusting his belt.

"We can talk later. I should probably dress and get back
out there before anyone knows I'm missing. But I really need
to find my panties." Had she flung them off when he'd offered
to put his face between her legs? It was entirely plausible.
Which meant she needed to find them before some poor janitor

uncovered them later. She stepped around Cade and peered into one of the buckets nearby. No panties.

"Kylie," Cade said, and his hand grabbed her wrist. "Look at me."

She frowned and looked over at him. "What?"

"We need to talk about you and me." His eyes were bright in his face, his mouth full and red from going down on her. And his gorgeous blond curls were mussed. He was frowning at her, too.

"What do you mean, talk about you and me?" She pulled her hand free from his grip. "There is no you and me, despite . . . this." She gestured at the closet, her face hot with a blush.

He stilled. "You're really going to start that again? After what we just had? After you begged me to put my mouth on you?" He grabbed a fistful of her skirt. "You want me to show you again just how much there's a you and me? Because I'm quite willing to plant my face between your thighs again and not come up until dawn."

She had to clench her thighs together to keep from shivering at the thought. Instead, she jerked her skirt out of his hands. "Stop it."

"Or what?" His mouth was harder than she'd ever seen it before. "You'll break up with me? You're already trying to ditch me. Your threats hold no weight. But I'm tired of trying to be nice and play by the rules with you, Kylie. I tried to give you space. Except the more space I give you, the further you push me away. So I'm not giving you space any longer. I'm taking space from you."

Oh no. "What are you talking about?"

His smile was cold. "Apparently I only get my way with you if I'm a bastard. So I guess I'll be a bastard." He leaned in. "You're going to finish work tonight, and then you're coming home. With me. And we're going to fuck until dawn and I'm going to make you come a dozen times, and then we're going to sleep in the same bed like a married couple does."

"No."

"You don't get to tell me no anymore, Kylie. I want you. And if I want something, I get it."

"Really?" she retorted. "You didn't get Daphne."

He stilled, and for a moment, Kylie wondered if she'd pushed things too far.

"I didn't mean that," she amended swiftly.

"You did," he told her, and his mouth flashed in a brief smile again. "Here's the thing, though. Maybe I'm starting to realize I didn't want Daphne half as much as I thought I did, because the thought of her brushing me off doesn't bother me. The thought of you brushing me off makes me go crazy." His gaze raked over her, and she felt scorched. "So. Tonight, you work. Then we leave together."

"Absolutely not."

He shrugged. "Then I go out and announce to everyone that we're fucking. You think I care if Daphne gets mad at me? More than that, you think Daph will be mad at me or at you?"

She knew the answer to that. "That is so freaking unfair."

"It is. And I don't even care." He grinned. "And it's going to work, isn't it? Because one of us cares very much if this information gets out, and one of us does not."

Helpless, Kylie could do nothing but glare at him.

"We'll continue this little charade if you want," he said, his voice silky and low. His fingers brushed over a lock of her hair, and then his thumb smoothed over her lip. "I'll ignore you until we leave, but when we get in that limo, you're coming with me."

She was fast running out of options. "Daphne will see—"

"No." His thumb ran over her lower lip again. "She won't. She only sees what she wants to see, and I'll play nice until we're alone."

Until they were alone? She shivered. "And then what?"

"And then I'm going to fuck my wife," he murmured. "And I'm not going to rest until she's screaming my name."

"And if your wife says no?"

"She won't," he said softly, and he moved in to kiss her. And she should have moved away from him, but instead, she turned her mouth up to his for his kiss.

"How do you know she won't protest?"

His lips moved over hers in a delicate caress. "Because," he breathed against her, "her mouth is going to be too full of my cock."

And she was unable to help the soft moan that escaped her. The mental picture of that was too damn delicious. "Just one night," Kylie murmured.

"Just one," Cade agreed.

———————

Kylie had to go back to work with her panties missing. It was an incredible distraction, because her skirt wasn't tight. Every time someone walked past, she clutched at the hem in fear it'd blow up and show that she was completely bare to her waist. She stood up and repaired her hair and makeup in her mirror, trying to hide the puffiness of her lips. She sprayed perfume and dabbed it at her pulse points so no one would smell the musky scent of sex on her.

Mostly? She fidgeted.

Cade sat on the greenroom couch that was dragged along to every one of Daphne's shows. True to his word, he paid not the slightest bit of attention to Kylie. Instead, he focused on his phone and sipped a whiskey he'd gotten from the bar.

At least she thought he was ignoring her. At one point, she ran to the bathroom because she could still feel her own dampness between her legs, and so she scrubbed herself as best she could and tried not to get aroused by the thought that Cade could drag her back to that janitor closet at any moment and prove to her that he could make her come in the blink of an eye.

The secret, naughty part of her rather hoped he would. She tried to shut that part of her mind down.

When she returned from the bathroom, though, her phone was back on her makeup table. Surprised, she picked it up and ran her fingers over the screen. She knew she'd left that in Cade's room this morning by accident. Unlocking the screen, she gazed at the text message on top.

> Cade: I have your panties. They're wet still, and if I put my hand in my pocket, it comes out smelling like your pussy. It's tempting to just shove my hand in there over and over again, mostly because I love your scent.

Lord have mercy, her nipples were hard. Kylie sucked in a breath and began to text back.

> Kylie: Please let me have my panties back.

> Cade: Convince me.

She licked her lips nervously, tasting the thick strawberry gloss she'd put on her mouth post-closet.

> Kylie: How?

> Cade: Get creative.

> Kylie: I'll . . . blow you in the limo once we get out of here.

She squeezed her thighs together tightly because just thinking about that made her wet again. Why did she like the thought of being on her knees before him so much? All he had to do was smile at her and she was practically reaching for his zipper.

> Cade: Tempting, but I feel I need more incentive. These are *very* wet panties.

She smothered a groan of frustration and glanced over at him to see if he was looking in her direction. The bastard was lounging, his pose as casual as could be. Meanwhile here she was with hard nipples and getting wet between her legs all over again. And no damn underwear!

As she watched, his hand shifted, and then he imperceptibly touched his fingers just above his mouth.

Smelling them again. Smelling her.

God. She was going to be so wet between her legs she was going to need to head back to the restroom and mop up again in a minute.

Stop that, she texted.

Cade: Or what?

This new side of Cade was driving her insane. Driving her mad with need, but also driving her crazy.

I'll . . . send you naked selfies, she offered.

Cade: That's an enticing proposal. Tell you what.
I'll let you have the panties back once I receive the pictures.

Kylie gritted her teeth.

I'll send you the selfies later. I need my panties back now.

"Who are you texting?" Ginger asked, appearing at her side.

Kylie jerked and nearly dropped her phone. "What? Huh?"

Ginger gave her another suspicious look. "What the fuck's your problem? You're as jumpy as Daphne."

"Sorry," Kylie said, putting a hand to her breasts. "You scared me."

"I bet," Ginger grumped. "You had this weird look on

your face and you were texting like no tomorrow. Who you texting?"

That was nosy. Kylie forced herself to give Ginger an innocent smile. "Just an old friend from school. She's trying to get tickets."

"Uh-huh." Ginger didn't sound like she believed her, but she didn't push. Instead, she showed Kylie one of Daphne's silvery kimonos for one of her midshow numbers. "Look, she's gotten purple lipstick on the collar of both of her backups and I can't get it out. Do you know how to remove this shit from fabric? Or maybe you have a good makeup remover? I'll try anything at this point, or I have to rip the collar out and redo it."

"Let me see," Kylie said, sliding her phone carefully into her purse and locking the screen again so no one could see the filthy texts she was sharing with Cade. Her fingers shook as she took the fabric from Ginger. "I do have a cream lip-stain remover that we could always try." She set the fabric down and began digging through her box of makeup removers.

Getting the stains out of the stage costumes provided a distraction for the rest of the show, and by the time the audience roared their way through the encore, Kylie was ready with Daphne's press makeup. She wasn't even thinking about Cade . . . much.

Okay, so she was, but she was under control now at least.

When Daphne tripped down the stairs in her platform heels, she took one look in her greenroom, squealed, and ripped off her bright pink wig. "Cade! Baby! You're here!"

Kylie watched as the billionaire stood up and Daphne launched herself into Cade's arms—into Kylie's *husband's* arms—and began to smother his face with kisses.

Kylie might have snapped the eye pencil she was holding, too. But she told herself that it was brittle and probably needed to be replaced, and stuck it back in one of her makeup totes. Goddamn cheap cosmetics. She fussed with her things, trying not to pay attention to Daphne and Cade.

After all, she didn't care if they kissed or got chummy, right? She was going with Cade tonight, but only because he was blackmailing her.

It'd be just one night.

Then she could convince him of the annulment and they could both be on their way.

———————

The only reason Cade let Daphne kiss his cheeks was because he loved seeing the mutinous expression cross Kylie's face. She might have been trying to hide their relationship from the world, but one only had to look at her aghast expression to see how pissed she was at Daphne's actions.

And really, Daphne was just being Daphne. Exuberant, silly, and charming.

She planted another smacking kiss on his cheek. "Look at you! Mister Sexy. Nice suit." Daphne grinned, wiping at a smear of pink lipstick she left on his collar. Then she shrugged and threw her arms around his neck again. "I missed you! About time you came to see me again."

Daphne was beaming so happily, her mood good. And Kylie was glaring, tossing makeup into one of her big containers as if it were full of poison. It made him feel curiously gleeful to see Kylie get moody and jealous for a change. She was the one that didn't want to say anything to Daphne, after all. And because she didn't, he had to continue the farce that he was here for Daphne, when he was only here for his new wife. So he put a fake smile on his face. "Yep. How was the show?"

"Didn't you watch? I got two ovations." She pouted and then flung herself off of him. "I need a towel, too. I'm fucking bathing in sweat here."

"Do you want to take your makeup off?" Kylie asked, her voice so carefully neutral that it made Cade grin, because he knew she was seething inside.

"Soon, Fat Marilyn. My boo here doesn't mind if I'm a little sweaty, right, babe?" And she winked at Cade.

Fuck. There was that *Fat Marilyn* comment again. "Daphne, that name's not appropriate and you know it."

"Boo?" She tilted her head at him. Before he could correct her, he watched as her face suddenly crumpled and she began to sob.

Kylie shot him an alarmed look, and Snoopy rushed to Daphne's side. The entire greenroom got quiet.

Everyone waited, tense, as Daphne scrubbed at her face, weeping. No one knew what to do. It was completely out of the blue. And everyone hesitated, because they were afraid that one wrong word would turn Daphne's crying into a firestorm of rage.

Eventually, her assistant stepped forward. "What is it?" Snoopy asked, putting a hand to Daphne's forehead. "Do you feel okay?"

Daphne shook her head. "No, I don't. I'm not okay at all."

Alarmed looks were exchanged. "What is it?" Snoopy asked.

"I'm just really tired," Daphne sobbed. She clung to Snoopy's hand. "I need some headache medicine. Can you get it for me?" She gave her assistant a plaintive look.

The assistant hesitated and exchanged a look with another person hovering nearby—someone that Cade assumed was the tour manager. He didn't like that look, either.

"Yeah, I'll go get your . . . headache meds," Snoopy said after a moment. "Be right back."

"Double dose," Daphne called after her, sniffling.

Quietly, Kylie handed her a face cloth and Daphne began to wipe makeup free from her sweaty face. Kylie shot him a worried look and tilted her head as if to say *See? See? This is why we don't say anything.*

"Are you all right, Daphne?" Cade asked, approaching his old friend again. He moved forward and put a hand on her shoulder, noticing that she was thin under the padding of her costume, and that when she removed her makeup, her face looked hollow and pale, with a fresh breakout of acne on her forehead.

She didn't look—or act—like someone who was getting clean. And that made him worry all over again.

Daphne waved an irritated hand at him. "Quit hovering, damn it. I'm just tired. Being tired makes me moody."

"Can I get you anything?" he asked politely. "Maybe a bottle of water or some cigarettes?"

"Snoopy's got what I need," Daphne retorted. "You're being a mother hen."

And that was more like the regular Daphne. He relaxed, stuffed his hand in his pocket . . . and froze when he touched the damp material there. He'd forgotten about Kylie's panties, and now he didn't want to take his hand out.

He noticed that Kylie stiffened, too. It was clear she was watching his movements.

"So," he said to Daphne. "Tell me about the show. Two ovations, huh?"

Daphne gave him a tired smile, tugging one of her legs up in her chair and unlacing her platform boot. "You should have seen it, Cade. It's like all of Vegas was out there tonight."

He chuckled. "They probably were."

———

They're just friends, Kylie told herself as she reapplied Daphne's makeup. Friends being friendly and hanging out together. That's all it was. Cade had told Kylie that he was interested in just Kylie, and not Daphne. There was no reason to be jealous.

But no matter how many times she repeated this to herself, Kylie got a funny tightness in her stomach when she saw Daphne had pulled a second director's chair next to hers for Cade to sit in. And that tightness returned every time the two of them bent their heads together and shared a joke or a laugh. And the tightness remained when Daphne insisted on dragging

Cade around the room with her as she did meet and greets. He wanted to be with Kylie, didn't he?

But . . . he sure didn't look unhappy to be Daphne's property all night, Kylie thought miserably.

She was relieved when the press thinned out and the staff started to head out. The dancers—all party animals—were hitting the open bar and getting their postshow party on. The rest of the crew—Daphne's personnel, chef, assistant, wardrobe, etc.—usually headed back to the hotel if they weren't sticking around for the party. When the first few people started to trickle out, Kylie was relieved.

She was tired, she was getting progressively crankier, and she just wanted to go home and curl up in a pair of pajamas and nurse her wounded feelings.

Except she wasn't home, she was in Vegas.

And she couldn't go home, because she had a husband.

And that husband was insisting she go home with him.

One thing was for sure, though—whatever Snoopy had given Daphne for her "headache" had cured Daphne's erratic mood. She was at her best tonight: charming and funny, the life of the party. Everyone was laughing at Daphne's jokes and she teased her favorite dancers, and erupted in giggles now and then. Snoopy wasn't happy, though, but Snoopy was discreet, and if she didn't like something Daphne was doing, she didn't say a thing.

Kylie tried to watch Daphne as the night wore on. She tried to see if Daphne went out to smoke cigarettes repeatedly, like Cade said she would do when she was finished with drugs. But she didn't see Daphne leave the room. She didn't see her light up. She didn't see her throwing up or clutching her stomach, or even looking the slightest bit sick.

Instead, Daphne looked happy . . . almost manically so.

She wondered if she should say something to Cade. Or would it come across as pettiness and jealousy instead of concern?

"We're heading back to the hotel," Ginger said, distracting Kylie. "You coming with?"

"No, uh, I think I'm just going to, you know, stay here for a bit." To her vast embarrassment, her cheeks kept getting redder and redder.

"Uh-huh," Ginger said, clearly not buying the lie. "See you tomorrow, then."

"Right," Kylie said vigorously. She gave her a thumbs-up. "See you then."

Ginger just rolled her eyes, picked up her own bag, and headed out with the others. It left Kylie in a curious predicament. Exactly how would she sneak out without alerting Daphne, who was currently clinging to Kylie's man?

And Jesus, what was wrong with Kylie that she was thinking of him as her man? He wasn't even paying a lick of attention to her, standing across the room with Daphne's posse. She doubted he'd notice if she exited and disappeared for the night, too.

He was probably bluffing about the panties thing, too, right?

Theoretically.

But even as she pondered making a swift escape, her cell phone buzzed. She checked the screen.

Cade: Go outside and head to the limo. My driver knows to expect you. I'll follow in about five minutes. When I get in there, if you're not there, I'm presenting Daphne with your still-wet panties.

God, he didn't play fair. Even as she thought it, she felt a shiver of desire. Why was she so insanely attracted to this guy? Why was it that having sex with him and being around him was suddenly trumping all common sense? It was maddening.

She should man up and confess to Daphne that she'd slept with Cade. Twice. And she might have married him by accident. And then let him go down on her in the janitor closet. But no, they were done. Really and truly. And she didn't want him, despite the fact that she'd promised to send him dirty selfies.

It would all be totally aboveboard if she just told Daphne, right? And maybe she wouldn't get fired. Maybe Daphne would still be on her manic shit and she'd laugh it all off. Maybe the best time to tell Daphne something bad was when she was on whatever uppers she was on. Brightening, Kylie looked over at Daphne's small group.

As she did, Daphne knocked a drink out of someone's hand and shot him the bird. "Get out of my party, asshole."

Everyone around her looked shocked. The room got quiet again, a sure sign that Daphne was lashing out unexpectedly.

Kylie swallowed. Okay. Maybe now was not the time after all.

As she watched, Cade leaned in and murmured something in Daphne's ear. His gaze caught Kylie's from across the room, and he oh-so-subtly pointed at the door.

Yeah, okay. For now, she'd go and have fabulous forbidden sex with the sexy rich guy. Like that was a hardship. She just wouldn't think about the bad things that could happen, like sending a junkie into a downward spiral . . . or losing her job and her senile Nana getting kicked out of her nursing home.

Not that Cade, Mr. Money himself, would let that happen. He'd probably swoop in and try and pay all her bills to rescue Kylie. But damn, she would be a horrible person if she just rolled over and let him. If she just threw her hands up and allowed herself to be a burden to him.

She didn't need rescuing; she needed to make better choices in life.

Besides, if she did let him swoop in and pay for everything, what was to stop him from holding that stuff over her head? Bad enough he had her panties. And then what? Throw the money in her face every time they disagreed? Remind her constantly that she owed him?

That she was a burden? And then when he was tired of

"supporting" her, would he toss her out on the street, too, leaving her humiliated and alone?

No, it was best if Cade didn't know about her Nana and wasn't involved, no matter how "easy" it might be to confess her money woes to him and let him handle things.

So she quietly slipped out of the room and headed to the front of the concert hall.

As was becoming familiar to see, a stretch limo waited at the curb in front of the building. The driver was leaning against the car and he straightened as Kylie headed toward him.

"I'm with Mr. Archer," she told the man.

He gave her a surprised look, and Kylie felt a flare of annoyance. What, a fatty like her didn't deserve a hot, wealthy guy? She hated seeing that expression on people's faces. Maybe that was why she was pushing so hard against Cade as he tried to get closer to her. At what point was he going to up and realize, *Oh, Kylie's not all that attractive*, and dump her? Everyone else seemed to be waiting for him to wise up, so why not her?

She got in the limo in a sour mood. It didn't help that her phone didn't have a single new text lighting it up. Maybe he'd changed his mind and decided to hang with Daphne after all. Even if he wasn't interested in her romantically, Daphne still had to be more fun than "Fat Marilyn," right? Maybe he was regretting his pushiness toward her. He could have anyone. Why was he working so hard to get *her*?

Kylie stewed for a few minutes, staring at her phone, wanting a text to appear. As five minutes dragged into ten, and then twenty, she contemplated texting him a snotty little *remember me?* sort of text.

But she knew Daphne, and she also knew how hard it was to sometimes detangle from her when she wanted you there. So she was patient. Sort of.

Just when her patience had reached its limits, the door to the limo opened and Cade slid in. The driver got in the front, and before Kylie could snap out some quip about how long he'd spent, his arms went around her and he pulled her close to him.

"Can I hold you for just a moment?" he asked.

And all of Kylie's anger melted, because of all things she'd expected to hear coming out of him tonight, that wasn't it. She nodded. His arms tightened around her and he buried his face against her neck.

She remained still, unsure what to think of this.

"She's using again," Cade murmured against her skin, and Kylie caught the notes of sadness in his voice. "I can tell by the way she acts. She says she's clean, but she's on something. And every time I tried to bring up the topic, she changed it."

Her hand went to his hair, and she stroked it. However turbulent and strange her own relationship might be with this man, she understood his frustration and unhappiness at seeing someone he cared for destroy herself. "I figured."

"You can't even talk to her right now. She just . . . refuses to hear it. Any of it. She acts like nothing is wrong, but she's not the old Daphne." His hands hugged her tighter. "The woman there tonight? I feel like she was a stranger. And it shouldn't surprise me, but every time . . ."

"You still hope for the best. I know." She felt that way with her nana. Every time she saw her, she went in hoping that this would be the time Nana would smile when she saw Kylie. Would feel real love and affection for her. Would view her as a grandchild and someone to love and not just an unhappy burden that cost money and a reminder of everything she'd lost. She knew how devastating it was to get your hopes up, only to have them dashed over and over again. "You can't be blamed for having hope, Cade." Her fingers brushed through his soft, soft hair. "You can be sad you want more for her than she wants for herself, but you can't get angry that you hope she'll change. The day we stop hoping is the day we stop caring, I think."

He lifted his head from her shoulder and gazed into her eyes. "You sound as if you're speaking from experience."

"Maybe I am." She tried to give a halfhearted little shrug. He didn't need to know about her personal sob story. Not tonight. So it was time for a distraction. "Does this mean I can have my panties back now?"

His eyes gleamed with that wicked edge she'd seen in the janitor's closet earlier that night. "Not a damn chance."

FOURTEEN

Kylie existed in a state of anticipation as the limo pulled up to the same hotel as the one she'd escaped from this morning. She'd left him hanging midsex over twelve hours ago . . . and she suspected it wasn't going to happen again.

And honestly? She wasn't sure she wanted it to happen again.

Their interlude in the janitor's closet had pretty much proven to her that all Cade needed to do was snap his fingers and her panties would practically melt off of her, legs springing open in eagerness for him. She wanted him more than anyone she'd ever dated in her life. It wasn't just because the sex was great—and it *was* fabulous. It was that Cade made her feel . . . well, beautiful. He never looked at her with that strangely questioning look that the limo driver had given her. He never made her feel like she was the ugly one in the relationship. He always made her feel desirable and perfect at his side.

Of course, that was what made this off-and-on relationship with him difficult. Because the more she tried to push him away, the more she wanted. The more she craved.

His arms were still around her when the limo stopped, though they hadn't spoken in several minutes. He was probably tired, she told herself. She knew she was. Her head hadn't stopped throbbing all day, and she'd been drinking water by the gallon in an effort to wash away her hangover. The weight of her new wedding ring was still heavy on her finger, and she couldn't resist twisting it occasionally, as if to remind herself that yes, it existed, and yes, she was married to Cade, however drunkenly spontaneous the ceremony had been.

She didn't recall the wedding. Okay, there might have been flashes of memory that included flowers and a drive-through wedding chapel and Elvis, but that was about it. Overall, the canvas was a big blank. It probably was for him, too.

And she felt a twinge at realizing that he'd drunk-hooked-up with her twice now. It seemed like every hookup they had was buoyed by alcohol, except for the interlude in the closet from earlier. And that had been fueled by anger.

What did that mean for tonight?

Kylie kept the doubts in her head as the driver opened the limo door on her side. She got out and waited for Cade, her big purse clutched to her shoulder.

Cade got out a moment after her, and pressed a wad of cash into the driver's hand. "Thank you, sir. We need you back here at . . ." He looked at Kylie. "What time does the tour bus pull out?"

"Ten."

"All right. We need you back here at eight thirty," he instructed the driver, then looked again at Kylie. "It'll give you time to pack up your hotel room and still be on schedule to leave with the others."

"Thank you," she murmured, and was a little pleased when Cade's arm went around her waist possessively. He began to steer her into the hotel.

They were silent as they went up to Cade's suite, and she wondered which Cade he'd be in bed tonight—the ruthless man he was in the closet earlier? Or the laughing, smiling man he normally was?

But when the door shut behind them, he took Kylie's purse from her arm and set it down on a nearby chair, then moved toward her and cupped her face.

And he began to kiss her. Softly. Sweetly. Tenderly.

It threw Kylie for a loop, and made her ache deep inside. Made her want things she couldn't have.

"Please," he murmured between kisses. "Let's not argue over whether or not I get to hold you tonight. Let me just love you, Kylie. Let me touch you and lose myself in you. I need that tonight."

He kissed her again, his eyes closed, and she saw the strain on his face, the worry and sadness for Daphne. Kylie might be jealous of her, but she was still a childhood friend of Cade's and she was still heading toward self-destruction. And if Cade needed comforting?

Kylie wanted to be the one to do it.

So she put her arms around his neck and kissed him back with all the pent-up longing she'd been fighting all night.

He groaned against her mouth, and then the two of them were staggering toward the bed as Cade shrugged off his jacket. She tugged at his shirt, and then they were both unbuttoning it together, anxious to get him free of his clothing. Within moments, Cade was undressed, and then it was Kylie's turn. She kicked off her shoes and tugged her top over her head, quickly followed by her bra and her skirt. Then she was just as naked as he was.

And Cade pushed her back on the bed, his gaze reverent as he stared at her breasts. "God, I love these," he told her, reaching out and caressing one nipple. It hardened against his touch, and Kylie shivered, gazing up at Cade as he moved over her. His knee pushed hers apart, and she spread her legs for him.

"You have the most beautiful breasts," he murmured,

cupping them in his hands and then leaning down to kiss the nipples. "I want to bury my face in them constantly. A man could lose himself in these gorgeous tits."

He made her feel pretty. Made her feel sexy instead of just fat. She loved that, and so she raised her arms over her head and clasped them there, knowing that the movement would make her full breasts stand at attention.

He groaned at the sight of it and leaned in to kiss the valley between her breasts. "So beautiful, Kylie. So soft and gorgeous and all mine." He raised his head. "If I go get a condom, are you going to abandon me again?"

She shook her head. She didn't think she could, even if she wanted to. And it was the last thing on her mind right now. At the moment? All she wanted was Cade, between her legs and thrusting deep inside her. "I need you," she whispered.

He kissed her skin again and moved off the bed. "Be right back."

She watched his tight ass as he headed for the bathroom and felt like a jerk when he kept glancing backward, as if uncertain if she'd try to escape again or not. She'd pulled a dick move on him, that was for sure. He needed her tonight, though. Needed comforting. Needed to lose himself in sex.

She wasn't going anywhere.

Cade's smile as he returned to the room with a handful of condoms made her chest ache with the beauty of it. He was so delectable, this man. So utterly gorgeous and completely perfect in every way. She sent a silent prayer of thanks for her being in the right place at the right time when he'd been discarded and needed scooping up.

Kylie licked her lips as he tossed all of the condom packets but one onto the bedside. He tore open the one in his hand, then carefully rolled the condom down his length. She watched him with fascinated anticipation, and when he looked up, she held her arms out for him.

He came to her, moving over her, and as she raised one

leg to go around his hip, he pushed into her with one swift, sharp stroke that left her gasping in surprise at the suddenness of it. She thought there'd be more foreplay, more kissing, more licking, but as he pressed his face against her breasts again, and then gave another rough, sudden thrust, she got it. This wasn't about mutual pleasure tonight. This was about comfort. He needed her, needed the distraction of sex.

Well, he wasn't coming without her. She adjusted her hips, rocking them with every thrust he made. She was still wet from before, so it hadn't hurt when he'd pushed into her . . . but she needed more if she was going to come. So she lifted a hand and licked her fingers, and the small movement caught his attention.

His gaze shot to hers, and she gave him a sultry smile just before she slid her hand to her pussy and began to tease her clit with her fingers.

Cade groaned. His fingers dug into Kylie's thigh, and he propped her calf up against his shoulder, her foot in the air. The angle left her wide open, and allowed him to thrust even harder, more vigorous than before. If his kisses had been sweet earlier, his thrusts were not. They were rough and full of need and power, and each one made her breasts heave and bounce. She tightened her arms against her sides to keep them from jouncing painfully, and her hand continued to work her clit.

"Goddamn, that's hot," Cade growled. "Why are you so fucking sexy, Kylie?"

She didn't answer. Instead, she raised her fingers to her mouth and licked them again, returning them back to her pussy a moment later and rubbing harder. His thrusts were slamming into her, shoving her back against the pillows in the bed, but the friction between their bodies was making her own pleasure ratchet up quickly. Moments later, her own orgasm blasted into existence, and she cried out, rubbing herself hard even as her pussy clenched around his pistoning cock.

Cade snarled and palmed one of her breasts, and she felt his entire body shake with his own violent release. Twice more, he pumped into her, movements ragged, and then he collapsed onto her, sweating and spent.

She sighed, a little surprised she'd come so quickly. That had been nice, though. His weight on her was nice, too. Heavy and pressing her into the mattress, and so good that she felt utterly replete. Her fingers went to the long, boyish curls of his hair and she began to toy with them, fascinated by his hair as always.

"Am I too heavy?" he murmured, and his hand went to her breast, teasing a nipple idly.

"Not at all."

"Then you don't mind if I stay here for a moment and just bask in you?"

Her lips curved into a soft smile. "Bask all you want."

They remained locked together for several minutes, Kylie idly playing with Cade's hair and feeling his breath strum across her skin. He rubbed his fingers over her nipple, but in an almost contemplative way. And though the touch was arousing, she wasn't sure if he was going to do more than just that.

"I have to leave for two weeks," Cade murmured, interrupting her thoughts.

"You do?"

He nodded against her breasts. "Meeting with a UNICEF group to discuss funding, and then after that, I have to attend annual board meetings in New York City for a week straight. It's going to be very, very dull." He lifted his head and gave her an apologetic grimace. "But it's also been planned for six months so I can't exactly get away."

"Oh," she said. Because what else could she say? It wasn't like she was in charge of his schedule. It wasn't like she knew anything about his schedule at all, really. And she should have been relieved that he'd be gone for two weeks so she could concentrate on work without having to worry if he was about to show up for a show and drag her into a closet for some mouth-on-pussy action. If he'd insist on her spending another night with him. And another. And another.

But she wasn't relieved. If anything, she was . . . sad. Unhappy at the thought of not seeing him for two weeks. And she kind of hated that. "Does this mean I get my panties back?"

His mouth quirked. "Not until I get my pictures of you. I'm going to need something to keep me company in the board room." He leaned down and tongued one of her nipples in a slow, delicious tease. "Something to look forward to when I get done with work."

"You know this was only supposed to be one night, Cade," she murmured. "Tonight only."

"I lied," he told her, and nipped at the tip of her breast. "I don't want just one night with you, Kylie Daniels. I'm pretty sure I want all of them."

She sucked in a breath. Because, really, what could she say to that? She wanted him, too. But she wasn't free until Daphne's concert tour was over. She didn't get her next payment until it was done, and she needed that money. "Well, you don't get the next two weeks," she said, forcing herself to be light and teasing.

"I suppose I should get two weeks of kissing in tonight, then," he murmured, and gave her breast another obscene, dragging lick.

"Guess so," she told him, and pulled him up for the first of many kisses.

———

Kylie's fingers were linked with Cade's as they rode in the limo the next morning back to her hotel. She stifled a yawn with her free hand, and blushed when he chuckled.

They had been up all night making love. Sometimes sweet and tender, sometimes fierce and almost brutal. Every time, though, Kylie came hard, and every time, it was utterly glorious. Between rounds of sex, they napped and talked, and sometimes they cuddled.

She was falling hard for Cade Archer, and that was going

to make things difficult. But she could deal with difficult, she decided. If she just kept her mouth shut and if Cade kept away on business for a lot of the next two months, they could probably make this work out. She could sneak away to see him between shows, and Daphne and the rest of the tour crew would never be the wiser.

After the tour was over, she'd pay Nana's nursing home fees for the rest of the year and then she'd see about getting some sort of long-term work in New York City, where she could be with Cade. Maybe something on Broadway. That might be fun.

They could make this work . . . couldn't they?

The limo arrived at the hotel far too fast. When the driver opened Kylie's door, she got out reluctantly, slinging her purse over her shoulder. Cade got out, too, and she turned to look at him, giving him a bright smile despite her gloomy mood. He stood in front of her, hands stuffed in his pockets like a little boy, and waited for her to make the first move.

Well, she would, then. Her own hands went to the front of his shirt, just so she could touch him, could feel his warmth one more time. She already missed him. "Two weeks is a long time. You're not going to forget me, are you?" Damn it, she'd tried to keep her voice light and teasing, but it'd come out shaky instead.

"Not at all," Cade told her, and kissed the tip of her nose. "I will text you so often that you'll feel like you have a stalker."

She grinned up at him. "And you'll send back my panties?"

The look he gave her was downright naughty. "You know what you have to do to get those panties back."

Kylie bit her lip. "You're incorrigible."

"Just determined to see you in a few pictures, that's all." His blue eyes gleamed wickedly.

"I'll see what I can do," she murmured, and tilted her face back for a kiss. Truth be told, she was already planning the series of pictures she'd send him. He was fascinated with watching her put on makeup, so she'd definitely have to have a naked shot of her putting on lipstick, or maybe just one of her breasts . . . the possibilities were endless.

He kissed her back, lightly sucking on her lower lip as she tried to pull away, making the kiss last even longer. When they finally pulled apart, he murmured, "I miss you already."

It scared her that she felt the same way.

————

When she boarded the tour bus, Kylie handed her suitcase off and held her purse close as she went to her regular seat toward the front. She had her potted violet in hand and set it carefully on the empty seat next to her. The smokers—aka the dancers—liked to hang out in the back, swapping cigarettes or weed while they wasted the hours between tour stops. Today, the bus smelled like weed, which was irritating. She stood up and pushed her window down to let in fresh air, then shot a glare at the smoky back of the bus. Kylie was in a sour mood. The thought of not seeing Cade for two weeks was already bugging the hell out of her, and it had only been an hour or so since she'd left him. How was she possibly going to get through two weeks?

As if he could hear her thoughts, her phone buzzed with an incoming text, and a smiley face popped up on her screen, which made her grin.

Two weeks might not be so bad if they involved constant texts. And if he was getting pictures of her? She wanted pictures of him, too. They didn't have to be nude pics; she'd settle for one of those early morning tousled hair glimpses that made her knees weak.

She was just about to text him that when someone picked up her flowerpot and sat down in the empty seat next to her.

"Hey," Daphne said, still wearing her wig from last night's show. And her makeup, too, if Kylie recognized that shade of eyeshadow. Which she did, seeing as how she was the one who applied it. Had Daphne not gone to bed?

Kylie slid her phone into her purse. "Hi, Daph."

"I'm glad you're here, Fat Marilyn. I need to ask you a question." She lit up a joint while sitting next to Kylie, took a puff, and then flicked the ashes in the aisle of the bus.

"Uh, what's that?" She waved a hand at the smell, trying to dissipate it.

Daphne shot her an annoyed look. "You know the blond guy in the suits that comes to the backstage area at some of my shows? Cade?"

Kylie stiffened, alarm flaring through her. "Yeah?"

Daphne crossed her legs and then recrossed them, flexing her foot back and forth in a rapid motion. Her pupils were dilated, Kylie realized, and she was on something. This early? Or was this an aftereffect of last night? Her mouth looked swollen, too, and she kept taking drags off of the hand-rolled weed cigarette. "You see him leave last night?"

She forced her attention back on Daphne's face. "Hmm?"

Irritated, the singer snapped her fingers in front of Kylie's face. "Pay attention, Fat Marilyn. Did you see Cade leave with anyone?"

Her mouth went dry. Was Daphne trying to suss her out? Get her to confess? *Yes, actually, I was in his limo and we went back to the hotel and had dirty sex for hours on end. I can still taste his cock if I lick the roof of my mouth.*

"Um, I don't recall," Kylie hedged. "I think I might have left before he did?"

Daphne's foot swung more rapidly in agitation. She flicked the ashes of her smoke again and then shot Kylie another irritated look. "I think the fucker's seeing someone behind my back."

"Th-that so?" Her stomach roiled nervously.

Daphne gave a sharp nod. "He's not answering my texts."

"Maybe he's just busy?"

"I don't give a shit if he's busy," Daphne said, her nostrils flaring with rage. She leaned forward and stubbed her "cigarette" out on the leather seat in front of her, careless of the damage she caused. "I'm doing my best to stay clean and he doesn't even have the decency to tell me if he's got a fuckpiece on the side?"

Kylie stared wordlessly at the blunt Daphne dropped to the ground and then back at Daphne.

"Oh, grow up," Daphne said with a sneer. "When I say clean, I mean the really hard shit. Weed is just weed. That's like saying you're an alcoholic if all you drink is beer."

Kylie didn't correct her.

Daphne gave a huge sigh. "I'm sorry to drag you in on my troubles, Fat Marilyn. I'm sure you've got issues of your own."

"No, it's okay," Kylie said, hugging her purse in her lap even as it buzzed with another text from Cade. "I understand if you're . . . upset."

"I shouldn't be, should I?" Daphne mused, brightening. "He'll probably dump whoever he's fucking as soon as I let him know I'm interested."

"Probably," Kylie whispered, her stomach clenching again. But then she remembered the ring on her finger, and Cade's sweetness and ignored Daphne's hurtful words.

"Well, I'm not doing my next show until Cade shows up and apologizes to me," Daphne said. "My fans can just fuck off until my personal life is all straightened out." She picked up her phone and began to angrily punch a text in, her twitchy foot motoring a mile a minute.

Kylie stared at her in horror. "You shouldn't do that. Daphne, think of your fans. The money it'd cost if you canceled—"

Daphne pressed her hands to her forehead. "I can't go on if I'm upset, though. I need my headache meds." She got up from the seat, kicking aside Kylie's potted violet as she did. "Snoopy! Where's my pills?"

"You just had some an hour ago," came Snoopy's quiet voice.

"Oh, I'm sorry, did I ask you to argue with me?" Daphne asked, her voice growing louder. "Or did I say hand me my goddamn pills?" She stormed to the back of the long bus.

Kylie leaned over her seat and scooped the dirt back into the tiny plastic flowerpot. This poor violet was never going to survive two months on tour. Good thing it wasn't a kitten.

"You need to shape the fuck up," a voice hissed at Kylie. She looked up at Ginger across the aisle. The older woman had her mending out and was shaking her head at Kylie as she fixed a button on a glittering costume. "I like you, Kylie, but that woman is becoming unbearable, and I'm not sure how much longer I'm going to hold your secret."

"Ginger, please," Kylie said. "Daphne's just being a spoiled brat."

"Yes, but that spoiled brat is also my boss," Ginger said. "And if she finds out you've been fucking her man on the sly, she's going to be worse than ever to work with. And here's the thing. If it comes down to you or me, I'm going to pick me." Ginger shot her a narrow-eyed look. "So don't make me choose, got it?"

Kylie nodded, clutching her plant. "I broke it off with him, you know," she lied. "Last night. After the show."

Ginger gave her a quick thumbs-up. "Atta girl. Once she starts hearing from him again, she'll calm back down."

"Yeah," Kylie said. She wanted to text Cade, let him know what was going on, but Ginger was watching her. It seemed she was *always* watching. Kylie glanced around and then got up to head for the tour bus bathroom, purse in hand.

The bathroom itself was a tiny cubby smaller than most airport bathrooms, and it currently stank of weed thanks to its close proximity to the back of the bus. It was also the only place she could have a moment's privacy. She sat down on the travel toilet and pulled out her cell phone and texted Cade.

Daphne's in a rage. She thinks you're dating
someone and doesn't want to do her next show
until she hears from you. Please please calm her
down and let her know you're out of town? Maybe
that'll soothe her. I have to go for now. People are
watching.

She stared at her text, and wondered what he'd think of
it. Would he think she was brushing him off again? Impulsively, she added:

Will send hot pictures later tho. XOXO

Then, she stuffed her phone back into her bag, turned the
ringer off, and doused her hands liberally with hand sani-
tizer before leaving the bathroom.

FIFTEEN

Cade: Hey, man. I can't be at the Brotherhood meeting tonight. I'm in the U.K. at the moment on business.

Reese: Jolly good!

Cade: I'm picturing you saying that in a horrible accent.

Reese: You should see the look my wife gave me, too.

Cade: How's the pregnancy going?

Reese: Her ankles are almost as big as her belly. And if she finds out I told you that, she'll kill me.

Reese: But she's gorgeous. I mentioned that, right? I mean, she likes pickles on everything at the moment. Like, if I want to get action, I need to douse my dick in pickle juice. But she's stunning. Radiant. We're trying to decide on names at the moment.

Cade: Good for you two.

Reese: So I guess that means you don't want to hear our choices? By the way, you're not going to miss much at the meeting. My sister-in-law's going to be there and Griffin's bringing his woman. Someone mentioned the dreaded words "bridesmaid colors."

Cade: When did our band of men turn into a hen party?

Reese: The moment everyone started getting their dick wet on a regular basis. Happens to all guys.

Cade: Guess so.

Reese: So . . . how's that Daphne thing going?

Cade: She's a hot mess. Still using.

Reese: You ever nail the other girl?

Cade: Better. I married her.

Reese: Bro . . . we got to talk about this playboy thing. You are doing it all wrong.

Cade: I will cheerfully give up all my playboy days if I can keep this one.

Reese: I'd say you're an idiot, but Audrey is here at my side and making little cooing noises about you getting married, so I get it. I really get it.

Cade: Tell Audrey it's a secret! We're not telling Daph. For reasons.

Reese: Shit. I'll make something up. Got it, bro.

Cade: Later, man. Have fun tonight picking out colors.

Reese: Fuck you.

————

Cade: Hey Daph, you there?

Cade: Daph? Answer me.

Cade: Come on. I know you're there. Don't be like this.

Daphne: Maybe.

Cade: I'm just checking in to see how you're feeling. How's the tour going?

Daphne: It's fine.

Cade: I'm sorry I won't be able to make it for a few weeks. I have business overseas. I'm typing this in London as we speak.

Daphne: ☹

Cade: I promise I'll come visit when I get back, though?

Daphne: I miss u ☹☹☹

Cade: I miss you, too, Daph. You're a great friend. Have some kickass shows, okay?

Daphne: Will do. ☺

————————

Cade: I just had to tell Daphne I miss her. Please don't hate me.

Kylie: Whatever you said was the right thing. She's smiling and happy at the moment . . . though that might be the weed she's smoking.

Cade: Ugh.

Kylie: I know, trust me, I know.

Cade: Feels like I've been gone forever.

Kylie: It's been three hours. ☺

Cade: Still feels like forever.

Kylie: I need to go—Ginger's coming back to front of bus. XOXO

Later that night

Cade: Can you talk?

Kylie: Wow, it's really late. You're still up?

Cade: Just woke up. It's seven a.m. London time. Did you miss me?

Kylie: I might have. Just a bit.

Cade: I missed you and those sumptuous breasts of yours. My pillow didn't feel half as good under my head as they do.

Kylie: Is this your way of trying to finagle a photo of them out of me?

Cade: Is it working?

Kylie: Are my panties still up on the table?

Cade: I'm afraid I have to keep them a bit longer. They . . . kept me company last night.

Kylie: You naughty boy.

Cade: Being with you makes me naughty.

Kylie: Just for that sweet comment, I'll attach a picture.

Kylie: Did you get it?

Cade: Christ almighty.

Cade: That . . . is incredible.

Cade: I think I need a moment. And a private room. And possibly a cold shower.

Kylie: They're just boobs. Big naked boobs. ☺

Cade: They are not just boobs. They are THE boobs. The best boobs I have ever seen.

Kylie: You're quickly earning yourself another picture tomorrow. But I want one of you, too.

Cade: Alas, my boobs are less magnificent than yours.

Kylie: First of all, "alas"?? You texted me "alas"??

Cade: You texted me "finagle" the other day!

Kylie: Second of all, I don't need a boob shot of you. I need a picture of your handsome face.

Cade: I can do that. Sending later . . . if I get another shot of your lovely face in with your boobs.

Kylie: I can do that. ☺

Next day

Daphne: My show was great tonight. Ur welcome!

Cade: Good job.

Daphne: So when r u coming 2 see me again?

Cade: Soon, Daph. I'm busy with work right now.

Daphne: Ugh. U and ur work. Why do I even bother?

Daphne: Ur not fucking around on me, r u?

Daphne: Hello? Cade?

Daphne: Cade?

Two days later

Daphne: I'm sorry. Talk 2 me.

Cade: Sometimes I don't know what to say
to you.

Daphne: Sometimes I don't know what goes thru my
head.

Daphne: Just be here 4 me, k?

Cade: Daphne. You know I care for you. But you
also know we're not together.

Daphne: Not . . . YET. But I'm working hard. Clean
as a whistle. Yessiree.

Cade: That's great. Has your manager been helping
you get clean?

Daphne: Naw, I got this covered.

Cade: Would you be willing to take a test just to
prove it?

Cade: Hello?

Cade: Daphne?

Daphne: Gotta go talk 2 u later bb!

———————

The last two weeks had been two of the longest in Cade's memory. Never before had he been so antsy to get away from business. Never before had he regretted the endless schedule of meetings followed by corporate dinners and happy hour cocktails. Never had he felt the intense desire to cancel his entire schedule and just say *Fuck it, you know what? Your schematics are fine. No need to have additional meetings.*

He couldn't, of course. There were always more meetings, more vendors to schmooze, more charities to talk with, more doctors to consult, more legal documents to review, more everything that required at least Cade's opinion on the subject.

And when there weren't meetings, there were presentations and spreadsheets to review, materials and numbers and findings and projections for the next year that had to be carefully consulted, questioned, and then more meetings to discuss all of that.

Thank God for his personal phone, at least. It was the only thing that kept his sanity.

"Where to, Mr. Archer?" the limo driver asked him as he opened the door.

Cade checked his watch. Nearly midnight. He'd just flown in to Dallas from New York after locating where Daphne's most recent show was at. Right about now, Kylie would be packing up her things and preparing to leave the backstage area and head back with the rest of the crew to the hotel. "American Airlines Center," he told the driver.

"Catching a show, sir?" the man asked.

"Catching someone that was at the show," Cade replied.

The car left the airport and started to weave in and out of the maze of Dallas streets. Cade pulled out his phone and thumbed through the pictures from the last two weeks. Kylie had sent him a new selfie daily, and each one was hotter than the last. The one from today had been on his phone when he'd woken up this morning. He'd masturbated to it.

Twice.

There was just something about Kylie that did it for him. He pulled up the photo, gazing at her in the see-through lacy black bra, kneeling on the bed. Her legs were folded, hiding her pussy, but it was clear she was wearing no panties, and her lush thighs were encased in silky black stockings. The shot was of her body, but he could just barely see her sexy red lipsticked pout in the corner of the photo.

He loved all the photos she'd sent him, though. He flicked through them, cock aching at the sight of each one. The first photo she'd ever sent had been nothing but a shot of her breasts, full and plump, the pink nipples taunting him. The next one had been her lovely face, her tongue out and licking a lollipop that made him imagine his cock instead of the candy. From there, it had been a mixture of face and body shots, and she was more gorgeous in each one.

Cade couldn't wait to grab her and drag her back to his hotel room with him and fuck the daylights out of her. He felt like the last two weeks had been priming the pump, and when he saw her, he was going to tackle her and screw her until dawn.

It sounded pretty fucking good at the moment to him.

You there? he sent, waiting anxiously to see her pinged reply. She knew he was on a plane earlier today, knew he was flying in to Dallas.

Here, she sent back immediately.

Cade: I'm in Dallas. Heading to American Airlines Center. Wanna meet me out front?

Kylie: You bet I do. ☺

"How long 'til we're there?" he asked the driver.
"Ten minutes."

Cade: I'll be there in ten. Will you be ready by then?

Kylie: Yup. Daphne's getting drunk with some of her fans, so I should be able to sneak away no problem.

His shoulders tensed. Does she know I'm in town?

Kylie: HELL NO.

Cade laughed. Thank God for that. He didn't want to deal with Daphne and her bullshit. Not tonight. Tonight? He just wanted Kylie.

Cade: Can't wait to see you.

Kylie: Ditto. XO

He watched the highways flash past, and since he was feeling antsy, he called Jerome.

"It's late, boss," Jerome said when he picked up.

"You still picked up on the first ring," Cade told him.

"That's because you pay me to."

"Did you get me a hotel for tonight?"

"Just like you asked," Jerome agreed. He gave Cade the details. "And a suite. And the other two suites on that floor are now rented out in your name. You will have complete privacy."

"Good. And the—?"

"The wine you requested is there, along with a tray of food. And an entire box of condoms."

"Perfect. You're the best."

"I know," Jerome said smugly before hanging up.

Cade grinned to himself.

After what seemed like the longest drive in all of history, the limo pulled up into the parking lot of the American Airlines Center. The driver navigated to the front of the building, a scatter of cars still in the parking lot and several buses waiting nearby. Cade could hear no music, so he knew the show was long over.

Sure enough, a lone figure stood on the curb, an enormous purse slung under one arm. She wore a short peacoat that went to her knees, despite it being August in Dallas. It was warm despite the late hour and her legs were bare, which meant she was likely wearing one of those old-fashioned skirts that drove him so crazy because they showed off the exaggerated hourglass of her figure.

"Stop here," Cade told the driver. "I see her."

The limo slowed to a crawl, and then parked, and Kylie looked his way, a smile breaking across her gorgeous round face. With a little hop, she stepped off the curb and glanced around, then crossed the street to the limo. She opened the door and got in before the driver could get out to open her door.

"Hey," Kylie said breathlessly as she slid in next to him.

He reached past her, dragged the door shut, and then pulled her into his lap.

Then they were kissing, her hands on his neck and in his hair and touching his face, and his lips were on hers, and she was making soft, hungry little sounds in her throat. And fuck, she was gorgeous. It was clear he wasn't the only one who'd thought the last two weeks were incredibly long and lonely.

"I missed you," she breathed between kisses, her tongue flashing into his mouth for quick, teasing licks. "God, I missed you."

"I missed you too, Mrs. Archer," he murmured, tugging at her bulky coat.

She giggled at his words, and showed him her hand full of rings. The enormous wedding ring was still on her finger, turned inward so the outside looked like nothing but plain bands. "Our secret is still safe."

He held up his own hand, showing he still wore his ring, and she linked her fingers in his.

"I was a little worried," she said, biting her full, ruby red painted mouth. "That you'd have two weeks away from me and realize you didn't want to be married anymore."

"Absolutely not the case," Cade said, shifting her on his lap so she was straddling his cock through his slacks. She must have been wearing a skirt—underneath the coat, he could feel the clench of her naked thighs against his pants. "If anything, I missed you more."

The smile she gave him was part shy, part vixen. "I'm glad," she told him, reaching for the ties on her coat. "Because I changed before you got here, hoping . . . you know. Just in case."

And she held open her coat.

Holy Mother of God, she wasn't wearing anything underneath. Her big, bouncy breasts were naked and ready for his touch, and in the shadows, her pussy was waiting for him.

Incredible.

"Where to, Mr. Archer?" the limo driver called, reminding them of his presence.

Kylie sucked in a breath and closed her coat, squirming on his lap.

And he wasn't going to last until they got back to the hotel. Seeing those naked breasts? Seeing Kylie sweet and naked on his lap? He needed her now. "Go ahead and drive around the city for the next hour," Cade instructed him in a surprisingly calm voice. "My wife wants to see Dallas by night."

"Gotcha," the driver said, and raised the tinted glass barrier separating the cab in front from the back.

Good man, Cade thought. He'd give him an extra-large tip when they were done. He pulled Kylie in to kiss her again. "I want you," he murmured against her mouth.

"God, I want you, too," she told him. "I've been horny all day, just thinking about you."

"Did you touch yourself?" he asked, tugging her coat apart again so he could see the swells of those incredible breasts. He palmed them and groaned, feeling the weight of them in his hands. So gorgeous.

She shook her head. "Wanted to wait for you. Did you like my pictures?"

"You can't imagine how much," he told her, pressing kisses to her neck and pulling her against him. "Your breasts fueled all kinds of fantasies for me."

"What kinds of fantasies?" she asked, breathless with curiosity.

"Fucking them," he told her bluntly. "I thought about fucking them a lot."

Her eyes lit up and she got a naughty smile on her face again. "Did you, now?" She reached over and picked up her big purse, digging through it.

He watched her, content to just admire the gorgeous figure she made, nude except for her jacket, straddling him, her mouth a red bow, her white and red hair in wild curls on her shoulders. He'd thought about Kylie night and day, but the reality was a million times better than his daydreams. Idly, he reached out and teased one of her breasts with his fingers, coaxing the nipple into a point. It hardened immediately and she moaned; he loved that she was so responsive, so completely into his touch.

Then, she held up something triumphantly—a small tube.

"What's that?" he asked.

"Lotion, of course," she told him, and wiggled her eyebrows. As he watched, she uncapped it and squirted a dollop into her palm. Then, her gaze locked on him, she rubbed it into the valley between her breasts and on the slopes of her tits, making them gleam wetly.

He bit back his groan at the sight of it. "What are you doing?"

She simply gave him another wicked look and slid onto the floorboards of the limo, kneeling in front of him. Now those wet, slippery breasts were practically touching his knees. She pushed his legs apart and grabbed his belt, hauling him forward a few inches. Then, she began to unbuckle him. When she pulled his cock free of his underwear, Kylie looked up at him again, that gleam in her eyes.

Then she leaned forward and wedged his cock between her magnificent breasts and began to rub him, back and forth.

Gliding over that slippery, warm skin? The sensation was pure ecstasy. The visual was even better. He flexed his hips and watched the head of his cock push between her breasts, nearly touching her chin.

She clutched her breasts and pushed them together, tightening the friction around him and then the sensations changed from good to mind-blowing. Cade's head fell back, his lips parting. Dear God.

"Does it feel good?" Kylie whispered.

"Incredible," he told her in a low voice. His hands moved over hers, clenching her big breasts together, and he kept driving his cock in the slick valley between them. The sight of the head thrusting forward to nearly hit her chin with each push was obscene . . . and utterly fascinating. It made him pump harder, his hips coming off of the seat with the force of his movements, and as he watched, Kylie's tongue darted out and tried to lick his cock as it shuttled near her mouth over and over again.

The sight of that made him lose control. With a muffled groan, he came, heat splashing across her chest, jets of milky white come arching over her neck, chin, and tits. And again, it was obscene and yet utterly beautiful.

Kylie grinned at him, pleased. "Glad you liked that."

"More than you can imagine," he panted, his cock throbbing from the force of his release. He glanced around, looking for something to towel her off with, and when she pulled out a packet of tissues, he chuckled. "I'm glad you're so handy."

She laughed. "I'd almost take that as a pun, except I'm pretty sure I didn't use my hands much."

He helped her mop up her front, and his cock, and by the time she was able to close her peacoat again, they had a stack of wadded tissue that Kylie stuffed in a plastic bag (found in the back of the limo) and down into her bottomless purse for disposal back at the hotel. Then, she sat next to him on the seat and he pulled her close, nestling her against him.

It felt good to feel her weight against his, to smell her hair, to hear her soft breathing. And as the city skyline of Dallas zipped by, Cade reached for Kylie's hand and twined her fingers in his.

Being with Kylie felt so good, so very right. It was nothing like his constant stress and unhappiness when he'd thought he'd wanted Daphne. With Kylie? He understood real contentment, real happiness . . . real lust.

Now he just had to convince her that they could make this crazy thing they had permanent.

Then again, judging by the way she'd greeted him tonight? Maybe she was thinking along the same lines he was. Cade grinned to himself and pressed a kiss to the top of her head.

SIXTEEN

Kylie enjoyed a week of perfection in her otherwise shit-sandwich life.

The tour ran smoothly—or as smoothly as a tour could run with a manic-depressive junkie at the center of it. Still, Daphne went on stage and sang her heart out every night, so her managers were pleased and money was being made. As long as money was made, all the other complaints just sort of fell by the wayside. Which was a little sad, but to be expected.

Kylie herself was on cloud nine. Were there clouds higher than nine? Maybe she was hanging out on number ten, because damn, she felt good. Her nana's nursing home bill was almost caught up. The job was fairly predictable, and predictable was good. Cade spirited Kylie away twice more that week for furtive hotel room sex and late-night dinners on the town. And when they couldn't be together because his business called him away, they constantly texted and sent each other goofy little notes.

She was happy. More than that, she was in love. Even when Daphne was irascible or got cranky when Kylie couldn't quite cover one of her many bruises and make it look natural, it didn't faze Kylie. This was just a passing thing. It'd get better, and the tour would be over in another two months. Surely she could hold out for two months.

"Not that shade, Fat Marilyn," Daphne said peevishly, knocking a tube of lipstick out of Kylie's hands before she could add the color to her makeup palette. "How many times do I have to tell you? I want red. God, are you fucking stupid?"

Kylie bent over and picked up the tube before it rolled under the makeup station, trying not to lose her temper. It was clear to anyone that Daphne was having a bad day. Even as she sat in Kylie's makeup chair, she was sweating. Kylie kept having to wipe her down to apply makeup, which didn't make things easy. She set the tube of tomato red lipstick back into her caddy. "Show me which color you want, then," she said, keeping her voice patient. It was like dealing with a child some days.

Daphne pointed at a terra-cotta shade. "Like that, but with more red." She pointed at a purple. "Mix it with that."

"That's not going to make a red—"

"Then it won't be fucking red. Just fucking do it, all right? Who's the goddamn star around here?" She picked up Kylie's sudoku puzzle and began to fan herself with the paper. "Christ, it's broiling in here. Someone turn on the air."

"I'll get on it," Snoopy said, jumping up and running off. Kylie guessed that she'd been waiting for an excuse to escape her irascible boss for a few minutes.

"All right," Kylie said, pleasant through gritted teeth. "Reddish brown and . . . purple." She picked up the tube and used her tiny makeup spatula to dab small amounts of both horrible colors on her makeup mirror, then used a brush to dab the two together. The resulting color looked rather . . . toxic, but hey. What Daphne wanted, Daphne got. "Part for me?"

Daphne parted her lips and tilted her head back, and Kylie noted with a bit of concern that she was clammy with sweat again, a bead rolling down one temple. Her lips were dry and cracked, too. Worst of all was her breath. Daphne's breath smelled like something had died in her mouth, and Kylie had to hold her own breath to lean in close enough to paint her mouth.

"There," Kylie said when she was done. "What do you think of that color?" She leaned back and let Daphne look in the big, lit mirror. Her phone buzzed with an incoming text, and she peeked at it, unable to resist looking.

> Cade: Thinking about you, sweetheart. I've got your panties out and I'm daydreaming about the taste of you. Can't wait for tonight. You gonna surprise me with another outfit?

Blushing, Kylie tossed her phone in her open purse at the far end of the table. She'd text him back a response as soon as Daphne got out of her chair.

Daphne perused her bruised looking mouth in the mirror. "This looks like shit. Not gonna lie." She snickered. "Maybe we should start over with a different color."

"All right," Kylie said, getting cleansing wipes and handing them to Daphne. Someone knocked at the door at the far end of the room—the one marked STAFF ONLY. Kylie looked over. No one was rushing over to answer it.

"I bet that's Snoopy," Daphne said, taking a sip of her drink and looking expectantly at Kylie.

"Okay," Kylie said. "Be right back."

She hustled over to the door, and sure enough, it was poor Snoopy, her arms full of Daphne's favorite brand of bottled water. "Thanks," Snoopy told her, staggering under the weight of the bottles. "They fucked up the tour rider again, so we're going to get stuff in piecemeal for the next hour or two." She pushed a case of water into Kylie's hands. "Help me shove these in the fridge?"

The two of them filled the fridge full of the water, and Snoopy shot Kylie a grateful look. Kylie hurried back to her makeup table. Daphne hated waiting and Kylie didn't want her getting bored and destroying some of her expensive cosmetics.

But as she approached the makeup station, her stomach clenched in dread. Daphne's mouth was smeared with the garish lipstick, as if she'd been distracted mid-cleanup. In her hands, she held a familiar phone with a bright red case.

Kylie's phone.

And she was flipping through Kylie's texts, her face unreadable. As she watched, Daphne's thumb slowly swiped across the screen again, in a motion as if she were looking through a picture album. If she did, she was sure to see the photos of Cade in bed that he'd recently texted her, shirtless and pointing at a pillow with the caption of *Missing you*.

She sucked in a breath and waited for the inevitable explosion.

Daphne's gaze flicked to Kylie. Her mouth flattened. "You . . . *bitch!*"

The singer raised her hand and grabbed something off of Kylie's table. A green object flew through the air. Kylie realized it was the heavy ceramic flowerpot moments before it cracked her in the head, just to the right of her eyebrow.

"You fucking bitch!" Daphne screamed as Kylie collapsed to the ground. The world was a blaze of red and black and pain. She put her hand to her face and realized it was wet with blood—her skin had split open. "Right under my nose?" the pop star shrieked. "Under my goddamn nose?"

Kylie just blinked at the ceiling. It was covered with small, exploding stars, her vision edged with black. Her mind was foggy and she couldn't focus. There was dirt everywhere, and her flower was probably dead . . .

Hands touched her arm, helped her sit up. "Oh my God, Fat Marilyn," Snoopy said in her ear. "Are you okay? She hit you right on the temple."

"She's a fucking man-stealing bitch!" Daphne screamed. The carefully organized makeup cases went crashing to the floor. Next, the cell phone smacked Kylie in the shoulder.

"Stop it, Daphne!" Snoopy yelled.

"She fucking stole him from me," Daphne screeched. Several of the dancers went to Daphne's side, and a moment later, Daphne burst into loud, noisy tears.

They spoke, but it all sounded like buzzing to Kylie. Snoopy's soft voice swam in and out. She was having a hard time focusing. Her head hurt madly, and she was having trouble concentrating.

"I'm okay," she mumbled to Snoopy. "Help me up."

But when she stood up, her knees went weak again, and she almost took a second tumble. "Get security in here," Snoopy said aloud. "I think we need a doctor."

When Kylie awoke again, she was lying in a hospital bed. Her head throbbed with a fresh, hideous kind of pain. "Ow?" Her mouth felt dry and she put a hand to her head—the pain seemed to be concentrated in one particular spot just to the right of her brow. Her head was bandaged.

"Hey." Snoopy peered over the bed and gave her a wan smile. "Can I get you something? Ice cubes? A hot nurse? A bedpan?"

Kylie chuckled, and then groaned because laughing hurt. "What happened?"

"Well, apparently you can give someone a concussion if you hit them in the head with a flowerpot in just the right spot. Who knew." Snoopy grimaced. "The doctors gave you two stitches and are holding you overnight to monitor things just to be on the safe side."

"A concussion?" Kylie echoed. No wonder her head felt like it had been cracked open. "What time is it?"

"Late. Like, ten-ish."

Her fingers gingerly touched the bandages. Each brush of her fingers seemed to bring fresh pain. "Who did Daphne's makeup tonight?"

"Well, that's the thing," Snoopy said. "Daphne has 'come

down with the flu.' " Snoopy made air quotes. "The show has been rescheduled for two nights from now."

"I see. Where's my phone?"

"Broken," Snoopy said. "Pretty sure Daph stomped on it after she pegged you with it. She was pretty pissed. I'm sure management will pay for a new one."

Yes, but Cade would worry as to why Kylie wasn't texting him. Oh God—a horrible thought occurred to her. "This isn't going to be in the tabloids, is it?"

"Nope," Snoopy said, texting something on her phone. ."Management's statement is that you were drinking too much and tripped. You know how everyone on Daphne's tour likes to party." Snoopy's voice was flat, and the smile she gave Kylie was thin.

Kylie snorted, and then winced because that hurt, too.

"Yeah, it's all bullshit," Snoopy said. "Everyone's tired of Daph's shit, but we're stuck because . . ." Her voice trailed off and she stood up. "Management's coming in. I need to vacate the premises." She looked over at Kylie and crossed her fingers. "Good luck. I'll be waiting outside if you need anything."

Good luck? Kylie stared after Snoopy's retreating back, confused. A moment later, the hospital door swung open again, and a tall, thin man in an expensive suit walked in.

Mr. Powers from the record company. Kylie recognized him and his small, bitter smile.

"Hello," Kylie said, touching her bandages again.

"Miss Daniels," he said by way of greeting. "How are you feeling?"

"Well, my head hurts," she said meekly. She wanted to ask *Why are you here?* But she had a feeling that'd be coming out soon enough. So she waited.

"That's too bad," he said in a voice that had zero emotion. He moved to the end of the bed and set a briefcase down. He opened it, pulled out a stack of papers, and offered it to her.

"W-what's this?"

"This is your contract," he said in a chilly voice. "I wanted you to read over it again so you could refresh yourself with things."

Kylie stared at the paper, but the words were so tiny and blurred together that her eyes couldn't focus. She put it down a moment later and shook her head. "I'm kind of unable to concentrate at the moment. Can you give me a summary?"

"I'll recap it in three words for you: You cannot sue."

Her head throbbed in time with his voice. Kylie squinted at him. "Huh?"

"I'll repeat it. You cannot sue, Miss Daniels. It says explicitly in your contract that any injuries or mishaps while on tour are paid for by the label. We'll cover your hospital room. We'll cover any prescriptions and the cost to get those stitches removed. But that's all we're paying for. And your contract states quite specifically that you cannot sue Miss Petty."

Not that Kylie was planning on suing, but this guy was making her feel like she was the one at fault, and she didn't like it. "You do know she hit me in the head with my flowerpot? And that was after she was caught going through my purse?"

He put the contract back in his briefcase and rustled a few papers. Just those small noises made Kylie's head throb. "I have spoken with Daphne prior to coming here. I am told by Miss Petty that it was provoked."

"P-provoked?" Kylie stumbled on the word. "You're kidding, right?"

"You agitated her, Miss Daniels. According to staff, you were arguing with her over makeup choices before she found your phone, and when she did, it set her off."

"She was snooping. As for what set her off, why not blame the drugs instead of me?" Kylie protested, shocked. Her head was throbbing even harder. "We were talking about shades of lipstick. That's not arguing." She shook her head. "You know she's on all kinds of things right now? Her mood's all over the place."

"That's another reason why I'm here. We need to discuss your agitation of Miss Petty."

"M-my *agitation*?" Was this man serious? He couldn't be serious.

"Yes. You signed a conduct clause."

Her head hurt. Her vision swam, and she wanted to rub her temples, but she was pretty sure that would only make things ache more. "I don't understand. What's a conduct clause?"

"It's a clause we've recently added into all staffing contracts. One, I might add, that you happily initialed without reading, I'm guessing." At Kylie's silence, he continued. "The clause states that if your actions or conduct interfere with the tour or Miss Petty's ability to perform, you can be held liable for damages."

Kylie felt sick. "Damages?"

"That is correct. As of right now, Miss Petty is refusing to perform her show tonight. We have rescheduled it for forty-eight hours from now, but if she still refuses to go on, ticket sales will be lost. The label will be looking to recoup those losses. And since you signed a contract stating that you would have no personal conduct that interfered with Miss Petty's ability to perform . . ." He gave her that horrible, thin-lipped smile again. "You see where I'm going with this."

She was going to throw up. Her stomach lurched unhappily, and spots were beginning to appear in her vision. Her head pounded like Daphne's drummer was behind her, banging away. "I don't have any money," she whispered.

"It's cost the studio several thousand dollars to reschedule the concert. Just so you know, we've taken that from your contracted fee. I'll leave the receipts here at the bedside." He pulled new documents from the briefcase and set them down on the table next to the bed. "You'll see that we've been quite fair."

"I—is that all you need from me?"

"No. Furthermore, I will do my best to convince Miss Petty that she needs to continue with the shows scheduled. Right now she is talking about canceling the entire tour. I'm sure you can agree that no one wants this. Since you are contractually obligated to act in a way that will not distress Miss Petty, I assume you will cut off all ties to Mr. Archer?"

"You mean until the tour is done?"

"I mean completely." He pulled out another piece of paper and put it in Kylie's hands. "This is the amount that the tour stands to make for the record company." He pushed another piece of paper into her hands. "And this is the amount that Daphne will cost us if she does not finish her tour. Which she is now threatening to do."

Kylie squinted, but she couldn't make out the exact number, just that it had lots and lots of zeroes. Way more than Kylie's bank account had. Her stomach roiled harder.

"In light of the situation, the label is willing to forgive all costs related to this incident as long as you promise to end all contact with Mr. Cade Archer, as it is upsetting Daphne."

Her head spun. So they were going to force her to give up Cade? "He's going to want to hear from me—"

"We can arrange for a new phone for you. You can send him a message telling him you no longer wish to see him."

Like Cade would buy that. Still, it was hard for her to think. Her head was throbbing madly, and there were papers with numbers and threats spread all over her lap. How could she possibly take care of her responsibilities if they were going to fine her this much money?

How could she possibly avoid becoming a burden again? At this rate, she'd be back in a cardboard box under a bridge once more.

She reached for her wedding rings, found them still on her finger, though all the others had been removed by hospital staff. Of course they had. She twisted the rings, turning the beautiful red ruby outward. Then, with a meek look, she showed Mr. Powers. "I married him."

"You *what*?"

She winced and clutched at her head. "Vegas. We got married in Vegas."

"Oh." Mr. Powers's shoulders relaxed. "That's easy enough to fix. I'll draw up annulment papers. Vegas weddings are discarded all the time." His glare fixed on her. "We don't need to inform Daphne of this, do we?"

"No," she breathed, wanting to cry and puke all at once. "I guess we don't."

"Good. I'll be back tomorrow with some papers for you to sign. Daphne's assistant is going to remain at your side to ensure you don't receive any visitors or call anyone." He gave her a tight smile. "I'm glad we could work things out, Miss Daniels."

"Sure," she said listlessly. Her head hurt so badly that she wanted to scream.

"Perfect," Mr. Powers said. He gathered his paperwork and returned it to his briefcase, and Kylie closed her eyes. She wished he would just go away.

She wished this entire situation would just go away.

But when she opened her eyes again, Powers was gone, and Snoopy was gazing at her, an unhappy expression on her face.

"I heard," she said, her voice sympathetic. "The label's giving you the shakedown because Daphne's being a brat, huh?" She tucked the blankets around Kylie's legs and then offered her a cup of ice chips. "While you're in the hospital, too? That's shitty."

Kylie took the ice greedily, putting a few flakes of it on her tongue to wet her dry mouth. She still felt as if she were going to vomit, but she wasn't sure if that was the concussion or just her general misery over the situation.

"So," Snoopy asked. "Did you really marry that guy?"

Kylie nodded, fighting back tears.

"Forgive me for asking, but . . . isn't he rich? Couldn't you go to him and say, 'Hey, the label's being a dick and I need help'? Wouldn't he help you?"

"It's not that simple," Kylie whispered. "The label would charge me for all of Daphne's tour. I don't know how many millions that would be."

"Oh Jesus," said Snoopy. "I'm guessing lots of them."

She nodded. "And we're barely dating, you know? The wedding thing was a drunk fluke, a mistake." Kylie twisted the ring on her finger. She didn't want it to be a mistake, but it couldn't really be called anything else, could it? They wouldn't have made the same decisions sober. "I don't feel like I can go to him with money problems when the money problems might run into the millions. Or tens of millions."

"Why not?"

"Because . . ." *Because then he might realize he likes me, but doesn't like me quite that much. And because I'll always owe him. He'll always have something to hold over my head, like the label is right now. And when things go south, as they inevitably do—always—I need to be able to stand on my own two feet.*

Because I'm tired of being someone's burden. "Because I'm tired of owing people."

"I understand," Snoopy said. She thumped into the chair next to Kylie's hospital bed. "I don't know about you, but I am mighty sick of this damn tour, Fat Marilyn."

Kylie winced and put her hands to her temples. Yeah, that small touch made her brain feel like it was about to explode. "Kylie. Call me Kylie."

"I don't blame you. Fat Marilyn's as shitty a name as Snoopy." Snoopy looked over at Kylie. "My real name's Carmela." She shrugged. "I guess it could have been worse. She could have called me Pig-Pen."

Laughing hurt. Kylie giggled, but it soon turned into too much pain, and fresh tears blurred her vision. She closed her eyes and lay back on the pillow, wishing the world would go away.

No Cade. Not for her.

She couldn't even call him to explain. To tell him that he

was wonderful, but she couldn't be a burden on him. Not like she was to Jerred. Not like her nana was to Kylie. She wouldn't do that to another person. Maybe it was stubbornness. Or pride. Or both. But there were no choices. Nana Sloane needed a safe place to live where people could look after her and care for her. And Kylie was her only remaining family left, so it fell on her shoulders. That was the least she could do for the woman who had worked two jobs she'd despised to give Kylie a roof over her head, if not love.

Then again, maybe it was a good thing that Nana Sloane hadn't known how to love Kylie. Sometimes it seemed like love was nothing but burdens. Maybe she was lucky in that the label was going to step in and force all responsibility for her relationship out of her hands.

But try as she might, she just couldn't feel lucky.

SEVENTEEN

Cade checked his phone for the dozenth time in the last half hour.

No messages. No texts. No e-mails.

Frowning, he pocketed his phone again and tried to concentrate on the philanthropist at the podium, who was droning on in a dry voice about the differences in solar energy versus wind energy and how they could utilize both for newly built hospitals in remote locations, such as Foula and McMurdo in Antarctica. It was good information, and everyone around him looked fascinated, but all Cade could think about was his too-silent phone.

It wasn't like Kylie to not even send him so much as a message. Or even a smiley face or two to let him know she was thinking about him. She had a lot of downtime on the tour, and so she tended to text on a regular basis just to chit-chat and check in.

But her phone had been silent for the last twenty-four hours. He'd tried calling but it had gone straight to her voice mail. Phone troubles, maybe. Maybe her battery had run out and she couldn't charge it until she got back to her hotel room. He glanced at his watch, trying to decipher what time it would be in Portland, where Daphne's next show was scheduled, and his location—Stockholm, Sweden. He was nine hours ahead. All right, then. It would be late, but Kylie tended to stay up late anyhow due to the tour.

Maybe she'd fallen asleep? He'd wait until later and call her, just to check in.

But eight hours later, the conference ended for the day. He shook hands and chatted with peers and other professionals. They'd all go out to dinner soon, and "work" would continue on into the night. This would be the perfect time to talk to Kylie. He excused himself from the crowd, wound his way through the busy conference center, and found a relatively quiet spot where he could get a few bars of signal for his phone.

She didn't answer when he called, though. Again, it went straight to voice mail. Again, Cade worried. He called Jerome.

"Hey, boss," Jerome said. "I was just about to call you."

"Oh?" Cade frowned, tensing. Jerome rarely ever called him, because he only liked to "bother" Cade for emergencies. "What's wrong?"

"Nothing's wrong," Jerome said. "Just that you got an envelope this morning. Looks like it's from a law office and it's marked extremely confidential. I had to sign for it, but I didn't want to open it if you were expecting some top secret information I shouldn't see."

"I'm not expecting anything of the sort," Cade said, fighting impatience. "Go ahead and open it. Listen, I need you to look up some information for me in regards to—"

"Huh," Jerome said, interrupting Cade's thoughts.

"What?"

"Well, this is weird. It's annulment papers."

His heart felt as if it had dropped to his feet. "It's what?"

"Paperwork to annul the marriage of Mr. Cade Christian Archer and Miss Kylie Anne Daniels. Reason: Impaired mental capacity due to drugs and/or alcohol."

He felt gutted. Completely and utterly gutted. "She won't call me. She won't text me. I don't know what's going on."

"There's a note in here, too," Jerome said, and Cade could hear him sorting through the paperwork. "Let's see. It's been printed on a computer. No handwriting or anything. And it's on the law office's letterhead. It says 'Dear Cade, I can't do this anymore. We both know we should have never gotten married. It should have been just the one night. I'm filing the annulment. Please respect my wishes and make no attempt to contact me. Yours, Kylie.'"

"Bullshit," Cade snarled.

"Whoa there," Jerome said, surprised at Cade's reaction.

"It's bullshit," he said again. "Someone must have gotten to her. They're pushing her to end this. We always say it's just the one night, and it never is." He shook his head, keeping his phone pressed to his ear as he began to storm down one of the hallways, heading for an elevator. "Kylie would at least talk to me. A text. Something. The fact that she won't even answer her phone tells me something's up. I need to talk to her in person. Can you book me a flight home?"

"How fast?"

"As fast as you can make it."

"You should probably charter something, then."

"Just do it," Cade said, hammering the elevator button. "I need to see my wife before I sign anything."

Sixteen hours later, an exhausted Cade arrived in Seattle, Washington. Daphne Petty's next tour stop was Key Arena and he dozed in the back of the limo while waiting for the box office to open so he could pick up his will-call tickets and backstage pass. When the ticket window opened, he waited (rather impatiently) for his turn in line, then got his tickets and practically ran to the backstage area.

Once there, though, he was stopped by a security guard.

"Daphne Petty is not allowing anyone backstage prior to the show," the guard said. "She needs her concentration. She'll meet all fans after the encore."

Gritting his teeth, Cade pushed his way forward again. "I'm a personal friend of Daphne Petty," he said, dropping her name even though he had no intentions of seeing her. "I'm sure she'd want me inside."

"I'm sorry, sir," the man said. "We have our orders. No one inside until postshow."

Fuck this. He'd been patient long enough. With a snarl of irritation, he pushed his way down another hall and out of the building, looking for the loading docks. Kylie had told him that the employees often went and found a Dumpster in the back area to have a smoke at throughout the night.

Sure enough, a woman with a "staff" pass was hanging out near one of the Dumpsters, talking to another girl. Both of them had cigarettes in their hands, and both of them stiffened at the sight of him. Encouraged, he rushed forward.

The women stubbed out their cigarettes and started to rush for a nearby door.

"Wait," Cade called as they hurried away. He raced after them and barely managed to get to the door before they could slip inside. Pushing his weight against it, he said one single word: "Kylie?"

They exchanged a look.

"She's not supposed to see anyone," the younger one said. "The label's clamping down hard on her."

"I just flew here from Sweden," he told them desperately. "And if I don't get to see my wife and find out what's going on, I'm going to lose my mind. Please. I will pay you. Handsomely. I will buy you cars. Private islands. Whatever you want. Just let me in this door, all right?"

They exchanged another look.

"No, Snoopy," the older one said. "You know this is some shit we don't want to get involved in."

"Snoopy," Cade said, seizing the opportunity. He pressed his back harder against the door, just in case they tried to move him. "You know my Kylie, right?"

She looked uneasy, crossing her arms.

"You'd tell me if she was hurt or unhappy, right? Because she's not answering my texts at all, and I'm worried about her. I just want to know she's okay."

The older woman stared at him, stone-faced, but he could see the younger one hesitating. After a moment, Snoopy said, "She can't text you because her phone broke."

The older one threw up her hands in the air.

"Her phone broke?" he asked, surprised it was as simple as that. If that was all it was, why all the subterfuge? Why the annulment papers?

"Daphne stomped on it," Snoopy blurted. "After she pegged Kylie with the flowerpot."

His entire body tensed. *"What?"*

"Jesus. Here we fucking go," muttered the older one. "Good luck getting rid of him now, Snoopy." She scowled at the younger woman and shook her head. "I'm heading around the front. Fuck all this. You want to do this? It's on you."

Snoopy looked uncertainly at the other woman as she walked away, but remained where she was. When the other woman left, she glanced at Cade. "My name's Carmela, not Snoopy. And shit's been bad for the last few days."

"What's going on? What happened to Kylie?" Fear and anger warred for dominance. "Why did she hit Kylie with a flowerpot?"

"Daphne's been uncontrollable," Snoopy—no, Carmela—admitted. "She has a doctor that gave me 'headache medicine' for her." She used air quotes and rolled her eyes. "Except I can guess that it's not really for headaches. Here's the thing, though. Up until last week, she was living on that shit. Now, though? She doesn't ask for them at all. Which tells me that she's got a new supply of something fun and it's making her nuts." She shook her head. "The other day . . . she . . . well, I think she grabbed Kylie's phone. Poked through it. Threw some shit at her. Kylie's fine, though. It was just two stitches—"

"What?" he blurted. *Stitches?*

"—and they said the concussion wasn't bad—"

"What?" A concussion? Was everyone out of their minds? His horror at the thought of Daphne seeing their private pictures and texts paled at the thought of Daphne attacking Kylie. He suspected she'd be jealous if she found out about them, but he never imagined that she would hurt Kylie.

Helpless outrage blasted through him. While his wife, his woman, was being attacked, he was overseas at a conference. He felt like a self-important asshole. He'd let her get hurt because of him.

Was this why she was trying to annul their marriage?

He pointed at the door, nearly shaking with rage. "If you don't let me in here, God help me—"

Carmela shook her head. "No, I'm letting you in. The label might lose their temper with me but I don't have anything to risk. I just hate seeing what they're doing. And you're not the only one tired of Daphne's bullshit."

With that, she ran her pass through the cardswiper on the back of the door and gestured for Cade to enter.

Cade surged his way into the building, slamming down the hall. The need to see Kylie—to know if she was all right, or if she was hurt worse than he'd been told—roared through him with an intensity that was shocking. For once, Cade was in danger of losing his cool. For once, he was about to lose his mind with rage. For once, he couldn't be the calm, easygoing guy.

His wife was threatened, and that meant all bets were off the table.

Then, he turned a corner and the room opened up. There was Kylie, her back to him as she faced a makeup mirror. Daphne was nowhere to be seen, and the room was deathly quiet, all lightness and sense of fun that normally pervaded the staff area completely gone.

"Kylie," he said, approaching her.

She turned, and he saw the enormous bruise on her forehead, the butterfly bandage covering the stitches. She was pale despite her makeup, and her expression was one of hesitancy. And the sight of her broke his heart. His loving, sweet, open Kylie looking as if she was frightened? Her spirit trampled? It filled him with even more anger.

Kylie hesitated at the sight of him, and that hurt even more. As if she shouldn't approach him. As if he was off-limits to her.

He opened his arms and waited, seeing how she would react. To see if she'd come to him or if she was already too far out of his reach.

She gazed at him for a long moment, clearly deciding.

Then her face crumpled and she flung herself in his arms, weeping.

Relief burst through him, and he stroked her hair, her back. "I've got you, sweetheart," he told her. "I've got you."

EIGHTEEN

It felt incredible to have Kylie in his arms. It didn't matter that she'd sent him annulment papers. It didn't matter that she'd hesitated.

The moment she fell into his arms and clung to him? He knew they were still good. He knew she still needed him just as much as he needed her.

"Love, don't cry," he murmured. He cupped her face in his hands and studied the ugly bruise on her forehead. It was purple and yellow at the edges, a sign that it had looked worse at one point and was now starting to fade. Just thinking about that made him even more furious than before. He forced himself to remain calm. "I'm here. I'll take care of you."

But she shook her head, and fresh tears poured forth. "I c-can't have you, Cade."

"Why not? Who's stopping us?"

She bit her lip, and for a moment she looked so sad that he thought she was going to burst into fresh tears. It was breaking his damn heart.

"Tell me," he said softly. "Trust me."

Kylie looked pained. Then she glanced around, her fingers curling against his shirt as if she were loath to let him go. "Cade. I'm . . . I'm supposed to tell you that you can't choose me. You have to choose Daphne, okay?" She gave a pitiful sniff. "You and I aren't supposed to happen."

Not the Daphne stuff again? Cade's temper flared once more. "Is that what this is about? About Daphne being a spoiled brat?"

Kylie was silent, averting her gaze. But he knew the answer, just from that small motion.

"Did someone find out about us, Kylie? Is that why the sudden annulment? The silent treatment? They're pressuring you to end it with me because Daphne doesn't like it?" he guessed.

A new tear rolled down Kylie's cheek. "I'm not allowed to say anything," she whispered. "It's in my contract."

And that banked fury just kept growing. "So that's what this is, then. It's not you deciding to break up with me, it's Daphne deciding that even if she doesn't want her toy, she doesn't want anyone else to have it, either."

The look Kylie gave him was pure misery and heartbreak. "I'm stuck," she admitted. "And I don't know what to do."

He cupped her gorgeous, beloved face. "Then you let me handle it," he told her in a soft voice, and kissed her sweet mouth. "You let your husband take care of you." The fact that she still looked skeptical after those words broke his damn heart. "You want me to choose Daphne over you? It's never going to happen. Not now. Not ever. And you know why?"

"Why?" Kylie's voice was soft.

"Because she's not one half the person you are." At Kylie's wince, he realized she probably thought of that as a size comment, and he continued on, determined to make her believe him. "When I was younger, I was in love with Daphne. She was bold, and brilliant, and could light a room up with her smile. When people said she was going to be a star, I believed them, because no one could meet Daphne and not fall in love with her. She was the most charming person I'd ever met, and

I was madly in love with her. Ever since I was a broke fifteen-year-old kid from the wrong side of the tracks, I waited for Daphne to notice that I loved her and for her to love me back. Half my damn life." His mouth curved into a wry smile. "Fifteen years wasted. You know why?"

This time, Kylie was silent.

"Because while I was busy working to become someone worthy of her, she became someone else. Someone mean. Someone who calls her staff stupid, hurtful nicknames because she can't be bothered to learn their real names. Someone who thinks about no one but herself. Someone spoiled and petulant and selfish. Someone that lashed out at people just to get attention. And I thought to myself, it's all right. It's a phase. She'll grow out of it at some point, and then we can be together."

Kylie closed her eyes. Her makeup, normally perfect, was smeared around the corners of her eyes and threatened to run down her cheeks. She'd never looked more beautiful to him.

"And then, that night that Daphne's tour started, I realized she was never going to grow out of it. That it was who she was now, and I was the blind one. And you know how I realized this? Because I met someone else. Someone who was thoughtful enough to see my pain and tried to keep me company, even though she didn't know me. Someone who drove me home to make sure that I wouldn't get hurt, because she cared what happened to me. Someone who gave herself so sweetly when I asked and wanted nothing in return." His fingers caressed her soft cheek, cupped her jaw. Forced her to look up at him. "And I realized that I'd been chasing the wrong kind of person all my life." He watched her lip tremble, her eyes close. And he kept speaking, because he needed to get it all out, needed to make her understand. "I thought I wanted a selfish brat because I remembered who she was once upon a time, and that under the glamorous shell, maybe she was still the same person. I forgot that people change, and maybe I did, too. Because even though I was supposed to be obsessed with her,

I kept thinking about Kylie. And Kylie's kisses, and the way Kylie always made me smile even when I wanted to be melancholy. How even when Kylie gave in to my bullying, she was never cruel or awful. She was always kind, and giving, and loving. And I find myself wondering what I would do if Kylie ever left me. And you know what I would do?"

"What?" Her voice was so soft, so small. So full of hope.

"I'd wait all my life for her to come back to me." He took her hand, kissed the palm. "I wasted fifteen years on someone that wasn't worth it. I can wait a lifetime for someone that is."

"Oh, Cade," Kylie said, tremulous.

"I love you, Kylie. I know the timing is terrible. I know I haven't been fair to you through things, but I love you. Not Daphne. Never Daphne. I love you because you're everything that she's not. You're the one I want in my life. You're the one I wake up wanting to see. You're the one I want in my bed every morning, and in my arms every night. And I certainly don't want an annulment."

For some reason, that made Kylie pull her hand free of his. Her face fell again. "I don't want an annulment, either. But my contract—"

"Are they holding you by your contract?" That blistering rage exploded through Cade's mind again. It wasn't Kylie that was the problem, then. It was Daphne. Always Daphne. "Goddamn that spoiled brat. She's the most miserable person I've ever met. I don't think she wants anyone to be happy if she's not. You don't worry about Daphne, love. I'll handle her."

"No need," said a curiously flat voice behind them. "The spoiled brat heard everything."

Kylie tensed in Cade's arms.

No. He wouldn't let her bully them any longer. Not with her actions, not with her words. He kept Kylie locked in his arms and turned, looking over his shoulder at Daphne. She was in her opening number costume, a spangly flapper dress designed to look a bit like the blue waves of the ocean, and her wig was a bright platinum. Underneath the thick, bouncy curls, though, her small face was sickly, her eyes hollow. Her twig-like arms hugged her torso, and Cade realized she was thinner than he'd ever seen her.

"Maybe I am a spoiled brat," Daphne said. "Maybe I am mean. And selfish. Or maybe I just need to know that no matter how awful I am, someone's going to be there for me." Her glitter-painted mouth quivered. "I . . . guess I was wrong about that, huh?"

She turned and stalked away, slamming through the double doors and heading for her private suite backstage.

Silence fell.

"Yo, should we go after her?" One of the dancers asked. "She's supposed to be onstage in five minutes."

"I'm not going after her," Carmela said. "I don't want a vase to my forehead like Kylie there."

Cade didn't blame her. "Everyone just leave her alone. Let her work off her sulk." He didn't care what Daphne did at this point. The livid bruise on Kylie's forehead—Kylie, who was nothing but kind and caring—had destroyed any sort of tenderness he might have felt for Daphne. Daphne had attacked an employee, and she should have been sued. Instead, they were pressuring poor Kylie to dump *him* to make Daphne happy. The ugliness of it galled him.

So did Kylie's next words. "You should go after her, Cade."

He looked at her incredulously, then shook his head. "I came here today for you and only you."

"I know," Kylie said softly. "But you haven't seen the way Daphne's been for the last week. She's crumbling, Cade. She's an utter mess and no one knows what to do."

"No. She had her chance. She could have apologized to you. She could have tried to make things better. Instead, she's letting her goons pressure you. I refuse to give in to her bullying."

But Kylie shook her head and clutched at his jacket. "It's not about bullying right now. Cade, I love you with all my heart, but I still think you should go after her, all right? She's not in her right mind lately."

"That much is obvious," he said, and brushed a thumb over Kylie's brow, just below the livid bruise. The sight of it made him furious.

"Exactly," Kylie said, her big eyes pleading. "It's not about sense any longer. It's not about who wants who. I'm just . . . I worry that she's going to hurt herself, all right? She's been raging unchecked and you were the only one she even halfway cared about. Now that she doesn't have you, I don't know what she's going to do. Just . . . go talk to her, okay?"

He hesitated. Then sighed. Cupping Kylie's chin, he gave her a soft kiss. "This is why I love you, Kylie Daniels. Because you have a soft heart despite everything."

"I love you, too," she whispered. "So much. Even though I'm not supposed to."

"That's bullshit. You are supposed to. I don't give a shit what the label says or what they think they can force you to do. Whatever it is they think they have over you, I'll handle it. Do you trust me to?"

Slowly, she nodded. "We'll talk about it later. For now—"

"Yes, for now, I'll see Daphne. For you." Cade gave Kylie another quick kiss, then turned and headed for the hall that Daphne had disappeared down. He noticed that no one in Daphne's staff volunteered to accompany him as he went, which told him volumes. Whatever loyalty or affection Daphne might have had from her people was long gone. Sad that she should have been on top of the world at the moment and now she had no one who cared for her.

The hall was empty except for a lone security guard at the end of the hall. It was obvious which one was Daphne's door. Cade headed toward the door, grimly determined.

The security guard gave him a carefully blank look as Cade approached.

"I'm here to see Daphne," Cade told him, stating the

obvious. "She needs to go up on stage and her assistants are worried she's going to hurt herself."

"I'm . . . not supposed to let anyone in," the man said slowly.

"Well," Cade said, pulling out his wallet. He peeled a few hundreds out of his pocket and held them out to the man. "I'm sure that's a good rule when she has rabid fans. But I'm not a fan. I'm a concerned friend. So we can do this two ways. We can either pretend I've overpowered you and pushed my way inside, or you can take this money and the knowledge that you'll have a job with me if Daphne should fire you. Either way, I'm getting in that door. You just let me know which one you decide, all right?"

The security guard hesitated, then grabbed the crisp bills from Cade's hand and stuffed them into his pocket. "I'm not paid enough for this shit, man. Eighty-fifty an hour doesn't cut it when you have to put up with this crap." He shook his head and stepped aside. "I'm going on a bathroom break."

"Thank you," Cade murmured, and tried Daphne's door. It was locked. He knocked as the security guard strolled away. "Daphne? Let me in. It's Cade."

Silence.

A hint of worry began to cloud his thoughts. What if Kylie was right and she tried to hurt herself? She'd overdosed before in front of him. "Daphne?" he asked, knocking again, this time more urgent. "Let me in. I'm serious. You need to get up on stage. There are two thousand fans out there waiting for you."

No response.

He considered the door. It was made of heavy industrial metal—there'd be no heroic breaking down of this door. Realizing that, he pulled out his wallet and shoved his black card into the doorjamb, trying to push against the lock. They made this stuff look so easy in the movies.

Five minutes later, his card was scratched to hell, but the

door fell open. Cade pushed inside, scanning the room for Daphne.

At the far end of the room, on a bright red old-fashioned sofa, Daphne's small form was curled up. He headed toward her. "Daph?"

No response. He sprinted the rest of the way across the room and rolled her onto her back. Her eyes were rolled back in her head, three empty pill bottles near her cheek. One pill was still stuck to the corner of her mouth, and drool pooled down her face.

Fuck. Kylie had been right. He shoved the pill bottles into his pockets and scooped Daphne's frail form into his arms. "Hang on, Daphne."

Cade carried her into the backstage area so they could call 911.

NINETEEN

⌒

Guilt was an extremely unpleasant companion, Kylie decided.

She sat next to Cade in the emergency waiting room at the hospital. Out of the rest of the staff, only Carmela and Daphne's manager had shown up out of loyalty to Daphne. The rest were calling contacts and pulling strings, because as soon as word got out that Daphne Petty's North American tour was canceled, they'd be out of jobs and it would be time to scramble once more.

Cade was quiet, a book in his lap, and he was scribbling notes on a piece of scrap paper. She rubbed his shoulder absently, being there for him while not trying to hog his attention. Weirdly enough, she felt . . . guilty about being here with him. That she shouldn't be so giddy to have him at her side while Daphne's stomach was being pumped in an effort to save her life. It almost felt like Kylie was profiting off of Daphne's troubles. After all, she was getting the guy, right? And Daphne was getting . . . her career destroyed.

Something about this didn't strike her as right.

A doctor emerged, and Cade jumped to his feet at the same time Daphne's manager did.

"She's sleeping," the doctor told them. "We'll keep her in intensive care for the next few hours, but she's in no danger."

Kylie watched as Cade's shoulders slumped in relief. Daphne's manager simply nodded and began to dial on his phone. Cade watched the man, and she could see his lip curling in obvious disgust. He shook his head and then sat back down next to Kylie, burying his face in her neck.

She hugged him, glancing over at Snoopy. She was deliberately not looking at Kylie and Cade, and she knew that she was probably feeling like Kylie was—conflicted in her loyalties. No one wanted Daphne to destroy herself for Kylie's happiness. Not even Kylie.

"You okay?" Kylie murmured, running her fingers through Cade's hair.

He nodded against her throat, and she felt his breath against her skin. "I should call Daph's family. Let them know she's out of danger. They should hear about it before they see it on the news." He straightened, pulled out his phone, and swore under his breath. "No bars."

Kylie gave him a gentle push. "Go find reception. I'll wait here and hunt you down if there's any change."

He gave her a grateful look, kissed her mouth, and then got up and headed down the hall toward the parking lot, Kylie guessed. The manager followed him, holding his phone in the air and trying to get reception also.

Then it was just her and Snoopy. Carmela. Jeez. Now she was as bad as Daphne.

Carmela looked over at Kylie. She hesitated a moment, then got up and moved to sit down next to her. "Can we talk?"

"Of course," Kylie said, trying to smile. She was pretty sure what this would be about.

"So here's the thing." Carmela squirmed uneasily next to Kylie. She chewed on her lip for a second, and then continued.

"Daph's not my favorite person in the world. I don't know that she's anyone's favorite person in the world at the moment. And I hate what she did to you. With that." She gestured at her forehead, indicating Kylie's bruise.

"But?" Kylie asked, sensing this was coming.

"But I am super uncomfortable about you and the guy being so kissy while she's in the hospital. It feels . . . I don't know. Disrespectful."

"I know," Kylie said, sighing. She kind of felt that way, too. Like she was being a dick by being happy.

"I mean, you couldn't wait until the tour was done to be all happy with each other? You both knew how fragile she is. It's not like all this," she gestured at the hospital waiting room, "is a surprise to anyone."

Kylie nodded, her guilt overtaking her happiness. Was she being that unfair to Daphne? No one questioned that she was troubled. Thing was, was it fair to ask everyone else to put their happiness on hold just so the precious pop star wouldn't be upset?

Then again, hadn't she signed a contract stating she'd do exactly that?

"I just feel . . . I don't know. Really bad for her. I feel like no one has her back at the moment." Carmela twisted her hands. "And part of me feels like she deserves it, and part of me thinks that no one deserves this, you know?"

"I know," Kylie said softly. Because she was thinking the same thing.

With every ring of the phone, Cade's stomach dropped a little lower. God, he dreaded calling Audrey and telling her the bad news. No one deserved to hear something like this over the phone. He thought of the last time he and Audrey and Daphne had been together. It had been in a hospital room then as well. Daphne had overdosed after sleeping with Cade because she thought she'd hurt Audrey and to get at the pills that Cade had been carefully hiding from her, doling out as her doctor prescribed.

Daphne had never really liked rules, though.

On the fourth ring, Reese picked up. "It's early," Reese groaned into the phone. "This better be important, man."

"It's Daphne," Cade said quietly. "Can you put Audrey on the phone? She should know that her sister attempted another overdose last night."

"Fuck!" Reese's expletive was loud enough to make Cade wince. "That selfish little shit. If she only knew what Audrey—"

A low, feminine voice murmured next to him, and then Cade heard the phone being transferred. "Hello?"

Even through the phone, Audrey sounded in control. Indefatigable. So very different from weak, brittle Daphne. "Hey, Aud," he murmured. "How's the baby?"

"The baby's fine, Cade."

"And you? How are you doing?"

"Great. Now how about you quit stalling and just spit it out? Whatever it is, I can handle it."

Somehow, he knew that. She could probably handle it better than her husband could. If there was ever anyone strong in a crisis, it was Audrey. "It's Daphne. She got upset prior to her show last night and locked herself away and took a lot of pills." There was utter silence on the other end of the line, so he continued. "We called an ambulance and her stomach was pumped, and she's going to be fine. I just didn't want you to worry."

"Thank you," she said, her voice flat. For a moment, she sounded just like Daphne.

"They say she's going to get out of the ICU in a few hours, and I'll go in and talk to her as soon as she can have visitors. But I'm sure if you came down, they'd let you in—"

"I'm not coming, Cade."

"Because of the baby? Is it not safe to fly? Let me talk to Reese and we can arrange cars so you—"

"No," Audrey said, her voice utterly brisk. "I mean, I'm not coming. I told Daphne that if she pulled this kind of stunt again, that I was done with her. I can't keep doing this. I can't keep running to her side every time Daphne can't handle real life and decides to take a bunch of pills to remind people how vulnerable she is. I'm not going to rush to her side and pat her hand and tell her everything's fine so she can do this all over again. Last time, I swore to her that this was it, and I meant it." Her voice wobbled, the strength leaving for a moment. "Have you called Gretchen?"

Daphne's older sister? "I . . . no, not yet."

"Good. Leave it to me. I'll handle Gretchen."

"Are you sure?" This was a hell of a load for a pregnant woman to handle.

"I'm sure," Audrey said. "We both know she's not good in a crisis. She'll just blubber like a baby, say a bunch of things she doesn't mean, and it'll just make things worse."

A half smile tugged at Cade's mouth. She had a point. Gretchen tended to speak first and think later. "Can I do anything for you, Aud? Friend to a friend?"

She thought for a moment. "Yeah." That quaver was back in her voice. "You can scare the living shit out of my twin so she never, ever does this again."

"I'll see what I can do," he said softly. "I promise."

"I know this is cruel, Cade," Audrey said. "But . . . we just can't keep doing this. I can't keep doing this." Her voice choked.

The phone switched hands again, and then Reese spoke, his normally carefree tone gentle. "Thanks for letting us know, man. I'll have Audrey call if she needs anything, okay?"

"Okay."

"You'll keep us posted?"

"Will do," Cade said. Damn. Why was Daphne so determined to ruin so many lives? He knew this was incredibly hard on Audrey . . . and at the same time he envied her for cutting all ties.

Time to cut a few of his own.

Several hours later, Daphne's doctor allowed visitors. Kylie had gone back to her hotel room to catch a few hours of sleep after waiting up all night, but Cade wanted to stay. Someone needed to be around for Daphne, and it might as well be him.

When they finally let him see her, he was relieved to see that they'd moved Daphne out of ICU and into a private room. She turned toward him, her smile wan, her eyes like bruises in her face. "Hey, you."

"Hi, Daph," he said, pulling up a chair and sitting next to her. "How are you feeling?"

"Like a shitstain on humanity."

He shook his head. "I'm sure you're expecting a lecture, but I'm not here to give one."

Daphne plucked at the tape on her hand that held her IV into place. "I'm sure you're saving that for Audrey, right?"

"Nope. Audrey's not coming."

Daphne's veiny, claw-like hands stilled. "She's . . . what?"

"She's not coming. She said that last time she warned you that she wasn't going to do this again." And he felt like an ass for delivering the painful message, but what else was there to do? "Gretchen's not coming, either."

As he watched, her eyes fluttered and she gave a loud sniff, then swiped at her nose with a hand. "Well, fuck them. I mean, hey. Don't support your sister when she's in her hour of need. Whatever. Fuck them both. I'm sure Miss Perfect Audrey just went on and on about what a screwup I am, didn't she?"

"Actually, no," Cade said. "She was very upset. She does love you, you know. And this is a stressful time for her, too. The last thing I wanted to do was to tell a pregnant woman that her sister tried to take her own life again."

Daphne sniffed. "At least I have you."

"You don't," Cade said. "Not after today."

Her eyes widened.

"I'll always love you as a friend, Daph. Always. But I'm

moving on, and I just wanted to let you know. That, and I wanted to see if this was okay with you." He handed her the piece of paper he'd been writing on all night. "Let me know what you think."

She took it and scanned the first few lines, wrinkling her nose. " 'I grew up with Daphne Petty back when she was a freckle-faced redhead who loved to take center stage. In all the years I knew her, that never changed.' " She dropped the paper. "What's this bullshit?"

"It's the speech I'm going to give at your funeral. Since apparently we're going to have it in the next year or so. I just wanted to make sure you were okay with what I had to say about you."

The hands clasping the paper began to shake.

"And since this is the last time I'm going to see you before then, I just wanted to make sure that you approved," he said softly.

"You're abandoning me, too?" Tears poured down her face, and her hands shook as if she had a palsy. "I don't have anyone left!"

"That's because you've driven them all away, Daphne. Were the drugs worth it? Getting high? Partying?" His voice sounded utterly cold, even to himself, but she was listening.

Daphne rubbed a hand over her eyes, looking childlike and very young for a moment. "I hate the drugs. You know that, right? I hate the drugs so much. I hate that I need them." Her voice became venomous. "I hate myself, Cade. I hate everything about me." A sob escaped her throat. "And everyone else hates me, too."

Poor kid. For the first time, he saw who Daphne really was. Not the teenage ingenue he'd longed for. Not the troubled innocent living her life on the stage. She was just a young woman with a massive sense of insecurity and isolation. Who didn't know what to do with herself. Who didn't know who to trust.

He reached out and took her hand. Squeezed it. "You're sick, Daphne. I say this as a friend, but you need help."

She gave a watery laugh. "Not more of those fucking idiots that want me to do Pilates and grow a plant and talk about my wounded feelings. Rehab's a fucking joke. You realize that, right? You know I scored drugs from my last nurse in rehab? He was a huge fan." Her mouth was bitter. "I can't even get clean when I go to the place to get clean."

"I'm not talking about just getting clean," Cade said. "I'm talking about who you are. The Daphne I knew growing up was magnetic. Lovely. Never cruel. The woman you are today . . . that's not her. You call your employees names, Daph. You gave one of them a concussion. They're all living in fear of you." He shook his head. "It's more than just the drugs. You need a life do-over."

"I would love a life do-over," she said, and for a moment, she sounded so wistful that his heart hurt for her. "I would love to not be me anymore. I'm so tired of Daphne Petty. No one likes me, you know? They just like who I am or what I can do for them." She squeezed his hand tighter. "I knew that, and I kept telling myself I didn't care. You know? But I do care." Fresh tears spilled forth. "Maybe the problem is that I care too much."

"Then do something about it."

She nodded, absently staring down at their joined hands. "You know . . . I always thought you'd be there to pick up the pieces for me. That no matter how awful I was, or how out of control I got, I could always have you to fall back on. Like a safety net." Her mouth curled. "Safety Net Cade, there to save Daphne from herself. But . . . you've moved on, haven't you? To Fat Marilyn."

His temper flared. He might have squeezed her hand a little hard. "That's not her name, Daph."

Her eyes grew unfocused for a moment. "Right." She grimaced. "I don't even remember her real name. Just that she's fat and nice and pretty, and I kind of hate her guts for having you at the moment."

"I love her," Cade said simply. "She's everything I've ever wanted, and she's a wonderful person."

"You love her," Daphne said, choking on tears. "She's fat and *nobody* and I'm famous and thin and no one loves me."

He was not going to feel sorry for her. Daphne fed off of pity. "Kylie's not thin. So what? I don't care. She's incredibly sexy and I love her figure. I love how lush she is and how much she adores life. Mostly, I love how giving and wonderful she is. I love how when I'm with her, she's the most important person in the world to me, and I'm the most important to her. That's what love is, Daphne. It's not lashing out and then hoping they'll stick around despite your behavior. It's trying to be the best person you can to make the other person happy."

She twisted her hands. "So are you two going to get married?"

He lifted his hand and showed her his wedding band. He had never taken it off. "Kinda already did."

Huge tears rolled down Daphne's cheeks. "I really have no one left, then."

You don't, he wanted to say. But he chose to be kind instead. "Go to rehab, Daphne. Get clean. Not for your label, not for your fans, not for your sisters. Not for me. For you. I'll help you, if you want. I'll pay for aides that will stay by your side at all times."

"And they'll just cave to the label," she said gloomily.

"Not if they work for me," Cade said in a firm voice. He reached out and took her small hand again. "But I'm not going to set people up for failure. You have to want this for yourself. And you have to treat these people like humans. No cute names. No going behind their backs. Because I'm going to ask them to report to me every week and if they say you're being cruel or ugly, I'll pull the plug and leave you without support, too."

Her lower lip trembled. "Why are you being so mean, Cade?"

"Because being nice and patient gets nowhere with you,

Daphne." His smile was apologetic but firm. "And I really don't want to give a speech at your funeral."

She looked at the paper on her lap, and then took a deep breath. "Okay. Okay. I can do this."

"It's going to be hard," Cade warned.

The look she gave him was scathing. "As if everything else in my life is easy? If you think that, Cade, maybe you don't know me at all."

He couldn't disagree with that. "I guess I'll see myself out, then. Like I said, my offer stands. I'll give you all the help you need." Cade inclined his head at the door. "Carmela's out there waiting to see you."

Daphne's brows drew together. "Who?"

"Your assistant? You called her Snoopy?"

Her expression softened. "She waited out there for me? Really?"

"Imagine that. Someone cares about you." He gave her a smile.

"Huh." She ran her fingers through her messy hair and gave him a tremulous smile back. "Well, send her in."

———————

Back at the hotel, the tour employees had been instructed to contact label management to receive their final payment and to arrange for a flight home. The news of Daphne's overdose was just now breaking, and employees were meeting with management in a conference room downstairs before being handed non-disclosure agreements to sign before receiving their last check.

Kylie emerged from her hotel room and ran into Ginger in the hall, and Ginger filled her in. "Just thought I'd let you know," Ginger said grumpily. "Since you don't have a phone and all."

Kylie gave her a hesitant smile. "Thanks, Ginger."

"It's Carol," Ginger said, and she scowled at Kylie. "And don't fucking thank me because I'm a decent human being and you're not. Because of you, I have to find a new fucking job. So thanks a lot for that. Thanks for driving Daphne insane by stealing her man." She shook her head and wheeled her suitcase down the hall, muttering to herself. "Should've spoke up when I had the damn chance."

Ouch. Shocked, Kylie watched the older woman leave. In a way, she supposed things were her fault. Indirectly, right? Sure, she had dated Cade, but they were quiet about things. It wasn't her fault that Daphne had hit her in the head with a pot and then decided to take a bunch of pills once she heard Cade say that he didn't want her.

But as she headed downstairs, she saw a few other tour employees in the lobby, and they all avoided eye contact with her. One shot her the bird before turning away.

Okay, so maybe everyone *did* blame her.

Uneasy, Kylie headed down to the conference room. Several employees were waiting by the door, and Kylie recognized two backup singers and a guy from lighting. They all gave her dirty looks. She ignored them, but it was difficult. She could deal with a few irritated people—poor Cade was having to deal with Daphne and her family.

By the time it was Kylie's turn to go into the conference room, she was getting tired of hearing the whispering and seeing the furtive glances in her direction. She'd pretty much heard a mumbled *whore* here and there. She ignored it, because what else could she do? For all they knew, Kylie had stolen Daphne's man. They didn't know Cade and his side of the story, only Daphne's. And Daph's was fueled by coke. Or meth. Or oxy. Or whatever she was on this week.

And why wouldn't they believe Daphne? Daphne was famous and beautiful and rich. Kylie was fat and broke and did makeup for a living.

She signed the clipboard in the waiting area, and then went through the doors into the conference room. She'd just get her check, talk to Cade, and get out of town and put this whole thing behind her. Maybe once everything had blown over, they could pick up where they were again, see how they felt after a few months had passed. Right now, though, it was starting to feel like a mistake. Like she was reaching too high. And she knew that was her self-confidence speaking, but it was hard not to be down on yourself when a pop star was in the hospital because of you and all the employees were calling you *whore* under their breath.

Things got worse when she walked through the door.

Mr. Powers was at the table, along with the tour manager and a woman Kylie didn't recognize. Stacks of papers were on the table, and the woman had a box of checks in front of her.

Mr. Powers gestured at the chair across from the three of them. "Please be seated, Miss Daniels."

Kylie sat, feeling like she'd been sent to the principal's office.

"This is Ms. Draper," Mr. Powers said, indicating the woman on his right. "She cuts all of the payments for Daphne's payroll. Now, before we give you your final payment, our lawyers are asking that we get all employees to sign a non-disclosure as a favor to Daphne. We'd prefer that this not hit the media any harder than it has." His smile was tight.

"Of course," Kylie murmured, taking the pen offered to her. They pushed a piece of paper in her direction, full of teeny tiny writing in a minuscule font. There was a signature line at the bottom, and she scanned the document. *Blah blah will not speak to media blah blah disclose any incidents on tour blah blah*. She signed and dated the document and handed it back. "I wouldn't talk to anyone."

They simply gave her a baleful look, and Ms. Draper began to flip through the envelopes in her box, looking for Kylie's name. She pulled it out a moment later and offered it to Kylie. "This is your net pay. The label is giving you a stipend for a ticket back home, plus the remainder of money you're owed for the tour, minus any contractual fees."

Contractual . . . fees? She took the envelope and because

they were all still watching her, opened it and looked at her check.

Twelve dollars and thirty-seven cents.

Her hands began to shake. She was owed several *thousand*. Tens of thousands. "Um . . . why . . ."

"Daphne's had two canceled shows, and this is your portion of the costs. In addition, you'll be receiving a bill for the additional fees that we are owed."

She felt faint. "You can't charge me for her shows. I had nothing to do with her overdose. I didn't force the pills into her mouth."

"Your behavior pushed her, however. Please consult your contract if you have any questions." Mr. Powers gave her a tight smile. "Good day."

Kylie stared at the three of them. She could sit there and argue with them about things, but that wouldn't solve anything, would it? She could fight this—hire lawyers to go over the contract and pore over every phrase. Interpret things differently. Take it to court and try to win some of that money back.

But all of that cost time and money. And while she now had nothing but time . . . she had no money.

Cade has money, her brain told her. *He can help you.*

And . . . then what? Be beholden to him? Allow someone else to control her life because she couldn't hack it financially? Be a burden like her Nana Sloane was?

In the end, she quietly left the room and went upstairs to pack her bags. Using the hotel phone, she called her friend, Star. Star was the only person saving Kylie from being homeless in L.A. by letting her sleep on her couch when Kylie was between tours. Occasionally, she let Kylie borrow money. Or rather, she sold off things of Kylie's on eBay and forwarded Kylie the funds. But it was easier to sell old family jewelry and heirlooms than to borrow money from someone that would hold money over her head.

So she called Star.

"Burger King," Star said as she picked up the phone. "We make it your way."

"It's me, Star," Kylie said. Star never answered unknown calls with her own name. She was a bit of a nut, but a well-meaning one.

"Sweetie! How are you? How's the tour? You will not believe what I saw in the news! Did you know—"

"Yep, I know," Kylie said tiredly. "And I'm under a gag order not to talk about it. I need a favor. You know the boxes I have in your storage closet?"

"Yup. What's up?"

"My nana's vintage mink coat is in one of them. Can you eBay that for me and forward me the money?"

"Sec," Star said, and put down the phone.

Kylie waited impatiently, twisting her finger in the curling phone cord. Star had an incredible eye for valuables, and could spot a dollar to be made at an estate sale. She could look at the coat and judge how much it was worth for her to sell. Hopefully it'd be enough.

Star returned a few minutes later. "All right, I took a look at it. Definitely vintage—at least eighty years old. Which is good because people like fur, but they don't like recently dead fur, if you know what I mean. Apparently it's okay if it died a hundred years ago, but not ten. Go figure. And the sizing is good, which means I can sell it. You know some of that vintage stuff is teeny tiny. I can probably get one or one point five grand for it on auction. You want me to advance you?"

They'd done this dance before, and at this point, Star didn't even ask why. Kylie could have kissed Star's crystal-rubbing horoscope-loving self. "Yes, please. One thousand should get me home."

"Can do, baby doll. You sound upset. You okay?"

Kylie smiled, fighting back tears. "Just having a rough week."

"Save all that for next week, honey! Mercury's not in retrograde until then."

"Got it. Just send the money, okay?"

They made payment arrangements and Kylie thanked Star profusely. Star was a bit of an eccentric, but a loyal and dependable one, and Kylie adored her for it. She called the nursing home next, and let them know that her next payment would be somewhat delayed, but she was making arrangements and if they could please just charge her a premium late fee until everything was settled, that would be wonderful.

She winced at the new monthly dollar amount quoted to her, but had no choice but to agree to it. She couldn't have her nana on the street, no matter how much it cost to keep her in the home. She'd luck into a job at some point. Hopefully sooner rather than later.

When all the arrangements were made, her flight booked, her nana handled, Kylie sat for a moment on the edge of the bed and pinched the bridge of her nose, trying hard not to cry. Everything felt so overwhelming at the moment.

It would be so easy to go to Cade, whine to him about her troubles, and let him fix it. Let him fling some money at it and make it go away.

And . . . then what? Be indebted to him? Wait for him to throw her a bone? Constantly be anxious about money and how much she owes him and how she'd pay him back? Wonder if he's going to get tired of having to clean up her messes and send her packing?

She'd been there before. And it was awful.

Never again. She'd just have to suck it up and figure out other ways to make things work. And if they didn't involve Cade, so be it. The timing was all wrong. She swiped at her eyes, hating the decision she was going to make, but knowing she was going to do it anyhow.

Still, she was unprepared when she opened the door to her hotel room, and Cade stood there, tired and rumpled and smiling at the sight of her.

"Hi, sweetheart," he said. "Can I come in?"

And she hesitated all over again. More than anything,

she wanted to throw herself into his arms. To say, *Yes, please hold me, Cade, and make it better for me*. Instead, she shook her head. "I need to get to the airport."

His face fell. "What? Kylie, why?"

"I'm going home." The words were strained, hard to get out around the knot in her throat.

Cade blocked the door, not letting her pass. "I don't understand. I thought we were good. I thought—last night, when I held you—"

She shook her head. "We can't be good, Cade." *I have the threat of a lawsuit hanging over my head and the timing's all wrong and I don't want to come to you as a burden.*

"Why not?"

"Because we're fucking everyone over by trying to be together," she snapped. "You choosing me publicly made Daphne go off the deep end."

His face grew red with anger. "We're not to blame for Daphne's actions—"

"And now there's an entire busload of people depending on this tour that are out of work." *And my nana needs me to come up with ten grand in the next two weeks or she's going to be out on the street.* "I can't keep being selfish about this, not when it costs the happiness of so many other people."

"What about my happiness?" he asked quietly. "Don't I count?"

Oh God, he counted. He counted so much. But she'd just had an entire day of people's hate and loathing in her face and her bank account had been more or less emptied by the label because she couldn't keep it in her pants when it came to Cade.

And how she'd end up being a burden to him.

A *burden*. A responsibility to be taken care of. Not a lover, but a millstone around his neck, always costing money.

A burden was the last thing she ever wanted to be.

So she shook her head. "I'm sorry, Cade. I can't do this. I care for you—"

"Last night you said you loved me." The pain in his blue eyes was stark.

"I do love you," Kylie said. "But that doesn't mean I can be with you. Not now. Maybe not ever. I'm sorry."

"I don't understand, Kylie." He shook his head, baffled. "Don't do this. Don't separate us again. Whatever it is, whatever's bothering you, I can help. Whatever your burdens, let me share them—"

But she went still at the word *burdens*. "I'm sorry," she said. She shoved her way past him, down the hall, and into the elevator that was just about to close.

He didn't come after her. Kylie squeezed her eyes shut, willing her tears to wait until she got into the cab waiting to take her to the airport.

She almost made it, too.

TWENTY

One week later

"How's Daphne doing?" Cade asked Carmela as he dodged taxis, crossing a busy intersection in Manhattan. "She adjusting?"

"She's doing really well," Carmela said cheerfully. "Smoking like a damn chimney, but I figure we can tackle one thing at a time. Oh, and she's cranky and irritable as hell, but overall, she's doing well." She paused for a moment. "She'd say hello, but she's currently got her head in the toilet."

He smiled to hear that. At least someone's life was turning around. "Tell her the vomiting goes away soon enough and she'll be happier for it."

A pause. "She says fuck you, and she can handle it," Carmela said, and chuckled. "Seriously though, things are good. Well, mostly. I'm going to go get you some more smokes, Daph," Carmela called, and he heard her walking on the other end of the phone. She must have had something to tell him that she didn't want Daphne to hear.

He'd hired Carmela onto his own payroll, doubling her pay so she'd report back to him no matter her loyalty to Daphne. He wanted the full truth of what was going on, not a glossed-over version. And Carmela was good at reporting back.

A moment later, he heard a door close on the other end of the phone and Carmela sighed. "Okay."

"What's wrong?" Cade asked, stepping into an alcove in front of a closed storefront so he could continue the conversation privately.

"So . . . it's that dick. Mr. Powers. Remember you hired a new manager for Daph last year? Well, the label didn't like him and booted him almost right away. They replaced him with Mr. Powers, and he's a bit of a control freak. Like, he's the one that had me give Daph the oxy to keep her on a leash. Said it was less dangerous than any of the street stuff she could score, and she could still perform with it." Carmela paused.

Cade frowned. "He's not trying to give her more drugs, is he?"

"No, not yet. But here's the thing. He came by yesterday and made her cry. Told her she was costing the label a fortune and she was a piece of shit, and how she was a drain on finances and she'd let down her fans. That she was a laughingstock. He said she had a week to get clean and then he'd expect her back in the studio if she couldn't finish her tour."

"What? She's supposed to be in rehab for at least a month."

"I know," Carmela said worriedly. "Daph said he was full of shit and just throwing his weight around, but he really upset her. Made her cry a little, and then she spent the rest of the afternoon chain-smoking and staring out the window. Took a lot of pep talks to get her in a good mood today." She sighed. "That fucking label, man. I knew the contracts were evil and all, but shit. I thought ours were bad just because we were the little peons. I bet Daphne's is horrible, too. She's hinted as much. No wonder she's such a stress monkey."

He frowned into his phone. "The last thing she needs right now is the label hounding her."

"I know. But what can you do? I'd say appeal to his higher-ups but I think he *is* the higher-ups."

He'd see about that. "Let me handle it."

"I just don't want them to do to Daph what they did to Kylie, you know?"

He stilled. "What did they do to Kylie, exactly?" He still ached every time he thought of her. Kept checking his phone in the vain hope that she'd text or call. Something. But it was utter silence on that front. And a week later? He still wasn't fucking over it. He was still raw and miserable and wanting desperately to understand why she'd abandoned him. He'd hoped for more from her.

"You know? The whole 'making her pay for the canceled concerts' thing. I know she was freaking out over the money. I think she must have big debts or something. She was really, really upset. Frantic, even."

"Was she?" He kept his tone mild. It was either that, or lose his shit.

"Yeah," Carmela said, obviously not realizing Cade's change in attitude. "I'm pretty sure they nailed her for both of Daph's missed concerts. Chewed her up and spit her out. And you know she doesn't like to be a burden."

"I know," he said softly. *There's nothing I hate worse than being an obligation to someone.* Her horrible ex had taught her that if she wasn't bringing in money, she was worthless.

Maybe this was why Kylie had abandoned him.

"Let me handle this," he said again, suddenly filled with a new determination to purchase a record company.

———

The good thing about being filthy rich? You got to take over the bad guys.

Oh, he didn't buy the record label outright. But he let the right parties know that he'd be buying enough stock for the majority share, and then when he'd acquired enough, called a meeting.

It gave him an intense amount of satisfaction to fire Mr. Powers. The man looked shocked, but Cade had also had his lawyers look over Daphne's contract and Kylie's both, and he learned a whole fucking lot in the next week. Like he learned that Daphne's album sales were better than anyone else's with the label, but the label was also taking a bigger percentage than with some of the other acts.

Cade installed one of his lawyers in management, set him to fixing a few things, and let it be known that he was taking a personal interest in Daphne Petty's career from this point forward, and no decisions were to be made without his okay.

And since he had enough money to throw around, they had to listen to him.

When he told Daph that he was shaking things up at the label and they'd no longer pressure her, she burst into tears. That told him everything he needed to know. He told her to take her time, get well, and she'd have her career—and the full support of the label he now ran—behind her when she was ready to return to it, be it in ten weeks or ten years.

It was the least he could do for his friend.

He also removed the atrocious clause in Kylie's contract, had the payroll office cut a new check for her, and had it sent to his office so he could personally deliver it, along with their apologies for the "misunderstanding."

If Kylie was so worried about money and wouldn't take his? He'd at least make sure she had hers.

But he wanted her to talk to him, first.

———

"You sure you're okay?" Star asked. "Your aura is very troubled."

Kylie resisted the urge to roll her eyes. Star meant well. She really, truly did. It was just that Kylie wasn't in the mood for anyone's concern, especially not a horoscope devotee's who was about to spout a pithy saying about her energies. Instead, she dug into her curly fries and tried not to think about it. "Just bummed," she told her. "I was hoping we'd find more stuff at estate sales today."

Her nana's coat had fetched double the expected price on eBay so she and Star had taken the additional money and hit up estate sales this morning in the hopes of finding new stuff to sell while Kylie was between jobs. Now, four hours and four dead people's houses later, they had a few trinkets and not much else to show for their trouble, so they'd stopped to grab lunch before heading home.

Star just shrugged, her fringed shirt shivering with her movements. "Sometimes you hit the mother lode, and sometimes you find nothing but smelly old shoes and Tupperware."

Well, that was certainly true. "Maybe I'm just not cut out to do the estate sale thing. I should probably take the rest of the money and see if they'll let me put a down payment on what I owe for Nana's living situation. I don't want her to be a burden." She choked on the word. Or at least, a burden to anyone else.

"They're not going to care unless you have the full dollar amount!" Star exclaimed. "Will you quit worrying? They're not going to toss your senile grandma out onto the streets because you're a month behind." She paused. "It'll probably be two months. Maybe three."

Kylie groaned. "Thanks."

But Star only smiled. "It's going to be fine. Throw positive thoughts into the universe and good things will happen."

She forced a return smile to her face and nodded. Positive thoughts. Right. Star would never realize how miserable Kylie was at the moment, how utterly lonely, unhappy, and despairing she felt. Star thought that sadness could be erased by a good round of meditation and consulting a star chart. She pretty much subscribed to everything nutty that people associated with Los Angeles, but she was a good friend.

"Well," Star said after a moment. "I think there's a dead adult film star's place on the other side of town if you want to hit up another estate sale?"

Kylie shook her head. "If it's all the same to you, I'd like to go home and mope, please."

Star stuck out her tongue. "Fine, be that way." But they packed up their trays and got back into Star's tiny beat-up Focus and headed back to her apartment.

By Malibu standards, Star's apartment was spacious. Sure, it was outdated, with popcorn ceilings and shag carpeting and not in the greatest neighborhood, but she had a large living area and a dining room which was currently full of packed items waiting to be auctioned. When Kylie wasn't touring, her "home" was Star's sofa, and as she set her purse down on it, she wanted nothing more than to be left alone. Unfortunately, that wasn't going to happen while she was living with Star. Her friend sat in her recliner across from Kylie and immediately flipped on the TV to *Antiques Roadshow*.

"You know what? I think I'm going to take a shower," Kylie said. She got up from the couch-slash-bed and headed for the bathroom. It was the only place where she might have a moment to herself.

Once she locked the door behind her, she started the shower and sat down on the edge of the tub. Hot tears pricked behind her eyes.

She missed Cade. Missed his smile, his hugs, his skin against her own, his teasing, his curls, his everything. She missed the way he kissed her like it was a special privilege bestowed upon him. She missed snuggling up to him at night, and the way he looked first thing in the morning, sleepy-eyed and smiling.

She loved him. She loved him, and because her life was

a mess, she couldn't be with him, because she'd be a liability to him, and he'd grow to resent her, the way she resented Nana Sloane. The way Nana Sloane had resented *her*.

It was the right thing to do, but that didn't mean she wasn't lonely. Didn't regret things. Didn't hate Daphne for taking the cheap way out and costing Kylie a small fortune because she'd signed a bad contract.

Actually, scratch that. She didn't even hate Daphne. She hated herself for leaving her phone in her purse and getting caught. That one small moment had cost her a wonderful man.

The tears flowed, and Kylie pressed her face into a washcloth, weeping.

A soft knock came at the door. "Hey, you all right in there?" Star asked.

"Fine," Kylie said quickly, swiping at her tears. "I'm okay."

"Well, I know you just got in the shower but there's some blond guy at the door asking to see you."

She bit back her gasp of surprise. Cade? But then, why was she surprised that he was here? Of course he was. She'd abandoned him so suddenly, and without explaining herself. She was such a jerk. "T-tell him I don't want to see him."

"Are you sure? He's got a pretty swanky aura," Star said. "And a limo. Those are two good things in my book."

"I'm sure," Kylie bellowed, and turned the shower stream up higher so she could hopefully drown out any further protests Star made.

An hour later, she'd put off getting out of the bathroom for as long as possible. She'd showered, scrubbed, loofahed, deep-conditioned, dyed her roots, shaved every inch, lotioned her skin, painted her nails, and would have blown out her hair if it wasn't so steamy in the tiny bathroom. So she hung up her towel, piled her wet hair into a clip, and then emerged.

Star popped her head around the corner. "Feel better?"

"Much," Kylie lied. Most of the swelling around her eyes had gone down at least. Most. And what the shower hadn't fixed, eyedrops had.

"It took me forever to get that guy to go away," Star said, shaking her head. "He seemed nice, though. Cute, too. He's a Cancer, you know. They're very supportive."

Count on Star to have someone show up at her door and get their star sign. "That's great."

"He'd be a great match for you since you're a Pisces," she commented.

"Not interested," Kylie said again. She was a terrible liar, but hey.

"Yeah, that's what I told him, too," Star said.

Kylie's heart skipped a beat and she forced herself to move to the couch and sit down calmly. "What did he say to that?"

Star shrugged her dainty shoulders. "He mumbled something about a band or singers or something and left."

A fierce pain stabbed Kylie in the heart. A singer? Was he deciding to finally choose Daphne instead of Kylie, who offered nothing in a relationship? Had he finally given up, figuring she wasn't worth it? God, why did it hurt so much to think about that? She wanted to run out the door after him.

That whole "burden" thing kept stopping her, though.

Numb, Kylie curled up on her end of Star's couch and hugged one of the throw pillows. She could get through this. She could. She'd had her heart broken once. It would mend again, right? She just needed time.

Even as she told herself that, fresh tears appeared.

Star gave her a stricken look. "Why don't I get us some Ben & Jerry's?" She didn't do well with touchy-feely emotional moments.

"Thanks." Kylie gave her a wan smile and swiped under her eyes again. She was such a mess.

The doorbell rang.

Alarmed, Kylie stared at it from her spot on the couch. "Star?"

"Just a minute," Star called from the kitchen. "I dropped the chocolate syrup on the floor."

Shit. Kylie contemplated leaving the door unanswered, but the doorbell rang again.

"Can you get that?" Star called.

Well, she kind of had to now, didn't she? Kylie went to the door, padding on bare feet, and peered out the peephole. A child was there. She squelched a flash of disappointment that it wasn't Cade and opened the door. "Can I help you?"

The boy standing there was dressed in a striped shirt and shorts, and had curly blond hair that reminded her too much of Cade. He gave her an angelic smile, his hands behind his back. "Are you Kylie?"

"Ummmm. Maybe?"

He grinned. "I'm s'posed to tell you to take this." He produced a flat box from behind his back, tied with a big white bow. "And that if you don't take it, the orphanage I'm from won't get any money."

Kylie's eyes narrowed. Her heart thumped. "Is that so?"

The little boy gave a slow nod and offered Kylie the box. And even though she knew she shouldn't take it, she couldn't help herself. With trembling fingers, she accepted it and pulled on the fluffy ribbon while the little boy scampered away.

Inside the box was a waffle, and a note.

Her choked sob turned into a laugh. A waffle. Typical Cade. The sight of it made her heart ache, and she thought back to those silly, wonderful late-night dinners. She picked up the card and flipped it open, holding her breath.

Just so you know, I have a marching band out here waiting to play "Pretty Woman" if you don't come out to the parking lot in two minutes. And more orphans ready to come to your door. I'm not playing around this time. We

need to talk, and I'm prepared to use billionaire guer-
rilla tactics if necessary.

—*Cade*

Exasperated, she dropped the note back into the box and
shut the lid. She didn't know what to do. Common sense told
her to go out and talk to Cade like an adult. To explain to him
exactly how she felt, and why she couldn't be with him. That
she didn't want to drag him down with her money troubles
and become a burden, someone he had to take care of and
rescue from herself constantly.

But the small, wounded part of her wanted to retreat
inside and pretend she never got the note. To call his bluff
and make him realize she couldn't be pushed around.

As she hesitated, strains of music rose from the parking
lot of the apartment complex. It sounded like . . . trombones.
Or a tuba. Her jaw dropping, Kylie headed for the parking
lot. He . . . he really hadn't hired a band had he?

As she turned the corner, an entire marching band
dressed in uniform with plumed hats burst into the chorus
of "Pretty Woman."

Sure enough, he had. And instead of being furious or
embarrassed, she couldn't stop laughing. It was sweet, she
had to admit. And no one could really stay mad at a marching band, could they?

The band began to move in formation, and as she
watched, they parted and revealed a long black stretch limo,
with a man in a gray suit leaning up against it. He held a
familiar African violet in a pot, and instead of his normal
welcoming smile, there was a wary look on Cade's face. As
if he wasn't sure what to expect.

At the sight of Kylie, though, the wary look disappeared
and his smile blossomed, and her heart gave a happy little
skip at the sight of his pleasure. It skipped again when she
saw the flower, and at this rate, she was going to pass out

from all the heart-skipping if he didn't stop looking at her with those soulful blue eyes.

He raised a hand and gestured at the band. They immediately stopped playing, the silence making her ears ring. "I figured you wouldn't believe me if I didn't show up with a band this time," he told her. "So I brought them."

She said nothing. The knot in her throat was too huge.

Her silence made him stand straighter. He put the violet on top of the limo and then stepped toward her. "Can we talk?"

Bad idea, her brain said.

Shut the fuck up, her loins said.

Kylie hesitated. Emotion warred with common sense. In the end, she listened to her loins. "Um, sure."

"You pick the place. Anywhere you like." He was now standing so close to her that she could smell his aftershave, and her knees went weak. Why did he have to smell so freaking good?

"Um." She gestured at Star's apartment. "In there, I guess." It was getting increasingly hard to focus with him so near to her. Longing was threatening to take over her brain and dump out all common sense and replace it with pure lust.

Which, honestly, didn't sound so bad at the moment.

He gestured for her to walk first, and she did, heading back toward the apartment. Her entire body was incredibly aware of his hand moving to rest at the small of her back. It was a simple gesture, and an utterly possessive one, and she couldn't stop thinking about it if she tried.

As they went into Star's apartment, though, she cringed at what he must think of it. Cade constantly wore expensive suits, and she'd never seen him in anything more casual than a sports jacket. Every hotel he'd stayed in was pricey and he normally had a suite. Star's apartment had blacklight posters of mushrooms, beads hanging from doorways, and smelled faintly of incense. Her couch was old and brown and ratty, and Kylie's blankets were still spread on it from when she'd woken up this morning. God, what must he think of them? She hurried forward and grabbed the pillow and blankets, piling them into her arms and rushing toward Star's bedroom. "Let me just clear you off a spot."

She quickly flung the blankets on Star's bed and returned to the living room, only to see Star holding up one of her rose quartz crystals and dragging it through the air. "You have the prettiest aura," she told him. "It's incredible."

"Thank you," he said, grinning. "Yours isn't so bad, either."

Star beamed at him and pocketed her crystal. "Can I get you something to eat or drink? Kylie and I were just about to drown our sorrows in ice cream."

"Is that so?" His smile turned to Kylie, and she saw it falter a bit. Just a bit. "Are there a lot of sorrows to drown?"

"Oh, you have no idea—"

"Star," Kylie barked. "Please."

Her friend blinked. "Oh. Of course. How silly of me. Mr. Fancy Aura, why don't you take my ice cream and eat with Kylie? I need to walk down to the store anyhow. I'm fresh out of, uh, packing tape." She gave him a brilliant smile, grabbed her purse, and then turned to Kylie and gave her an exaggerated wink. "See you in about three hours."

As Star left the room, Cade turned back to Kylie, his hands shoved into the pockets of his jacket. "Does she need a ride to the store? I hate to think of her walking so far."

"The store's around the corner," Kylie corrected, heading to the kitchen to retrieve the ice cream. "She's just being a good friend."

"Ah," Cade said. "I have a few of those."

"I bet they've never analyzed your aura," Kylie grumbled as she picked up the two bowls of ice cream from Star's avocado-colored countertop. God, Star had made the servings absolutely huge. "Um, so this looks like a lot of ice cream but it's also dinner," she explained, handing him a bowl.

"Would you like a waffle to go with this?" he asked as he took the bowl. "I know where we can get one."

Her laughter came out of her nose as an embarrassing snort. *Way to go, Kylie.* They held the ice cream bowls in front of them, standing awkwardly and staring at each other. Finally, Kylie decided to break the silence. "I'd offer for us to sit in the dining room, but that's Star's work area."

"Is she . . . a fortune-teller?" Cade asked.

"You'd think that, but no, she's just a flake." Kylie smiled. "She goes to estate sales, scrounges through dead people's stuff, and resells it on eBay."

His brows rose. "Sounds morbid."

"She says it's an adventure and beats working in an office." Kylie shrugged and gestured at the old brown sofa. "Shall we?"

They both sat down, and Cade gamely ate a spoonful of Cherry Garcia, his gaze on her the entire time. Kylie couldn't eat. She was too nervous, too awkward, too ready to fling herself into his arms and sob that she wanted to love him desperately but fate was a cruel bitch.

"Are you . . . not hungry?" Cade asked, glancing at the bowl clutched in her hands.

Dutifully, she put the spoon in her mouth and took a bite. Phish Food. Her favorite. Today, though, it tasted more like Phish Glue. She forced herself to swallow, and gave him another awkward smile.

"Daphne's good," he volunteered, taking another mouthful of ice cream. "She hates rehab but we've got new people around her and she's determined in a way I've never seen before. Carmela's sticking at her side, too."

"Good," Kylie said. "That's good." Great, now she was just parroting back his words. *Way to be a stunning conversationalist, Kylie.*

"Good," he agreed.

Silence fell again. Kylie twisted her spoon in her melting ice cream. The bowl was cold against her thighs, but she didn't have any other place to put it. Cade was still cradling his bowl in his hands, glancing around Star's shabby apartment. God, this was all so awkward.

Then he looked at her with those gorgeous blue eyes. A hint of a smile curved his mouth. "You know, I pictured this reunion with a lot more making out."

For some reason, that struck her as insanely funny, and Kylie began to giggle.

He grinned at her, visibly relaxing. "It's true. I thought maybe you'd see the band and fling yourself passionately in my arms and we could ride off into the sunset. Or down Sunset Avenue, at the very least. And I'd hold you close—much, I imagine, like a spider monkey would—and tell you all about how much I love you and miss you, and we'd kiss and I'd end up with most of your lipstick on me and it'd be pretty damn great."

More giggles erupted from her, and she stared at her bowl. To her horror, her laughter turned into a sob, and she started to cry. Shit, not again.

"Please don't cry, Kylie. Please. God, I can't stand to see you hurting and not be able to do anything about it." Cade set the bowl down on the floor and moved closer to her. His hand went to her waist and he pulled her close, burying his face in the curve of her neck. "Please. I'll go if you want me to, okay? Just don't . . . don't be so sad. Tell me to go and I'll go."

"I . . . don't want you to go," she admitted softly. She wanted to burrow against him and forget the world.

He took the bowl of ice cream out of her lap and set it on top of his. Then he shifted closer to her on the couch and began to kiss her neck, her ear. "Tell me to stop and I'll stop."

Her breath shuddered in her lungs. "I don't want you to stop, either."

His fingers moved to her chin and he tilted her face until she was looking at him. "Tell me not to love you."

She . . . couldn't tell him that, either. "Oh, Cade."

"That's not a *no*," he told her.

"I love you," she admitted. "I just . . . I'm trapped, Cade." She shook her head, feeling a bit hopeless. "I love you. I want to be with you more than anything, but with circumstances how they are, I just can't. I can't be a burden to you."

"A financial burden?" he guessed.

Her entire body stilled. "You . . . how . . . ?"

"Carmela mentioned that the label had put the screws to you in your contract and they were doing something similar to Daphne." He smiled broadly. "So I bought myself a record label."

"You *what*?" Her heart pounded.

"I bought the label. Reviewed the contracts for myself and found them rather unfriendly. Daphne's now in better hands, and I have this for you." He pulled an envelope out of a pocket inside his jacket.

Her stomach dropped. "I don't want your money, Cade."

"Well, that's nice, but this isn't my money. This is yours." He pressed the envelope into her hand. Wary, she opened it.

Inside was a check on the record label's account. It was the exact amount they had charged her for Daphne's concerts.

"How . . ."

"Like I said, I now own the label." He corrected himself a moment later, tilting his head. "Well, actually, I own the majority share. But they wanted to make me happy and this was what I insisted upon."

"Th-thank you." She stared down at the check, numb.

"Don't thank me," Cade said. "Talk to me. Make me understand why you keep running away." He clasped her hand in his. "I'm pretty sure I mentioned the part about me being rich, right? You could have come to me. I would have gladly given you the money."

She flinched and pulled away from him. "That's just it. I don't want a handout. I don't want to be a burden."

"There's that word again," he said, and his voice was hard. "I don't know why you seem to think that supporting and helping someone you love equates to a burden."

"Cade," she protested. "They were coming after me for thousands of dollars. Hundreds of thousands if what they told me was right."

"Then it's a good thing I have billions." He shook his head. "It's not about the money. Tell me what it is, Kylie. Make me understand."

Kylie stared down at the check, then looked over at him again. "I . . . told you I grew up with my grandmother, right?"

"You did."

"Well." Her lips were dry. She licked them repeatedly, feeling uncomfortable and anxious. "My nana isn't the most . . . happy of people. Her husband died when she was fifty, and then her only child died ten years later. So when she inherited me and I was all of ten years old, she really didn't know what to do with me. Not only that, but her husband didn't have life insurance, and neither did my parents, so not only did she have me to take care of, but she had to work outside of the house for the first time in her life. She hated it. And she hated me because of it." Kylie's stomach churned uncomfortably at the memories. "She always reminded me that I was fat and ugly, and she had to work two jobs because of me. I was nothing like my mother, who was beautiful and smart and thin. I was a burden, and she told me that constantly. And as I grew up, well, I decided that I'd never be a burden to someone like I was to her." She gave him a faint smile. "Want to know the ironic part? When I hit twenty or so, Nana Sloane slipped into full-on dementia. She has to stay in a locked-down nursing home with round-the-clock care because her mind can't stay focused on the present. Now she's *my* burden." Her laugh was bitter. "And she's a really expensive one. I can't seem to make ends meet caring for both her and myself, so one of us has to give, and she can't work, so it falls back to me."

"Oh, Kylie." He gripped her hand in his. "That's a horrible story. Didn't anyone love you, growing up?"

She shrugged, feeling uncomfortable. "My parents did. I never felt unwanted with them. And I always had friends in school. It was just hard after they died." Because Nana Sloane hated Kylie.

Such a burden. So useless. Look at how fat she is. She's not even trying to take care of herself. I can't believe I got stuck with her. I should have just called the state and had them take her away, but family always handles their own, no matter how awful it is. She's my own albatross, a fat little liability that means I'll never be happy again.

Cade's look became knowing. "That night we went out for waffles . . . You told me about the ex that dumped you on the street. Does this have to do with him, too?"

"Boy, I'm really not good at hiding my issues, am I?"

"Are you afraid I'd do the same to you?"

"I don't think you would," Kylie said. "Then again, I didn't think he would, either. I just . . . I can't be someone else's problem." She rubbed her forehead. Talking about all the hurting, ugly things in her past was giving her a headache. But she had to. She had to make him understand that it wasn't him, it was her. All her and her baggage.

"I'd never—"

"But you did blackmail me," she pointed out with a rueful smile. "I still don't have my panties back."

Cade's expression grew sad. "I was ruthless with you because I needed to see you. Had to have you in my bed. I suppose that was the wrong thing to do, given your past."

"It's just . . . hard for me to trust," she admitted. "Hard for me to go to sleep at night and know everything's handled, and I'm not just a responsibility to you. Not financially or emotionally. For once, I'd like to be in charge of my own life, you know?" She looked around Star's shabby apartment and sighed. "It's sad, because I'm taking advantage of Star, really. I pay her two hundred a month to sleep on her couch when I'm home and to have my mail sent here, but I'm still imposing on her."

"I'm sure Star doesn't look at it that way," Cade said. "She's helping a friend. And I bet she loves the company. Because no matter what you might think, Kylie, you're wonderful to be around. You're caring and kind and utterly loving. And my life isn't the same if you're not in it."

She looked into his blue, blue eyes, and then down at the check clutched in her hand. "This . . . helps," she admitted. "I was going to use this money to pay for Nana Sloane's next year of care and couch surf with Star until my next gig."

"I have a new proposal," Cade said, dragging her against him. He pulled the check from her hand and set it down on the floor. Then, he had her breasts pushed against his chest and his arms around her waist and his mouth was so close to hers that she thought he'd kiss her.

"What's that?" she asked, feeling breathless at his nearness.

"I know this great townhouse in Manhattan with a very lonely bachelor who's looking for a roommate. I hear he's going to charge very reasonable rates if he can find the right woman willing to put up with him and all his money." His mouth crooked. "See, he travels a lot, so he needs to know that his girl won't be too lonely when he's gone."

"I imagine she'd be working her own job," Kylie said breathlessly, heart thudding. "So she could pay her portion of the rent."

"That sounds perfect," Cade said. "He's going to want rent on the first of every month, of course. But the perks are pretty good."

"What kind of perks?"

"Well, he likes his coffee black. I hear it's very important to have similar tastes in beverages. He's got a pink roadster he doesn't know what to do with, a really big bed, and a really great shower. No grand piano, though."

She giggled, thinking about his first hotel room with the absurd piano.

"But if it's important to his roommate, he'll get one," Cade continued. "And best of all, he has good contacts at a lot of local hospitals and nursing homes so he's sure he can help her find the perfect one for her relative to stay in and be comfortable. It's one of the benefits of being a billionaire who made his money on medical patents."

"He sounds ideal," Kylie murmured. His mouth was so close to hers. She wanted him to kiss her. Hell, she wanted to throw him down on the couch and make love to him.

"I wouldn't say he's completely ideal," Cade told her. "He's a workaholic and a bit pigheaded from time to time. And he snores."

She giggled. "He does, indeed."

"But he loves you very, very much, and he's willing to do whatever it takes to ensure that you feel comfortable in the relationship, Kylie. And if that means charging you rent and insisting you work instead of using his money, then that's what he'll do." Cade's eyes were so blue as he gazed at her. "Say you'll come home with me."

Kylie was terrified. Terrified that this would be a mistake, but even more terrified that Cade would walk out the door and she'd never see him again. "Tell me you love me again?"

"I love you," he told her, leaning in and brushing his lips over hers. "And rent's five hundred a month."

She giggled again. "That's a lot of money just to couch surf."

"Ah, but I have a really awesome couch," he told her, kissing her mouth again. "And an awesome bed." His tongue flicked into her mouth, slicking against her own, only to pull back a moment later as he continued. "And an awesome kitchen. Really, I'm just awesome all around." He kissed her again, longer, slower, sweeter. "But . . . only if I'm with you."

Damn it, there were the tears again. Kylie blinked rapidly. "I love you. So much."

"Then come home with me. Take a chance on me."

She nodded, taking a deep breath. "Yes. Okay. I'll do it."

He grinned, his smile so dazzling she felt as if the entire room lit up. "You sure you don't need more convincing? I came armed with an entire box of condoms."

She laughed, feeling light and carefree, and her hands went to the buttons of his shirt. She wanted this man desperately, and loved that he wanted her just as much. "I hear that my roommate isn't going to be back for at least two more hours."

"Then let's get your money's worth out of this couch," he told her, his grin fading and his mouth seeking hers. All of the playfulness was suddenly gone, and the hunger resurfaced. Cade's mouth devoured hers, and Kylie whimpered as his tongue swept into her mouth again. His hand went to her breast, cupping it and rubbing her nipple through the fabric of her top.

She moaned, tearing at his shirt now. "I want to feel your skin against me, Cade. I need you so desperately."

"Then quit leaving me," he murmured against her skin. "I'm all yours."

"I won't leave again," she told him.

He raised an eyebrow.

"I'll *try* not to leave again," she amended, smiling. "And the next time I freak out, I promise I'll share why."

"Fair enough," he said, his fingers still gliding over her nipple, back and forth, coaxing it to aching hardness. "Now, I need to put my mouth on all this gorgeous skin," he told her. "Undress for me."

She did, pulling off her clothing with haste, anxious to feel his weight on her, to have him between her legs, his warm flesh touching hers. How long had it been since they'd last had sex? Too long, she decided. She cringed when she revealed her serviceable, ugly beige bra and her cotton briefs.

"I wasn't expecting company," she told him. At least her legs were shaved.

"You could be wearing rags and you'd still be utterly gorgeous to me," he told her, and the sincerity on his face made her believe it. It was hard not to feel pretty when a man like Cade was gazing down at you as if you were a work of art.

But then she was naked, and he was mostly naked, and their clothes were flung somewhere on the shabby carpet in Star's living room, and Cade's glorious, naked chest was there for her to touch and lick and caress at her leisure. And she did, murmuring her pleasure at touching him, and moaning when he reciprocated. As always, he paid attention to her breasts—he seemed to love them, despite the fact that they weren't firm or perky; they were too big for that sort of thing. All of Kylie was. But he made her feel pretty nevertheless, and when he looked up at her with heated eyes and parted lips as he took her nipple in his mouth, she'd never felt sexier.

"Condom," she told him breathlessly. "Now."

He nodded and leaned over the side of the couch, searching through the discarded clothing. A moment later, he produced one packet and held it aloft.

"Can I?" she asked. Just the thought of rolling it down his length was making her ache between her legs.

The hot gleam in his eyes was answer enough. He gave her the package, and she opened it, carefully removing the condom. It was slick with lubricant, and her own fingers were shaking with need so much that she dropped it on the floor.

Right into one of the melting bowls of ice cream.

Kylie blinked at it, then giggled. "Houston, we have a problem."

"Do we?" he asked, burying his face against her breasts again. "Or are you still on the pill?"

No condom? Her breath rushed out of her at the thought.

Cade with a condom was good. Cade without a condom felt . . . intense. So intense. "I'm on the pill, yeah."

"Then, can we . . ." He let his words trail off, his gaze asking the question even as he continued to kiss and nuzzle her breasts.

She nodded, her hands going back to him. She laid back down on the couch, ignoring the fact that the pillows were sliding around a bit with all the moving Kylie and Cade were doing. It didn't matter. Nothing mattered but Cade over her, and his knees parting her own, his hips settling between hers, and then his cock pressing against her pussy and stroking through her folds, teasing her clit. She moaned.

"My sweet Kylie," Cade told her. "So damn wet for me. God, I love you."

"I love you, too," she told him in a shaky voice.

And then he pushed into her, and she gasped at how big he felt, and how tight she was. She spread her legs wider, and his hips fit between hers perfectly, and they began to move together. Kylie's hips lifted with Cade's thrusts, and before long, the friction was building between her legs, making her cling to him with breathless need, crying out his name as he hammered into her. She came with a wracking cry, and moments later, he came, too. He pushed into her a few times more, their joined bodies wet with mutual pleasure, and then he slid on top of her, all sweaty skin and muscle.

And perfection. Cade was pure, utter perfection. From the dark blond lashes framing his gorgeous eyes to the loose curls now sticking up from his head, to the way he kissed her neck, her arm, her skin, everywhere he could, even though they'd both come.

Perfection.

Her perfection.

"I love you," she told him again. Just because she felt like it. And maybe because she could. Because they were together now, and he wasn't going to hold anything over her, and she'd never be a burden. Unwanted, unneeded burden. Because she realized something as he moved onto his side and curled on the narrow couch with her. Burdens had nothing to do with love. As long as there was love, there would be no resentment, just a desire to help.

Maybe that was what had been missing all along.

Maybe that was why, in Cade's arms, she was no longer afraid.

TWENTY-ONE

Two weeks later

Kylie's hand was clammy in Cade's as they headed into the nightclub. "Are you sure your friends are going to want to meet me?" She asked for what felt like the dozenth time that evening. She'd fussed and worried over dinner, fixing her makeup over and over again even though in his eyes, she was utter perfection. He knew his Kylie had confidence issues, and she was working on them.

He'd just have to keep loving her and making her feel as utterly beautiful as he knew she was. *Not that it was a chore,* he thought with a grin, giving her hand a squeeze. He'd gladly do so every day for the rest of his life.

Moving Kylie and her Nana Sloane to New York City with him had been one of the happiest weeks he'd ever had. While he wasn't a big fan of Nana Sloane—not after some of the stories Kylie had told him about her childhood—he couldn't help but feel sorry for the frail lady with the confused mind. They'd moved her into one of the best nursing homes Cade could find, and he'd used his name to finagle a discount for Kylie, since she insisted on paying. That was fine with him. She could pay until she was used to him and his money. It was actually kind of refreshing being with someone who didn't give him an expectant look every time the check arrived at a restaurant.

If anything, his Kylie laughed and teased him about his wealth. She'd burst into a fit of giggles when he'd shown her his Manhattan townhouse and the Monet—a real one—above the fireplace. "What, were there no Picassos available when you were decorating?" she teased. "Museum fresh out of Van Goghs?"

He'd tickled her straight into bed for that one.

She'd teased him about the thousand thread-count sheets, too. Were three hundred threads not enough for a billionaire? And she'd poked fun at his marble-tiled bathroom and all the other expensive trappings in his townhouse. Kylie was cheap, she declared, and if she was going to live with him, he was going to eat off-brand groceries and shop at the local Super Saver because no one really needed to spend eighty dollars on a hand towel. He was fine with that. He didn't care if she turned the entire place out with plastic furniture and red Solo drinking cups. Just as long as she was in his arms every night, it was fine. Cade preferred to donate to charities anyhow. Billions of dollars were far too much for one man to have, and he'd told Kylie that once. Her eyes had gleamed so happily that he felt like giving all of his money away.

He didn't, though; he was saving it to spoil his woman whether she wanted it or not.

Like tonight, they'd gone out to one of New York's swankiest restaurants so Cade could show off to Kylie a bit. They'd ordered a moderately priced wine so Kylie wouldn't feel obligated to drink the entire bottle and he didn't let her see the menu so she wouldn't exclaim over the prices. Still, he had a suspicion she was eating on the cheap when she ordered chicken instead of the lobster he had. That was fine. He made her eat a dessert with him anyhow, just so he could lick some of the chocolate off of her decadent, full mouth.

Now it was time for his weekly Brotherhood meeting, and he was bringing Kylie to meet his friends. She didn't know it was a secret society meeting. Actually, most of the *secret* had gone out of the society once Gretchen had started showing up on a regular basis, and then the other men had one by one started bringing their wives and fiancées around. Last week, Audrey had made a genius suggestion that the men were anxious to implement, and Cade was curious to see the results.

As he led Kylie into the club and down one of the back halls, she ran a finger under her lip, checking her lipstick once more.

"You look fine, love," he told her. "Better than fine. Utterly beautiful." She was, too. Dressed in a tight black sheath that wrapped below her breasts, the dress showed off the exaggerated hourglass of Kylie's lush figure and emphasized her glorious breasts. Her golden hair had been freshly retipped with flame red, and was pulled back from her face into glam waves.

But she gave him an uncertain look. "Won't the others be expecting you to show up with Daphne? After all the history you guys had?"

Was that what was troubling her? Cade smiled, imagining the reactions of the others if he *had* showed up with Daphne. "I think they'd question my sanity if I'd brought her. No one thinks Daphne and I belong together. And they can't wait to meet you. Really."

"Even Daphne's sisters?" she asked, ever skeptical.

"Especially them," Cade declared. Once she met brash Gretchen and efficient Audrey, she'd realize she was worrying over nothing. Neither one was a bit like Daphne.

Kylie's hand tightened in his again, and he looked over at her. She was staring down the hall, where Hunter's enormous bodyguard stood, guarding the door to the basement.

"I'll get this," he told her, and approached the door. He

knew the man recognized him, but they still used the Brother-hood's signal, since he had a guest with him. Two fingers, swept over his shoulder, then resting over his tattoo of the Brotherhood's symbol on his bicep.

The guard nodded and stepped aside.

"Come on, love," Cade told the hesitating Kylie. Wide-eyed, she followed him in.

Down below, he could already hear strains of conversation. Maylee's thick southern drawl was mixed in with Gretchen's louder, more boisterous tones to the right of the stairs. To the left, he could hear Reese smugly announcing his hand of cards. They'd already started without him. That was fine—he knew he and Kylie were late. And as they came down the stairs, he grinned at the changes below.

The men's enormous basement room had been neatly halved. A wall had been erected on one side of the room, and the women's voices could be heard from that newly created room. The walls of the men's room had been painted a dark Kelly green, and inside the new "women's room" he saw the walls were a fresh baby pink. An identical card table with six chairs had been placed in the new room, and he could see the alcohol and refreshments cart in their room, just like in the men's.

They'd given the ladies their own club, so they could quit crashing the men's. Everyone was delighted at the thought.

But before he turned Kylie over to the women, he wanted her to meet the guys. His brothers. So, squeezing her hand to reassure her, he led her down toward the table where the men were seated.

At the sight of them, five chairs scraped back and the men stood. Cade felt proud at the sight of his friends—here were five of the most influential men in the world, and they were standing up to greet Kylie and smiling. Smiling at her, though he noticed Reese had eyed her figure appreciatively. He'd have to knock Reese in the head for that, he thought with good-natured jealousy.

"Boys, this is Kylie. Kylie, these are my brothers."

She gave them a shy, charming smile. "Hello."

"It's very nice to meet you," Logan began, only to be interrupted by a feminine cry.

"They're here," Cade heard Gretchen bellow. "Everyone out! We need to meet the fresh meat."

The women piled into the now-smaller men's card room, and from there, things were a little chaotic for the next half hour. He introduced Kylie to his friends one pair at a time. There was Hunter and Gretchen, who insisted on going first (Gretchen more so than Hunter). He could tell that Kylie felt awkward meeting Gretchen, who looked extremely similar to Daphne, but when Gretchen gave her a bear hug and squealed with delight at meeting "Cade's new boo," he saw Kylie visibly relax. Then, he introduced Kylie to Maylee and Griffin, because Maylee's sweet southern charm made her easy to talk to, and Griffin had unstarched quite a bit since meeting her. Brontë, Logan's new wife, then gave some pithy quote about friendship, and Violet and Jonathan were polite and friendly. Jonathan gave Cade a knowing, approving look at the sight of Kylie. Jonathan knew all about Cade's long-term despair over the Daphne situation, and it was clear he approved that Cade had moved on.

Then, Reese and heavily pregnant Audrey came forward. Kylie did a double take at the sight of Audrey, who held up a hand. "I know. I get that from some people," she said wryly. "We're twins."

"I just . . . Oh." Kylie bit her lip and looked at him helplessly. "It's very nice to meet you."

"You sure?" Audrey said. "It's probably awkward as hell, considering that my sister beaned you with a flowerpot. Cade told us all about it."

"She wasn't in the right frame of mind," Kylie said, her voice gentle. "I don't hold it against her."

"Which is why you're a better person than me," Audrey said, and patted her belly. "Can we all sit down now? My back is killing me."

"Of course," Cade said, and rushed into the ladies' side of the basement to get Audrey's chair for her.

The women headed back into their room, all chattering. Maylee had already linked arms with Kylie's and was exclaiming over her hair and makeup, and Gretchen was talking up a storm. Kylie was still smiling, but it wasn't the helpless, unsure smile. She looked at ease.

"Thanks for bringing her, Cade." Audrey said as she settled into her chair. "I'm so glad to see you settled and happy. I almost thought Daphne was going to keep you miserable and strung along for the rest of your life."

"I almost thought that, too," Cade admitted. "Then I met Kylie, and everything changed overnight."

Audrey's expression softened, and she smiled. "Just like me and Reese."

"Just like," he agreed, grinning. He moved to the far side of the table and gave Kylie—who was now wedged in between Maylee and Gretchen—a kiss. "Will you be all right? Can I get you anything?"

"She's fine," Gretchen said, waving a hand at him. "Quit being a helicopter boyfriend."

Kylie stifled a grin. "I *am* fine. Thank you, love." She beamed up at him. "Go and have fun."

"All right," Audrey said as he exited the room. "First order of the Ladies Club—changing the color of this room."

"Hear hear," Gretchen said. "Who the hell decided pink?"

Chuckling, Cade shut the door behind them.

"A ladies club is genius," Griffin said as Cade sat in his customary chair between Reese and Jonathan. "I always felt bad leaving Maylee at home, knowing I'd be out late with the boys."

"And now we can finally play cards in peace," Jonathan agreed.

Just then, a raucous shout arose from the women's room. "Bras off if you lose," Gretchen shouted. "Ante up, bitches!"

Silence.

Reese raised an eyebrow to Jonathan. "You were saying?"

Cade just grinned. He had a sneaky feeling that Kylie was going to get along just fine with the other women. "We should play, too."

"Speaking of bras," Reese began. "May I just say on behalf of all of us, that you made the *obvious* choice, Cade?" Reese gestured in front of his chest, clearly referring to Kylie's assets. "I mean, damn. I thought Audrey had some impressive tatas, but you got a good one there, buddy."

"I'm glad you remembered that she's mine," Cade said, pulling his chips toward his spot with one arm. "Because now I don't have to kill you."

Logan tossed his ante into the pile and then lifted his glass. "Someone pour Cade a drink so we can start this meeting, already."

A shot of whiskey was set before him a moment later, and all the men raised their glasses, some drinking water, some alcohol. They clinked them together and said the motto that had gotten them through college, through years of hard work and financial success . . . and now, love. The motto had made them who they were today. *"Fratres in prosperitum,"* they chanted.

Looking around the table, Cade had never felt closer to his Brotherhood.

Life was good. Life was very, very good.

EPILOGUE

Six months later

Oh my God, would you quit squirming?" Kylie exclaimed as she leaned in to add more glitter to eyelids. "It's impossible for you to sit still, isn't it?"

The man sitting in the chair pouted. It looked rather funny, given that he was wearing a pink feather boa and mile-high heels. "I'm sorry."

"Don't be sorry," Kylie said with a grin. "Just stop freaking wiggling and hold still so I can draw your eyes."

Obediently, the drag queen closed his eyes and leaned forward. "Just glitter me up and let's get this show going."

Several minutes later, she'd transformed the dark-haired lithe young man with the five o'clock shadow into his stage persona. They were trying a new type of eye makeup tonight, and Kylie saw with approval that it looked great on Carl, aka Carla the French. "I like it. What do you think?"

He opened his eyes with a dramatic flutter of his sweeping

lashes, then looked critically in the mirror. "Needs more glitter."

She studied him, then nodded, dipping her brush into the paint. "More glitter it is."

Kylie had been working a popular drag show Off Broadway for the last two months, and she had to admit that she absolutely loved it. There was not an audience more appreciative of makeup than drag queens, she mused as she added more glitter to Carla the French's eyelids. It was a bit like coming home. They loved her makeup, loved her, and loved to experiment with new and dramatic looks, which Kylie also adored. The men were pretty fricking fantastic, too: funny and sweet and no one had thrown a flowerpot at her head. Nothing like her last job, Kylie thought with amusement.

She finished and leaned back for Carl/Carla to inspect. He peered in the mirror and then nodded. "Good job, babe."

"Thanks." She felt a bit like preening. "Go out there and wow them."

"I always do," Carla the French said, getting up with a flourish of pink boa.

Kylie grinned and began to tidy her station. She could put away her things and leave for the evening now that the makeup was done, though she always left extra cosmetic sponges and makeup remover for the men once they finished the show. The stuff they'd been using in the past was crap, and Kylie was particular about her canvases, and the men definitely qualified as canvases.

She was just putting away the last of her bottles when someone knocked at the makeup room door. "Knock knock," said Tessa, the stage manager. "You have visitors."

When Kylie looked up, she sucked in a breath.

There, in the doorway with a stranger at her side, was Daphne Petty, global superstar.

The last six months had been rough for Daphne. Kylie hadn't seen her, but she knew from Cade's reports that rehab was an uphill climb, and the tabloids had been crawling all over her, determined to be the ones to catch her when she slipped. Then, she'd left rehab three months ago and put on weight, and the tabloids had gleefully reported that, too. There wasn't a day that Daphne wasn't in the tabloids in some negative fashion or another.

But . . . she looked really damn good.

Daphne had put on at least twenty pounds from when Kylie had last seen her. Maybe thirty. The hollows were gone from her face, and she looked more like her twin, Audrey, now. She wore a brown wig with a thick fringe of bangs, and her skin was clear of makeup. Her figure was no longer twig-thin, but had curves to it. She wore a plain black sweater and a pair of jeans, and gave Kylie an awkward smile. "Hey there. Long time no see."

"Oh wow," Kylie said, moving forward to hug Daphne. "It's so good to see you! How are you?" She wrapped her arms around Daphne and held her tight for a moment, pleased to see that Daphne no longer felt brittle underneath her grip, and that she actually hugged Kylie back.

"I'm doing great," Daphne said as they pulled away. "And I should probably introduce you to Wesley. He's my life coach slash bodyguard slash slap-my-hand-away-from-bad-things guy." She gestured at the Goliath behind her.

Kylie eyed the man. He was well over six feet tall, had a body like a pro wrestler, and looked rather . . . strict. She offered him her hand. "It's nice to meet you."

"Likewise." He scanned the room and moved protectively closer to Daphne, which Kylie thought was rather sweet. It was nice to see someone looking out for her for a change, instead of leading her down a bad path.

"So," Kylie said, "I'm surprised you're here in NYC." She tucked a stray lock of hair behind her ear, hating that it'd been a few weeks since she'd colored her hair and her ends weren't as vivid as they could have been. She'd just been . . . busy. When she wasn't working, she was running around the city with the ladies of their Ladies Night Table. She and Maylee had grown exceptionally close and traded recipes back and forth.

And when she wasn't with the ladies? She was with Cade. Glorious, wonderful Cade. Cade, who had a crazy schedule between charities and foundations and his business—Archer Industries—and going overseas for ambassador programs—but who always managed to find time to make her feel pampered and loved and utterly, completely adored. Sometimes she went with him on his trips, but after three dry, obscenely boring medical conferences in a row, her eyes started to cross and she stayed home. When he was gone, though, her phone exploded with pictures and texts . . . and she reciprocated. They lived through texts and phone calls until he got home—and then they spent the entire night in bed, loving and reconnecting.

It was wonderful. Perfection, even. And seeing Daphne looking and feeling better? Instead of making her wary and jealous, she was just really happy for her that she'd found some measure of peace.

"Well, I'm working on a new album," Daphne said. "The label suggested Christmas songs. Something low-key that doesn't require a ton of touring."

Kylie blinked. "You don't want to tour?"

"She's not ready to tour," Wesley said protectively.

"Oh."

"I'm not," Daphne said with a grimace. "The day-to-day temptations are still hard for me to shake, but it's getting easier." She patted her stomach. "And I'm eating like a pig since Wes here won't let me smoke."

He gave Daphne another one of those stern looks, but Kylie thought it looked a little . . . adoring, really. "Smoking's the gateway drug to smoking other things," he chastised. "You can have carrot sticks if you need something for your mouth."

"Hear that?" Daphne teased. "He thinks I'm a rabbit."

Kylie couldn't stop smiling. Daphne just looked so happy, so at ease with Wesley at her side. Healthy, too. "Cade's in town right now. He'd love to see you if you're free tonight."

"Oh." Daphne looked surprised for a moment, and she glanced at Wes. "We do have tickets to the show, but I'd rather see Cade, honestly. Do you mind, Wes?"

The beefy guard crossed his arms. "Do I look as if I'd mind missing a drag show?"

Daphne patted his arm cheerfully. "I won't answer that."

The thing with Daphne? She was just as charming and funny as Cade had always sworn she was. Now that she was clean, she was fun to be around. Kylie had brought her home to surprise Cade, and had been genuinely touched by the tears in his eyes as he hugged his longtime friend. They'd had dinner at home, and instead of drinking wine and sitting by the fire, they'd had hot tea (Wes's orders) and Cade and Daphne caught up, sharing stories of their childhoods and some wild auntie stories with Audrey and Reese's new baby.

Eventually, they hugged again and Daphne left for the evening, promising to have dinner again next week since she was in New York City for the foreseeable future. And Kylie was left with the dishes and a lot of swirling thoughts in her head.

"You're quiet," Cade said as he wrapped his arms around her from behind as she stood at the sink.

"Just thinking about Daphne and you," she admitted. "Think about it. You could have waited six months and had the Daphne you always wanted. Do you regret not waiting for her?"

"Are you kidding me?" Cade pulled the dishes out of her hands and turned her to face him. "Kylie, I love you. I love you more and more each day."

Her smile was soft, rueful. "I know. Just old insecurities popping up." She'd been gaining a lot of confidence by being with Cade, but seeing Daphne tonight had made certain things rise to the surface. "She was so happy tonight."

"She is happy, and I'm happy for her," Cade agreed, holding Kylie against him. "But I can't imagine dating Daphne now. Old Daphne or New Daphne, she doesn't hold a candle to Kylie. And Kylie's the one I love with all my heart."

She wrapped her arms around his shoulders and tugged him down for a kiss. "I love you, too, babe."

They kissed for a long moment, and then he broke it with a chuckle, pulling away. "You know, I was going to give you this tomorrow when we met for lunch, but it seems appropriate now." He reached into his pocket and pulled out a tiny pale blue box.

Tiffany's.

Kylie's eyes went wide. "W-what?"

"Now I suppose I have to call off the marching band that's due to appear tomorrow," he said. Since she wasn't moving, he popped open the box and showed Kylie the new ring. Big. Sparkly. Ornate. Huge diamond, oval cut. "Marry me again? For real this time? Not Vegas, but a real, honest-to-goodness ceremony?"

Kylie's squeal of happiness was all the response he got.

"I take it that's a yes?"

"Yes, yes, yes," Kylie said, covering his face with kisses. "A hundred thousand times yes."

Cade's smile was brilliant. "You know I'd marry you over and over again, Kylie Daniels?"

She knew. Oh, she knew. It was in every touch, every glance, every caress. And as she flung her arms around his neck again and dragged him to the floor for a spontaneous round of lovemaking, she felt silly for ever pushing him away.

A burden was never a burden as long as there was love. And she loved Cade so much that she'd have followed him anywhere, done anything for him. Because that, she'd realized at some point, was love. It wasn't fear. Wasn't regret.

It was pure happiness.

It was Cade Archer, her husband.

Keep reading for a special excerpt from

the next title in the Hitman series

LAST KISS

by Jessica Clare and Jen Frederick

Available now from Berkley!

One Month Ago

VASILY

"You think to lead the Petrovich *Bratva*?" Georgi Petrovich cries from far down the table. He is so far removed from the main branch of the Petrovich family tree he barely warrants a place here. "You aren't even blood Petrovich!"

"Am I not?" I ask. There's no need to raise my voice. Any emotion indicates weakness. I am not a weak man. "What makes a Petrovich?" I stand then and begin to walk around the table. "Is it blood? Then half of you should be executed on the table for failing to have the requisite DNA. Who shall go first?"

I point to Thomas Gregovorich, a loyal member of the *Bratva* for at least two generations. His father served in the KGB during the Cold War.

He gives a small nod in deference acknowledging that the *Bratva* was a true brotherhood made up of allegiances rather than blood.

"Or you, Kilment, when we took you and your brother in when you were left orphaned on the street, did you believe you became a true Petrovich when you made your first kill? Conducted your first job? When we speak of the *Bratva*, we speak as one voice. What is done to one, it is done to all. Or does that maxim no longer hold true, Georgi?"

There are low murmurs of approval and Georgi sits back, folds his arms, and looks petulantly at the table. We are meeting today to discuss the future of the *Bratva* after the death of Sergei Petrovich. A death I helped orchestrate, and many suspect it, which makes it difficult for me to enact my next step—to kill Elena Petrovich. Two Petrovichs dead so close together smells of a coup. We are an unstable lot, and lopping off the head of this snake would result in chaos. In order to achieve my ends, the *Bratva* must be stabilized.

However, in this den of iniquity, it is not love that holds the loyalty of each man. It is fear. The Petrovichs have held power over us all by setting us one against the other. To rise above, I have eliminated all weaknesses.

What sets me apart is all that I am willing to do. Each of these men at the table has had limits. I have none.

The men that sit at this table are divided. Some view me with awe and respect, and others with disgust. The latter are the ones I respect, because a man who would kill his own sister, a man such as I, deserves to be in a dungeon, locked away from all of humanity.

Instead I stand here as the potential leader of this room of villains and thieves. And it is a position I seek, not because I lust after power, but because if I control the *Bratva*, then nothing is out of my reach. I have one goal now.

"Will you kill your mother to save the Bratva, Thomas? And you, Pietr, when your sister whispers to her lover Pavil Ionov, do you worry that she's telling secrets? Or Stefan, your son, I saw him the other day holding hands with . . ." I stop behind Stefan's chair and rest both hands on the back. I can almost feel him inhale the fear. ". . . a smart young thing. They looked to be enjoying themselves."

Pietr coughs. "So you are willing to kill us all to maintain hold of the *Bratva*? That is not a good reason to follow you."

"No, but you all know that I will sacrifice everything and everyone to protect the brotherhood."

They are all silent because unlike the others, my sister, Katya, is gone. Disposed of by my own hand at the order of Elena Petrovich.

I end my stroll around the room behind my chair. "I am the one who led us away from munitions and dirt to telecom interests. In less than a decade, the *Bratva*'s primary businesses will be legitimate, which means that you no longer have to hide behind your armored vehicles. You no longer have to rely on bodyguards that could be bought off. You need not fear the KGB or the *militsiya*. You can invest in your *futbol* teams and mansions in Londongrad without fear of reprisal."

Leadership means effective utilization of the carrot and the stick. I lead with the stick. Always. The Petrovichs believe in only the stick. For them the carrot does not exist or is viewed with suspicion.

The *boyeviks*—the young muscle our old warlord Alexsandr groomed from urchins on the street to protect the brotherhood— grow tired of the constant threat to their homes and family. They sleep with one eye open, their hand over their heart, wondering if the brother next to them will be killing their mother or raping their sister in retribution for some *Bratva* infraction.

The older generation such as Thomas and Kilment and those who sit on the Petrovich *Bratva* council are loath to hand over the power of this organization to me, a mere foot soldier sold by his father to repay debts. With Sergei dead and the vicious Elena the only real Petrovich remaining, I am left with a choice. Attempt to wrest control of the brotherhood from the old guard or walk away.

And I would walk away. I have some money stored but I've

been a Petrovich for a long time and there are many enemies that would crow over my death. No, in order to survive, the Petrovich *Bratva* must remain strong.

If I have learned anything, it is that people with nothing are victims. It is those with power and money and might who have the ability to protect others.

Thomas rubs a hand across his jaw. "There is one thing you could do."

"That is a legend, Thomas," Kilment groans.

"I will do it." Legends persist because people believe, and if belief means I can bring down Elena Petrovich and secure a peaceful future, then I will pursue this foolishness until the painting is mine. Their desire to recapture the past is absurd and yet another reason the old guard should be replaced. "You wish me to procure the Caravaggio."

Cries of wonder and confusion fill the room.

"So you know," Kilment says flatly.

I pretend no ignorance, for it is a story that Alexsandr shared with me long ago. "I know that a famous triptych painted by Caravaggio once hung in the palaces of the Medicis in Florence, perhaps the Careggi Villa. It was commissioned as an altarpiece but considered to be too profane, as many of his pieces were judged. It was gifted by the Medicis to Feodor the First, who then lost it, and Russia entered the Time of Troubles. When the Boyars rose to power in the seventeen hundreds, it is rumored the painting was recovered by Peter the Great. Citizen Petrovich's grandfather was gifted this set of three paintings and it hung in the great hall of the Petrovichs until it was lost, sold, stolen during Sergei's time. Many say that he who holds it, holds the world."

Thomas nods at this recitation, but Kilment looks unconvinced.

"It is known as the *Madonna and the Volk*," I conclude. The Petrovichs loved the painting because the woman who sat for Caravaggio was purportedly a true Mary Magdalene— a whore. And the *Volk*? It is a man wolf who is eating Mary, and despite the gruesomeness of the depiction, there is an expression of ecstasy on her face. *Volk*, too, was seen as a play on the old Russian criminal rank of *vory*. Thieves, wolves at the door. We were the predators. Everyone else is prey. I saw it only once, when I was given to Elena Petrovich like some birthday treat. It seemed fitting that Sergei sold it to fund some sordid perversion of his own. "But why is it that it is of any importance? It is a mere painting."

Thomas stares at me. "It is a symbol of our wealth and power, and we have lost it. And no Caravaggio, one of the greatest painters of all time, can be dubbed a mere painting. It belonged to Peter the Great. It is priceless, one of a kind. Why would we not want it? That it is in the hands of someone else is shameful, a blot against the Petrovich name. Now more than ever, we must show our enemies we are strong."

"So you want it, but why is this your loyalty test? Have I not proven myself again and again? Have I not shed the blood of my own family for the brotherhood?" I spread my scarred hands out as if they hold the proof of my allegiance.

"The Caravaggio has been lost to us for years. Many of us have tried to find it but have failed," Thomas admits. "If you find it, you will show yourself to be a man of resource and cunning, a man who is unafraid. You will restore the pride to the brotherhood and prove your worth as a leader."

I hold back a lip curl of disgust at this. Leadership is not running around the world seeking one painting. Leadership is moving our assets out of dangerous and risky ventures and into more stable enterprises. Leadership is generating loyalty by providing a way for the members to feed their families and protect their loved ones.

This is a snipe hunt, an impossible task designed to make me fail and appear weak amongst those who would support me. Or worse, in my absence they will eliminate those they deem a threat. To kill me here would generate a revolt.

No, this is not about a painting. This is punishment, revenge, retribution. But I am one step ahead of them. I guessed that this is the task they would set before me. They think I will be gone long, chasing my tail for months. I will be happy to prove how wrong they are.

Thomas sits back and looks around the table. He has been a member of the *Bratva* for a long time. They respect his voice. "Bring us the Madonna, and the Bratva will be yours."

I smile and raise my palms in a gesture that says *fait accompli*. "Then it is done."

I am not so sanguine two hours later as I sit across the table from Ivan the Terrible. Ivan Dostonev is the leader of the Dostonev *Bratva*, an organization whose base is in St. Petersburg. The Dostonevs posture that they are descendants of confidants of the tsars. Perhaps they are, but we are all criminals. We bathe in the blood of our enemies and eat our own young.

"I hear the Petrovich *Bratva* is troubled, my friend," he says with studied casualness. Ivan has held power not because he is particularly clever but because he is a man of his word—a rarity in these parts. People trust him—and fear him. He trades in favors and you do not know when your favor will be called in, only that when the time comes you must heed his call or reap terrible consequences.

I owe this man a favor, and I knew from the moment I saw his name on the screen of my phone that my reckoning had arrived.

"When there is a change in leadership, some are disconcerted. That will change," I reply.

"My people tell me that the council has set a challenge for you. Meet it and the Petrovich brotherhood is yours."

I meet his boast that he has infiltrated our organization with my own. "And my people tell me that your son has no interest in following in your footsteps. What will happen to the Dostonevs then?"

"Bah! Vladimir is young. He wants to drink and fuck. Let him have his fun." He swallows his vodka and gestures for me to drink. I do, tipping the glass and allowing the clear liquid to coat my tongue and glide down my throat. "Enough of the niceties. Fifteen years ago, you asked a favor of me. I granted it. Now it is time for you to repay your debt."

"Of course." There is relief in finally discharging my debt. For so long I've wondered, not what I would be asked to do, but when. The uncertainty will soon be behind me. "What is it?"

"I want you to bring me the Caravaggio."

His request astonishes me.

"Why does everyone love this painting?" I'm truly bewildered.

He holds out his arms; heavy jewels adorn nearly every finger. Put him on a throne and one would easily mistake him for a prince of old. "I've always wanted it. It hung in the palace of Peter the Great. It was commissioned by the great Cosimo de' Medici."

"And you thumb your nose at the Petrovichs."

He grins. "That too."

"No." I refuse tersely. "Ask something else."

"I want nothing else." He waves his hand. "You know they are setting you up. This painting means nothing to them. They want you out of Moscow so that they can weed out those amongst your young soldiers who look up to you. The old guard will not give up power so easily."

I stare impassively. The old guard is senile. Their plays are so obvious they are read by outsiders. "I did not know you had interest in the Petrovich holdings. You've always said Moscow is full of peasants."

He flicks his fingers in disgust. "I do not want your precious *Bratva*. I have no interest in your businesses. And frankly, Vasya, neither should you. Let the Petrovich *Bratva* burn. Find me the painting and you can bring her home. Fifteen years is a very long time to have not laid eyes on your precious sister. What would you do to have your family restored to you?"

I fight not to bare my teeth at him, to not jump over the table and strangle him until pain replaces his smug smile.

"I know they expect me to fail and be distracted for months, but when I return with the Caravaggio, they will not be able to deny me. They have prepared their own shallow graves."

"So you have found it?" He quirks his eyebrow.

I shrug but do not answer.

"Well, well. I am impressed, Vasya. It is a shame I did not find you all those years ago. You would have made a marvelous part of the Dostonevs. Still, I want the painting. You will have to find a way to bring me the painting and still gain power within the *Bratva*. For you see, Vasya, if you do not bring the painting to me, I will summon your sister home and she will become exactly what you do not wish—a target for all your enemies. I helped save your sister once. It is easy enough to help kill her, too. Choose your course wisely."

"They are setting you on a fool's errand," Igorek announces as I enter my office. He is standing next to the single window that overlooks a dirty alley and the brick wall of the building next door. Igorek is a young warrior with a brother and a mother to protect. He worries, for good reason, that he and his loved ones would be imperiled if I am gone for a long period of time. He is not the only one who has invaded my sanctum. Aleksei, an enforcer whom I trained with as a boy, is also present.

"Only if I cannot return with the Madonna. When I present the painting to them, they will be forced to back me. I will remove Elena to some dacha in northern Russia, and we will jettison any who would hew to the old ways."

"Merely remove her?" Igorek raises an eyebrow.

"What else would I do with her?" I meet his inquiry coolly, for speaking out loud of the murder of Elena Petrovich would not be met in all quarters with approval. She needs to die, but

I cannot kill her until the *Bratva* is firmly under my control.

"*Mne pofig.*" He shrugs. *I don't care.*

Of course he cares or he would not suggest it. I, too, care, but it is not the time or place. "Once the *Bratva* is mine, then we will talk about protecting our own."

"Fine, so you look for a painting that has been lost for decades?" Igorek is skeptical.

Aleksei, whom I've known longer, is much less circumspect. "The Madonna? Holy Mother of Mary, are you crazy? Did killing Sergei cause you to lose your motherfucking mind?" Aleksei kicks at a chair and stomps around the room, looking for more things to break. I pull down a Meissen vase that is part of a set we'd recently discovered being transported inside a large set of ornamental—but very cheap—concrete dogs imported from China. Peddling antiques is more lucrative than I had anticipated. We started just a few years ago, as part of my goal to supplant income from the sale of krokodil and humans.

Sergei had been lured to the easy money, but trafficking in drugs and people is not only dangerous but also short-lived. The problem with Sergei was that he lacked vision. Now he's dead, his body dumped in a hog lot so that the only thing he's possibly seeing now is the inside of a pig's belly. An ignominious end to the crime boss of one of the largest brotherhoods in Russia, but a fitting one.

"It's out there." I sit at my desk and check my e-mails. I've been searching for the Caravaggio for months now and while I have not found it, I believe I have discovered a person who can.

"You should shoot yourself now and save yourself the misery." Aleksei exhales grumpily and seats himself in one of the two low-backed leather chairs in front of the desk. I suppose it is my desk now. Once Sergei sat here and before him Roman Petrovich.

I hate the Petrovichs, all of them, both dead and alive.

They had promised me safety but delivered only fear and torture. But my revenge will be to rule over this entire *Bratva* until the Petrovich name will be known only in connection with me, Vasily.

"What is your plan?" Igorek asks.

"There are rumors on the deep web of a collector who has not only the Madonna but the Golden Candelabra as well as a few other holy relics."

"Wonderful," Aleksei scoffs. "You know not but of rumors. Even if these rumors are true, one would have to assume that these artifacts are owned by a capitalist and are held in a safe that is virtually impenetrable. Just shoot Elena Petrovich and be done with it."

"If I kill her, who else will I have to kill? Thomas? Kilment? All of them? How about you, Aleksei? Or Igorek? And do I just kill the male members or every issue to the fifth cousin?" Aleksei pales at his name, at the mention of his family. "While it is better to be feared than loved, each act of ill will toward one's own people must be done only when there is no other action. If bringing this painting back means new leadership without bloodshed, it is worth the risk."

He is unconvinced by my speech, but he has a new wife and a child coming. Either of those could be used as bargaining chips against him.

"Igorek, you talk to the others, prepare them for my absence and be on watch." He nods. "How long will you be gone?"

"Not long." My inbox dings and I read the e-mail swiftly. Finally. I give the two a ghost of a smile. "There is one person who can find the source of the postings on the dark web. One person who can lead us to the Madonna. And one person, I suspect, no modern security system can withstand. The Emperor." I lean back in my chair and point to the computer. "The Emperor appeared out of nowhere eighteen months ago and built an untraceable trading network for drugs, guns, flesh. And each of these transactions were paid in digital currency that flowed back to the Emperor in the form of tribute. He has made a fortune. A man who can create that? There is no bit or byte that can hold secrets from him."

"And you think you've found him?" Igorek asks.

"I know I have. He is in Brazil. He is in the employ of the Hudson gang or perhaps another local. But Brazil is the base according to the information we have been able to glean. I have paid for information that should be delivered to an associate of mine. With that, we should be able to locate and extract the Emperor."

"And how will you get the Emperor to work for you?" Aleksei is still dubious.

"By giving him whatever it is that he wants."

FROM *NEW YORK TIMES* BESTSELLING AUTHOR
JESSICA CLARE

The
WRONG
BILLIONAIRE'S
Bed

A Billionaire Boys Club Novel

It's a dream come true for successful, dependable Audrey Petty when she thinks she'll be spending a month with her childhood crush, Cade Archer, at his remote cabin retreat. But instead of a romantic escape with Cade, Audrey ends up crashing billionaire playboy Reese Durham's getaway—and Reese isn't above tormenting Audrey for her sudden intrusion.

Audrey may think she knows what she wants, but Reese is determined to show her what she needs. And as Reese discovers the volatile minx behind the buttoned-up exterior, he starts to think maybe she's just what *he* needs, too.

jessica-clare.com
penguin.com

  Penguin
Random
House

M1622T0115